DRAWN
AND
BUTTERED

Also by
Shari Randall

Against the Claw
Curses, Boiled Again!

DRAWN AND BUTTERED

Shari Randall

St. Martin's Paperbacks

This is a work of fiction. All of the characters, organizations, and events portrayed in this novel are either products of the author's imagination or are used fictitiously.

DRAWN AND BUTTERED

For information address St. Martin's Press, 175 Fifth Avenue, New York, NY 10010.

ISBN: 978-1-250-11674-1

Our books may be purchased in bulk for promotional, educational, or business use. Please contact your local bookseller or the Macmillan Corporate and Premium Sales Department at 1-800-221-7945, ext. 5442, or by e-mail at MacmillanSpecialMarkets@macmillan.com.

Printed in the United States of America

St. Martin's Paperbacks edition / March 2019

St. Martin's Paperbacks are published by St. Martin's Press, 175 Fifth Avenue, New York, NY 10010.

10 9 8 7 6 5 4 3 2 1

For Bill, my favorite sailor

Acknowledgments

Special thanks to the Cozy Mystery Crew. They came through with dozens of wonderful suggestions when I needed just the right name for a very unusual character. I'll be using some of the names in the future, but for now, many thanks to Meg Gustafson and Traci Lowder for the perfect name.

Chapter 1

"Allie, what on earth is going on out there?"

Excited chatter, laughter, and then a shrill scream flowed in the screen door of my aunt's Lazy Mermaid lobster shack. I joined the customers who stood to look out the windows toward the river. A group from Bertha Betancourt's Learn to Lobster tour streamed from her boat, *Queenie,* and surged up the dock toward the shack.

Aunt Gully set a steaming bowl of creamy clam chowder in front of a man in a Red Sox shirt. He rubbed his hands and dug in, ignoring all the excitement outside.

"Let's go see." Aunt Gully and I hurried out the front door behind several customers. Our cook, Hector Viera, all six feet four of him, followed. Gold and brown leaves swirled around us in a cool breeze off the Micasset River as the screen door banged shut. I shaded my eyes. It was two days before Halloween and the sky was that deep shade of late October blue that's so bright it almost hurts to look at it.

When I saw all the kids surrounding Bertha, I remembered that her Learn to Lobster tour became the Local History Field Trip once a month for school groups. The crowd bubbled with excitement, with kids jumping up and down to see what was being carried in a large plastic tub by several teachers and Bertha.

A very tanned and skinny ten-year-old boy with an armful of knotwork friendship bracelets loped up to us with surfer-dude grace and pulled me into the crowd. Bit Markey lived across Pearl Street from the Mermaid in a prerenovation 1840s house with a pink and purple color scheme and a marijuana-leaf flag in the window. After years of begging, Bit's parents had finally relented and let him go to the public school. "You've got to see the giant lobster Bertha hauled in!"

I greeted the teachers and Bertha as they struggled to carry the plastic tub. One of them had been my science teacher almost twenty years ago at Mystic Bay Elementary. They parted so we could see the prize catch. The tub was barely big enough to hold a huge lobster, its tail and lower body set in water, its upper body and claws curved against the side of the tub.

"God bless America!" Aunt Gully peered over her rose-rimmed glasses. "That's one of the biggest lobsters I've ever seen."

"He's impressive," I said.

The crustacean, mottled brown and black, was easily over three feet long, the same size as a little girl who gazed at him with adoration. "He's so ugly but I love him. Can I take him home? Please, please, please?" She leaned closer.

I pulled her away. Much of the lobster's weight was in his claws, which he suddenly thrashed, opening and closing them with menace. Several people screamed.

"Whoa!" Bit said.

The little girl's mother hurriedly picked her up.

"We have to get him banded," I said. Lobsters' claws

are closed with thick rubber bands to keep them from at-
tacking other lobsters or those who are trying to cook
them.

"I didn't have any bands big enough for this bruiser,"
Bertha said, her ruddy, weather-beaten hands gripping
the tub. "I called Fred Nickerson at Graystone." Professor Nickerson ran nearby Graystone College's marine
biology program. "He'll bring some. Don't get too close,
folks. Those claws will snap your hand off!"

One little boy wailed, "It's scary!"

The crowd murmured assent.

"He can't stay out of the water long. Let's put him in
one of the saltwater tanks in the shed," Aunt Gully said.

"After we clear one out for him." I turned toward Hector. "Hector, what do you think? How about a private tank
for this guy? Otherwise, he'll tear the other lobsters to
shreds with those claws."

"I'm on it." Hector dashed to the buoy-covered shed
where we stored our live lobsters.

"He's a monster!" Bit's green eyes gleamed with ad-
miration. He and a friend had slipped closer through the
crowd and now helped carry the tub, not minding the
water dripping onto their sneakers.

"Like Godzilla," his friend said.

"Relax, Lobzilla, we'll get you a nice home," Bit
said.

Laughter rippled through the crowd. "Lobzilla!" Kids
pressed close, forcing a stop. Tourists gathered around,
taking selfies with the crustacean.

"There is something prehistoric about him, isn't
there?" I said.

Someone in the crowd murmured, "That bad boy
would make one big lobster roll."

A white sedan with a *Mystic Bay Mariner* logo

stenciled on the driver's door pulled into the parking lot. A man whose flowing gray hair, parted in the middle, was at odds with his khakis and button-down shirt jumped out and ran over as he steadied a digital camera against his chest. "Bertha, that's one heck of a lobster! Thanks for texting me." Johnny Sabino, longtime reporter for our local paper, started shooting photos.

"Hi, Johnny." Bertha's broad smile brightened her round, sun-reddened face.

Hector ran out from the shed. "The Presidential Suite's ready for you, big fella."

The crowd followed Bertha, a denim-clad Pied Piper with a giant lobster. The customer Aunt Gully had served just before running outside now lounged against the shack's cedar shingles with his bowl of chowder, eating as he watched the parade pass.

After a few minutes, Bertha emerged from the lobster shed, where we stored live lobsters in several bathtub-sized saltwater tanks. Bertha's Bruce Springsteen T-shirt was spattered with salt water but she was smiling, no, more than that. She was star struck.

Johnny turned to Aunt Gully and me, flipped open a notebook, and took a pen from behind his ear. "Let me get your names right."

"Oh, Johnny, you've known me since kindergarten at Mystic Bay Elementary!" Aunt Gully said.

"Gotta spell things right. Otherwise folks get mad." He nodded toward me. "You're one of the Larkin girls."

"Allie Larkin." My older sister's Lorelei, who prefers to go by the more professional-sounding Lorel.

"That's right, you're the ballerina who fell down the stairs and broke an ankle then came home to help at the shack. I remember the story we did on you in the spring. 'Pirouettes to Pier.'"

"That's me." Not much longer on the pier, I hoped. While I loved helping Aunt Gully at the Lazy Mermaid, I couldn't wait until the doctor cleared me to return to my job dancing with the New England Ballet Theater. "Allie's short for Allegra."

"A-L-L-E-G-R-A," Johnny spelled.

I steeled myself as I waited for him to ask me about some of the other incidents—murder and mysteries—that had gotten me in the paper over the summer, some of which I'd rather forget.

To my surprise he flipped his notebook closed and called to Bertha, who was posing for a photo with some students. "Hey, Bertha, can you answer some more questions?" Johnny jogged over to her. I exhaled.

Bertha straightened her black paisley neckerchief and smoothed her pewter plaits. "Don't mind if I do."

Aunt Gully and I headed into the kitchen.

"You know, Aunt Gully, it's kind of nice to be ignored by the press."

Aunt Gully patted my arm. "Nice to be back to normal, isn't it?"

A half hour later, a rusted blue Volvo station wagon sped into the parking lot, scattering gravel as it jerked to a stop by the front window. As I wiped down the counter, two men got out of the car. The first was a tall guy swinging a black backpack onto his shoulders, a Graystone College T-shirt taut across his broad torso, his sandy-blond hair cut long on top and close to his head on the sides.

The other man was older, slight and stooped, wearing a wrinkled T-shirt and baggy jeans cinched at his waist with a worn leather belt. He had bushy gray hair and over-sized glasses swung on a lanyard around his neck. Johnny Sabino and Bertha ran up to them. Excited conversation ensued, with Bertha spreading her arms in a "this big" gesture. They headed toward the lobster shed.

I recognized the older man. My dad had taken Professor Fred Nickerson out several times on his lobster boat, *Miranda,* and Fred was a regular at the Mermaid, too.

"Aunt Gully, Fred Nickerson's here."

"Your aunt's on the phone." Hilda Viera took a plate with an overflowing lobster roll from the pass-through, her black hair sleek despite the warm air of the kitchen. Hilda, along with her husband, Hector, helped Aunt Gully run the shack. "Why don't you and Hector go check it out. He's dying to get further acquainted with Lobzilla."

I guess the name's going to stick. Hector and I hurried to the shed and crowded in.

The shed was small, with a row of tanks on one wall. Hoses pumped fresh seawater into the tanks, so we all had to raise our voices to be heard over the sound of gushing water.

Fred looked at me over his half-moon glasses, raised his bushy eyebrows, and smiled, a crooked grin like one of the Halloween pumpkins by the front door of the shack. "The Lazy Mermaid herself," Fred shouted over the rushing water.

"Hi, Professor."

"This is Max Hempstead." The guy smiled and shook hands firmly, his smile wide and brilliantly white. His name fit. He was handsome and ingratiating to the max.

"Max is a student at Graystone. What are you, Max, a sophomore?"

Max opened his mouth to speak, but Fred continued. "We were chatting when I got your call and he offered to come help."

Max nodded as he took measurements on Lobzilla. I was relieved to see they'd banded the lobster's huge claws.

"Glad you had bands to fit him."

"One of the biggest I've ever seen! A lobster of this size is very unusual, especially for our area. The biggest lobster ever found was three and a half feet."

Max showed Fred the measurement on his metal ruler. We all held our breath.

"Just an inch shy of the record." Fred shrugged. "Well, well, so this fella's not the largest, but he's still magnificent!" Fred laughed and his glasses slid off his nose—his lanyard just barely kept them from hitting the water. Fred settled them on his head.

Bertha and Johnny shouldered in. With Hector, well over six feet, Fred, Max, and me in there, it was a tight fit. I was mashed up against Max's backpack, and I angled myself to avoid getting poked by the Swiss army knife, keys, and marlinspike that hung off his key chain along with an orange foam key fob. He must be a sailor—marlinspikes were a tool used to untie knots and sailors used foam key fobs so if they dropped their keys in the water, they'd float.

It was funny that Max left his backpack on. Maybe he was nerdier and more excited about the lobster than I'd assumed from his model good looks.

"Oh, you do go on." Bertha gave Fred a friendly punch on the arm.

He winced and rubbed his arm, but beamed at her. "Isn't he wonderful? Just wonderful?"

"Yes, indeed." Bertha's eyes shone. She was looking at Lobzilla the way she looked at her beloved cats, Big Man and the Boss, named in honor of her Bruce Springsteen infatuation.

I looked at Lobzilla and saw an angry brown and black mottled crustacean with claws so big he could snap off a careless finger. "Question is, what to do with him?"

"I'll take him back to my lab as soon as I can," Fred said. "This guy's going to need special care."

"A feather in your cap," Bertha said.

"Sure is, Bertha, and yours," Fred murmured. "Highlight of my career."

The reporter's phone buzzed and he stepped into the relative quiet of the doorway to answer. "Yeah." He listened. "Where? Rabb's Point. I'm on it."

"What's happening on Rabb's Point?" I squirmed past Max's backpack toward the door. Rabb's Point wasn't far from the Mermaid, a peninsula where some of the oldest and most expensive homes in Mystic Bay and the exclusive Yacht Club were located.

Johnny hung up. "Burglary at the big house there, the Parish place. Gotta run. Fred, I'll call with follow-up questions."

Max dropped the gauge he'd used on Lobzilla into the tank. "Sorry, Professor Nickerson."

Fred swooped it up. "No worries, Max. Oh, this one is a keeper."

"Professor Nickerson, don't you have a class this afternoon?" Max said.

"Oh, my, you're right!" Fred's glasses slipped again.

"He'll be safe in our tank until you can get back," I said. "We can lock the door."

"I'll arrange a pickup tomorrow. Is that okay? I'll call to let you know when I'm coming." Fred and Max gathered equipment.

Hector nodded. "I promise not to cook him."

"That lobster wouldn't go down without a fight," I said.

"He's old, but feisty." Bertha sighed.

"Lobzilla wouldn't be the best eating," Aunt Gully said. "An old lobster is a tough lobster."

A little girl with tumbling brown curls knocked on the door of the shed. "Is this where the Lobzilla lives?"

We parted so she could peek into the tank. She squealed with glee and ran back to the door. "Mom, come quick!"

I stepped outside. A line had formed outside the shed and cars poured into the parking lot.

"News travels fast," I said.

"Oh, my!" Aunt Gully pulled her cell from her pocket. "I'll call some of my gals to keep an eye on Lobzilla while he has visitors." Aunt Gully had an inexhaustible supply of friends who liked to help at the shack. They referred to themselves as Gully's Gals.

Fred threw a longing look back at Lobzilla as he stepped from the shed. "Maybe we should move him this afternoon."

"Your class, Professor." Max's words were gentle.

"We'll take care of him for as long as you need," I said.

"I'm going to make some arrangements at the lab," Fred said. "I'll get back as soon as I can."

As Max herded Professor Nickerson out the door, he gave me a broad smile. "Nice meeting you."

My phone buzzed with a call from my sister, Lorel. She'd probably already heard about Bertha's find. I suspected that Lorel, who was in Boston working at a social media marketing firm, would milk Lobzilla for all he was worth. I debated answering. This guy was old and had survived many years on the sea floor. He deserved a nice, quiet retirement. I hoped Fred would get him settled in his new home before Lorel got him on a TV show.

I answered the phone as I went into the kitchen.

"I heard about the giant lobster. Why didn't this happen during the summer?" Lorel said. "Imagine the crowds!"

I put her on speaker as Aunt Gully, Hector, Hilda, and I prepped lobster rolls for the hungry hordes crowding into the shack while they waited to see Lobzilla. Hilda and I shared a look. "We could barely handle the crowds we had this summer." *Which Lorel wouldn't know since she was in Boston, not sweating in the kitchen at the shack every day.* "We'll talk later." I hung up.

I, for one, was grateful that fall had brought slightly smaller crowds to the Mermaid.

The summer tourist hordes were gone, replaced by visitors who weren't quite so, well, touristy. The crowds at the Lazy Mermaid and walking the uneven brick sidewalks of historic Mystic Bay had changed: more bed-and-breakfast and less T-shirt and clam roll. Schools were back in session, so our visitors were more likely to be couples looking for a quiet weekend getaway. With the leaves changing into their fall colors, leaf peepers were taking to New England's back roads.

But with one of the biggest lobsters ever caught in New England in our saltwater tanks, the Mermaid was hopping like the Fourth of July weekend.

Chapter 2

The next morning Lobzilla made the front page of the *Mystic Bay Mariner.* A photo of Bertha hefting the giant crustacean, a beatific smile on her face, ran under the headline LOCAL WOMAN SNARES MONSTER LOBSTER.

"He has a certain *je ne sais quoi*," I said as I wiped down the pink Formica kitchen counters in Gull's Nest, Aunt Gully's cozy Cape. "Ugly, but in a swaggering, 'I don't care what you think of me' way."

Aunt Gully smoothed her thick silver hair, then packed fresh aprons in a lobster-print canvas tote bag. "I thought for sure Fred would come back for him last night, but he called to say he needed a special tank from the research institute at Woods Hole. He'll come this morning. And burglars did break into Royal Parish's house on Rabb's Point!" She tapped the newspaper that lay on the kitchen table. "The police think the thieves got in through an unlocked window."

Unlocked doors and windows were a point of pride in Mystic Bay. People bragged that they didn't lock their doors. Just asking to be robbed, I thought, but I'd lived in Boston and experience had shown me what an unusual little town this was.

"'Mrs. Kathleen Parish said her husband, local lawyer Royal Parish's, home office had been ransacked,'" Aunt Gully read over her pink-rimmed glasses.

"Wait, this guy's name is Royal? Really?"

"Name's been in their family for generations. They don't want people forgetting that they're descendants of British royalty. Well, pretty minor royalty, way back when."

Our family, the Larkins, had been lobstering in Mystic Bay since way back when. "What did the burglar take?"

"Kathleen Parish said nothing of value. Her husband was away and will make an inventory when he returns." Aunt Gully folded the paper and tucked it in her bag as we left the kitchen. "Maybe she scared away the burglar before he could get anything."

"You'd think they'd have security in that big house."

Aunt Gully shrugged as we got in her van and headed to the Mermaid. She was Mystic Bay born and bred and though she locked doors now that Uncle Rocco had passed, it was only when I bugged her about it. Our doors were solid oak, but the locks were old and I was pretty sure I could kick them down, even when my broken ankle had been in the boot. It dawned on me that Aunt Gully only locked the doors when my sister, Lorel, and I were home. I guess we were her things of value.

I parked the van in the Mermaid parking lot. Aunt Gully and Hilda had decorated the shack for Halloween. Orange tinsel hung from the roofline, along with lights and miniature skulls that I was certain would not just light up, but strobe. Over-the-top was how Aunt Gully decorated. Hilda had planted orange and purple mums in huge half barrels to which Aunt Gully had added spinning purple and orange pinwheels and miniature headstones. Scarecrows and skeletons in pirate vests sprawled on hay bales, and tiny white tissue-paper ghosts dangled from the roof.

A wooden mermaid figurehead, which had once graced the prow of a ship, had stood by the front door of the shack ever since the Mermaid opened in the spring, a gift from one of Aunt Gully's friends who'd found her at a barn sale. Aunt Gully had dressed the mermaid in an orange bikini top and she'd gone on to star in hundreds of vacation photos.

Since September, well before Aunt Gully started decorating for Halloween, someone had started looping colorful plastic leis around our mermaid's neck. Today, she was covered with so many her head was completely hidden. Several other leis were scattered at her feet along with a dozen empty whiskey and beer bottles.

"God bless America!" Aunt Gully huffed. That was her catchall phrase, as close as she came to swearing. "They've gone overboard this time."

"Not cool." At first it had been cute—mystifying but cute. One day a customer or a neighbor, we had no idea who, had left a single lei around the mermaid's neck. Then a few days later, there was another and then, somehow, it exploded, and every weekend since September we'd cleared a pile of leis off the Mermaid's front porch. Aunt Gully collected the leis and gave them to squirmy or bored kids. But now, with all the liquor bottles, the prank crossed a line.

"Probably kids from the college," I said. Graystone College, just fifteen minutes away, had a gorgeous campus situated on a hill overlooking the river, its buildings constructed of the granite that gave the college its name.

Aunt Gully surveyed the scene, hands on her hips. "With all this liquor, I hope it's not high school kids."

"I'll get the flag and a trash bag."

Every morning Aunt Gully put an American flag outside the front door of the shack. It was her tribute to her deceased husband, Uncle Rocco, a lobsterman who had proudly served in the Marines.

Aunt Gully raised the flag and blew a kiss. I swallowed a lump in my throat as she made sure the flag hung straight. Then we gathered up the leis, cans, and bottles. We looped the leis on our arms. She caught my eye and we both flapped our wings. "Polly wants a cracker!" she said, laughing.

My smile faded as I picked up a beer-soaked lei and stuffed it in the trash bag.

We tossed the bags in the recycling bin behind the shack, then went into the kitchen to start prep work. I dropped the clean leis into a carton that was close to full already.

"Good morning." Hilda stood at a wooden chopping block, her knife flying as she prepped cabbage for coleslaw. "With Lobzilla on the front page of the paper, we'll have more customers today."

"I hope Fred gets him to his forever home soon." Aunt Gully slipped an apron over her head. Like our T-shirts, the apron was also pink with strategically placed red clamshells on the front and the Mermaid's motto, NO FUSS FINE FOOD, on the back. The only staffer who didn't wear the T-shirt uniform was Hilda, who always wore a fresh white blouse that somehow never got a spot on it, plus matching necklace and earrings.

"Hector's been dying to see Lobzilla. It's all he's talked about since yesterday." Hilda shook her head. "I swear he'd turn our bathtub into a home for that giant."

A muffled cry came from outside, then a loud bang.

"My stars!" Aunt Gully said.

"Was that the door of the shed?" I hurried toward the kitchen door.

"What on earth?" Hilda laid down her knife.

Footsteps pounded across the gravel. Hector banged through the kitchen's screen door. "Lobzilla's gone!" he shouted.

Chapter 3

"Gone? Well, Fred Nickerson did say he'd come back to get him." Aunt Gully frowned. "Wait a minute, he didn't call here first?"

Hector wiped sweat from the top of his bald head. "Nobody called. He's been kidnapped. Er, stolen. The lock on the shed door was broken. Fred loves his lobster, but he wouldn't break into the shed."

We all pushed through the kitchen door. Aunt Gully, Hector, and Hilda ran into the shed. I paused to look at the shed's door frame. I ran my finger along splintered wood where there had been a sturdy Yale padlock. Someone had pried off the lock and hasp. It would have taken some strength and a crowbar to do the job. I walked around the shed, scanning the ground, but didn't see anything in the gravel and patchy grass. The lobsternapper had taken the lock with him or more likely had thrown it off our dock into the dark waters of the Micasset River.

I stepped inside the shed and let my eyes adjust to the dim light. The only sound was salt water pouring from plastic hoses into the tubs. Hector, Hilda, and Aunt Gully had gathered by the empty tank, their heads bowed. Lobzilla was gone.

Ten minutes later, police cars screeched into the parking lot. Johnny Sabino from the *Mystic Bay Mariner* was already at the shed, coffee cup in hand, examining the splintered door frame while he talked on a phone cradled between his shoulder and chin. Aunt Gully told me she'd tried to reach Fred, but his phone had gone to voice mail.

Back in the Mermaid's kitchen, I tied an apron behind my back and went to the counter to take orders. For once, I had nothing to share with the police. I had no idea who would have wanted to steal a giant lobster.

A tall woman dressed entirely in black approached the counter, smoothing her stick-straight, almost waist-length black hair. She wore a black velvet jacket nipped at the waist with a studded metal belt. Her pasty white face was devoid of makeup except for heavy kohl eyeliner and black lipstick. She craned to look past me into the kitchen.

I steeled myself. Beltane Kowalski managed the Mystic Bay Historical Society. She'd asked Aunt Gully to do a cooking demonstration there a month ago and now came into the Mermaid at least once a week. She gave me the creeps. I took a deep breath and pasted on a smile.

"May I help you?" She pulled her gaze to me. Her eyes, black and glittery like a crow's, traced around my head and shoulders. *What is she looking at?* Something beyond my wavy, copper-red hair, something only she could see. My smile faltered and I suppressed a shudder.

"Blue," she muttered.

Blue? Beltane always said something weird and cryptic, in a low, deadpan voice.

"Curiosity, creativity, power," she intoned.

"I'm sorry?"

She blinked, pulling herself back from whatever spiritual plane she'd gone to. "Is Gina here?" She used Aunt Gully's given name, Gina Fontana, which no one did.

"She's a bit busy now." *What does Beltane Kowalski want with Aunt Gully?* I made my voice firm. "May I help you?"

She sighed theatrically and smoothed her hair. Even the polish on her dagger-sharp nails was black.

"This time of year. It makes one melancholy. Death is in the air. Literally. The mold, the corpses of dead things. Nothing you can do, it is a dark time. I'll have a cup of chowder, please."

"Here or to go?" *God, this woman is unreal.*

She cast her eyes on the other diners and sighed again, Marie Antoinette forced to eat with the farmhands. "Here."

"That will be $3.50." I clipped the order on the wheel, then spun the wheel into the kitchen.

A gray-haired man in a blue Mystic Bay VFW ball cap eyed Beltane. "Hey, sister, you're early. Halloween's not till tomorrow!" He nudged the man sitting next to him at the counter and chuckled.

Beltane's control was impressive. She didn't just ignore him, he was simply Not There. The man's laughter trailed off. He cleared his throat, hunched his shoulders, and turned back to his lobster roll.

Beltane paid me and I handed her the chowder. She sat at a counter by the window, not far from our ceiling-mounted TV.

Past her out the front window, I saw Fred get out of his station wagon, a lanyard with keys swinging around his neck. He was smiling. My heart dropped. *Oh, no. He doesn't know about Lobzilla yet.* Then he pulled up short, his forehead furrowed. He must have seen the police cars.

I ran into the kitchen. "Fred's here. Hilda, would you cover for me?" I rushed outside, right behind Aunt Gully.

Fred's head swiveled from the police cars, to the reporter, to us. "Good morning, Gully. What's going on?"

Aunt Gully laid a gentle hand on his arm. "Fred, I'm sorry to tell you, but someone's stolen Lobzilla."

"What!" Fred shouted. He dashed to the shed, shouldering Johnny aside.

Aunt Gully tsked. "What a blow for Fred. I'll bring him a cup of tea."

Aunt Gully and her tea. To her a cup of hot tea was a cure-all.

"I'll get it for you."

Poor Fred. He'd been so happy. What had he said? Finding Lobzilla was the highlight of his career.

As I returned to the kitchen to make the tea, I noticed a beer bottle shoved behind one of the bright orange mums Hilda had planted in a half barrel by the back door. I tossed it in the recycling bin where it crashed against all the others.

The leis. The bottles. My mind churned as I went back into the kitchen.

Through the pass-through window between the kitchen and the dining room, I watched the scroll across the bottom of the TV screen: CELEBRITY LOBSTER ON THE LAM—LOBNAPPED? UPDATE AT NOON. News traveled fast.

I remembered letters we'd once received from a Lobster Liberation group. Could someone have liberated Lobzilla? I made a cup of tea and brought it out to Fred. He, Aunt Gully, and Johnny Sabino sat at a picnic table. Fred held his head in his hands, mussing his already messy hair.

I set the cup down on the table in front of Fred.

"Thanks, Allie." Fred's voice was a whisper. I hated to see him like this.

"Aunt Gully, Beltane Kowalski asked to speak to you," I said.

Aunt Gully waved me away. "She knows my answer. I'll talk to her next time I'm at the historical society."

My answer? What did Beltane want from Aunt Gully?

Johnny Sabino stood and focused his camera on the shed's splintered door frame. Aunt Gully'd never even wanted a lock on the shed but was convinced by Lorel to get one earlier in the summer. Aunt Gully said if someone was desperate enough to steal a lobster it meant that they were hungry and really needed one. Not a born businesswoman. That was Lorel's job.

As if summoned by my thoughts, my cell phone rang. Lorel.

I stepped away and told her what happened.

"You still have photos of Lobzilla," she said. "I know. Make a Wanted poster and put it on the Mermaid's Instagram."

I rolled my eyes—Lorel and her crazy publicity stunts.

"I'll let you know what happens." I hung up and went back inside.

Cars flowed into the parking lot at a steady pace—probably folks who hadn't heard about the theft, lobster lovers who wanted a photo taken with Lobzilla.

Reluctantly, I returned to Beltane. "Sorry, Aunt Gully's still busy. She said she'd talk to you at the historical society."

Beltane stared at something over my left shoulder. I whirled but saw nothing but a crowd of contented diners. "One must wait for the opportune time," she said, and turned back to her chowder.

I rolled my eyes and went back to the counter. Lobzilla's fans streamed in. Their disappointment didn't seem to affect their appetites.

Three guys in Graystone College sweatshirts pressed up to the counter. "We're bummed about Lobzilla. Any word?"

I shook my head. They ordered two lobster rolls each.

The whole situation was so odd. People came here to eat Lobzilla's smaller relatives. Maybe even Lobzilla's own kids. But Lobzilla's size and age made him something special.

Who would want to steal a giant lobster? As I served the guys their lobster rolls, I saw Hilda drape a little boy with one of the leis we'd collected from the mermaid figurehead. A thought began to take shape.

I went outside and greeted an officer standing by a Mystic Bay police cruiser. His eyes were hidden by black aviator glasses; his bristling mustache made me think of a walrus. Officer Petrie was a regular at the shack.

"Allie, I see you got both your legs back." He jutted his chin at my ankles. I'd been wearing a boot or a high-tech polymer wrap on my healing ankle all summer.

I flexed my foot. "Feels good to get back to normal. I've even been helping teach a dance class at the college. Just can't dance on pointe yet."

Almost normal. I'd be seeing the doctor who worked for New England Ballet Theater for a consultation in the afternoon. He had the answer to the question that had burned inside me since my fall in the spring: was my ankle sufficiently healed for me to return to my job, full-time, dancing with the company?

I pulled my thoughts back. "This morning Aunt Gully and I cleaned up a dozen empty booze bottles and leis from around the mermaid statue." I walked him to the front of the shack and then back to the recycling bin. I lifted the lid. Officer Petrie's eyebrows flew up over his sunglasses. "I mean it's pretty harmless with the leis, that we don't mind, but the bottles and drinking . . ."

Officer Petrie stroked his mustache. "We'll increase patrols. We did have a complaint from a neighbor last night about noise. Maybe your aunt should get security cameras. Lotta businesses are getting them. May be a deterrent. You know, some folks just put up signs that say there are cameras and sometimes that's enough. Your aunt could try that. Too bad she didn't have them last night."

I was thinking the same thing. "This lei thing started early in September. I'm wondering if it isn't kids from the college."

He nodded. "Timing's right. And there's a fraternity there. Seems like a fraternity prank."

A thought struck me. "Wouldn't stealing a lobster, a giant lobster, make a great fraternity prank?"

Officer Petrie stopped stroking his mustache. "I think you're on to something, Allie. I'll give the Graystone College security team a call."

Chapter 4

I'm so good at making lobster rolls that many are surprised to learn that underneath this pink Lazy Mermaid Lobster Shack T-shirt I'm actually a ballerina. After years of study at the conservatory, hours in studios, and several dream-come-true seasons with New England Ballet Theater, I managed to trip and fall down the stairs of the home I shared with dancer friends in Boston this spring. My ankle broke in two places. I still don't know how that fall happened.

After months of rehab and physical therapy, this afternoon I had an appointment with the company doctor to see if he'd sign off on letting me return to dancing. Aunt Gully, Hilda, and Hector hugged me as I left the shack to get the news.

Hilda embraced me, her big brown eyes shining with tears and her lower lip trembling. I could feel her heart throb through her pink Lazy Mermaid apron. *Aye, caramba*.

"Call me first thing." Aunt Gully smiled and squeezed my arms, her brown eyes warm behind her pink-framed glasses, her red sequined lobster earrings swinging.

"Back on your toes," Aunt Gully murmured as she hugged me. "Where you belong." I could practically feel her strength and positivity flow into me.

Hector swatted me on the bottom with a towel. "Go get 'em, Allie!"

I headed to Boston, Aunt Gully's van complaining like a built-in backseat driver every time I tried to go over the speed limit. The old purple van had started with its usual shudder and cloud of smoke. We'd catered a huge fancy party on the Fourth of July and made a ton of money, but Aunt Gully was allergic to spending it. Part of me prayed that I'd get to Boston and back without breaking down. The other half wished I wouldn't, because if Aunt Gully thought I was in danger, that would prod her into car shopping.

At the medical center, I met with our company doctor in his office, where the walls were covered with signed photos of dancers and athletes, a Who's Who of Boston sports and theater.

After he greeted me, my doctor's eyes flicked away from mine a little too quickly.

My heart dropped.

He had been very happy with the condition of my ankle but said I had to start back slowly. My disappointment turned his words and the MRI images into a blur . . . *jumping and pointe work, dancing on the toes . . . especially brutal to a healing body . . . healing is a process that can take a while. Patience.*

He'd been gentle giving me the news, but it still stung. I could dance, but not full-out, and definitely not on pointe. Not yet.

In the parking lot of the medical center, I got in the van and stared at my phone. I'd promised to call Aunt Gully with the news but I couldn't make myself move.

A text buzzed. *Allie, I heard from doc. Come see me. Serge.* I'd forgotten that I'd given permission for my doctor to share my prognosis with Serge Falco, the director of my ballet company. My thoughts raced as I drove to the South End of Boston. What did Serge want? *Probably going to give me my walking papers. What good is a ballerina who can't dance on pointe?*

New England Ballet Theater was housed in a nineteenth-century brick mill building that had been gutted and turned into an airy and light-filled company headquarters. Trepidation slowed my steps as I walked to Studio F where we did company class. It was my favorite space—the ceiling was two stories high with exposed brick walls and towering windows overlooking the Boston skyline.

Serge was bent over a page of music with one of our pianists. He was a legend in the dance world, a wiry sixty-year-old man with a mop of gray curls. "Allie!" He rushed over to me, took my hands, and kissed my cheek. A former dancer, his every move was elegant and precise.

I started to speak but my disappointment stopped the words in my throat. He squeezed my hands.

"Allie, I'd had you all set to be my Dewdrop." Dewdrop was a featured role in *The Nutcracker*. "But Doc said no pointe work." My heart plunged as Serge paced. I could tell he was already recasting the role in his head. As he pushed back his mop of curls, his forehead furrowed.

"Merde." Serge used the dancer's traditional swear word. "Allie, you know how much I wanted you in that role."

I tried to swallow the lump in my throat. "Yes, Serge." I didn't trust myself to say more.

"How about a character role?" he said carefully. "I still need you. *Non*. I want to use you. I'm thinking of making a bigger dance for one of the party guests in act 1."

Character roles are those not danced on pointe. I'd be playing a regular person, background to all the fabulous fairy-tale characters in *The Nutcracker*. But excitement kindled in me. Who was I kidding? Serge was creating a dance just for me? Of course I'd dance. "Of course."

"Good, good." Serge rubbed his hands. "I'm glad you said yes because I've already put you on the rehearsal schedule."

The pianist and I burst out laughing.

"We'll do it when you come up next week. Oh, Allie, it will be wonderful."

So many emotions vied within me. Disappointment that I couldn't dance Dewdrop. But having Serge, one of the most famous choreographers in the world, create a role just for me, even a small one, was beyond my wildest dreams.

I hugged Serge and ran from the studio, excitement speeding my steps.

If Aunt Gully's van didn't complain too much, I'd be on time for my dance class at the college.

Chapter 5

The entry to Graystone College was a sweeping S-curve through high stone walls topped with ornate cast-iron lanterns. Students turned up the collars of their jackets as they emerged from one-hundred-year-old buildings built of the college's namesake granite. Crimson and orange leaves scuttled across emerald lawns bordered by spreading oaks and maple trees.

In preparation for my return to the stage, I'd started working as a teaching assistant in an advanced class taught by my first ballet teacher, Madame Svetlana Monachova. Madame was an elegant woman in her seventies who still danced several hours a day. After having her own studio in Mystic Bay for decades, she'd been offered a spot as artist-in-residence at the college. She was tough on me, but she also watched me like a mother hawk, keeping me from any moves that would put too much stress on my ankle. She wanted me healed as much as I did.

I turned toward the Arts Center, a modern building of cement and dark glass at the far end of the campus. It was hidden in a sheltering grove of old oaks, well away from the more picturesque part of campus. Modern sculptures dotted the path to the entrance. One was a favorite of mine, a large cube almost as tall as I was, resting on a pointed edge. It was so perfectly balanced that you could spin it with just a touch. The tradition was to make a wish every time you spun. I took it by the rough metal edge and pushed with all my might.

I checked the time on my phone. I was early. Not only had Aunt Gully's van held together, traffic had been surprisingly light. Once inside, I stopped to fill my water bottle from a drinking fountain and greeted a student from my class. He pressed up against a glass door into another studio. "Check it out. Some girls from the fencing team are practicing."

He made room for me to peer in.

Two fencers in padded white uniform jackets and knickers saluted each other by holding their swords up in front of their faces. The swords were very thin and surprisingly flexible, bending almost like whips.

The girls bent their knees, at the ready. One of them shouted, "Fence!"

The fencers moved toward each other, one stepping forward boldly, the other with small, tentative steps. Fascinated, I drew closer to the window.

The bold fencer attacked with a shout that was almost a scream. She drove her opponent back with such ferocity that the girl tumbled to the floor. The attacker pushed her sword tip into the fallen girl's chest. Thank goodness it was protected by a padded chest plate.

My student said in a low voice, "Someone's got anger issues." He shouldered his dance bag and went down the hallway.

I shifted my bag and angled to get a better look at the fencers. The victor raised her black mesh visor, revealing brassy blond hair with bold black roots. She tilted her head back, looking down her long thin nose at her opponent on the floor. Her chin was prominent, her eyes large and heavy lidded, her lips turned down in disdain.

The fallen fencer got up and shook herself, but her hunched shoulders telegraphed her fear.

An older man I assumed was the instructor and two more students entered the building and hurried toward the studio door. I stepped aside so they could go in. As I hurried to my own class, the attacker's cry rang down the hallway.

In the dance studio, tall windows overlooked a broad lawn and two dorm buildings that made me think of the mansions on the covers of the romance novels Lorel liked. Instead of Regency gentlemen, kids in shorts carrying lacrosse sticks jogged down the steps on their way to practice.

Golden late afternoon light died in the west-facing wall of windows. The room filled with students—they set bags against the wall, stretched on the floor, and draped themselves over the barres as the pianist prepared her music.

Madame Monachova stood reflected in the windows at the far end of the studio. She spoke with a tall, broad-shouldered woman in a colorful abstract print tunic and black leggings. Their heads were close together, Madame Monachova's gray hair pulled back into a ballerina's bun, the other woman's glossy brown hair cut short in an angular modern cut.

I warmed up at the barre, too far away to make out their words, but the tone of the tall woman's voice was terse, intense. Still, her bowed shoulders mirrored Madame's.

Why did Madame look so upset? I didn't want to eavesdrop, exactly, but stepped closer to them as I stretched.

"At the grant presentation Saturday" were the only words I could make out before the pianist started playing a bit of music.

Madame wore glasses on a long lanyard. She tapped them against her palm, with a faraway look in her eyes. The other woman spoke urgently, but Madame patted her arm. They walked together to the door, kissed each other's cheeks, and the tall woman left.

Madame stood for a beat, looking at the floor. The sunlight outlined the wrinkles at the corners of her eyes and her furrowed brow. With a pang, I thought she looked old, worried. She slid her glasses back on and looked up.

"Allegra, what happened at the doctor's office?" She took my hands in hers as I told her the news.

"It's like Aunt Gully being told she can cook, but she can't make lobster rolls. It's her favorite thing." Dancing on pointe made me feel—how to put it in words? Floating wasn't enough. When a ballerina's *en pointe,* she's no longer an everyday human. She's a character in a fairy tale, a princess in an enchanted world, a goddess.

I pulled my thoughts back to earth. I still had some good news to share.

After listening, Madame embraced me. Her fragile frame made me think of a baby bird, and for a second my composure cracked and I wanted to lay my head on her shoulder and cry. "I know it's hard, my dear. Very hard. But you can still dance, and what a coup, a dance created just for you by Serge Falco.

"Still." The way Madame pronounced the word, it sounded like *steel.* "A dancer's life is ups and downs. We ask our bodies to do too much. But the body will heal. You will grow stronger. The answer, as always, is the same."

I nodded. "Work."

"Look at the time! Five after five!" Madame strode to the center of the room. "Good afternoon, class. Places." Everyone took their places at the barre and Madame demonstrated our first exercise combination. She nodded to the pianist.

Music filled the studio. As I moved, I wondered about the woman Madame had spoken to. Who was she? Why had Madame and she looked so unhappy, so angry?

After class, I meant to ask Madame, but she was surrounded by students. I waved and slung my dance bag over my shoulder. I was determined to ask her at the next class.

In the hallway, I stopped to refill my bottle from the water fountain and took a sip. Angry voices made me raise my head.

Down the dimly lit hall where I'd stopped to watch the fencing class, a young woman and man stood close together. I recognized the intense girl I'd seen fencing earlier. Her frame was the same, with the same strong carriage, the same blond hair with dramatic jet-black roots. The guy's back was to me—he was tall and golden blond, with a black backpack slung over his shoulder. Something jogged my memory. Where had I seen him before?

Then with an explosive action and cry, she pushed him away. He stumbled and fell against the wall. She ran down the steps and through the exit door.

"Isobel!" He scrambled to his feet and ran after her.

I hesitated. This was a private moment, but this was also the way to the parking lot. I jogged down the steps pulling my phone from my pocket as I exited into the dark.

Sunset was coming earlier; the streetlights were on.

A crisp leaf skittered down the sidewalk. A woman's voice swore. I turned. The couple had turned north, walking back toward the main campus.

"Max, I hate you," she shouted.

Max? The guy stood under a streetlight. Yes, it was Max Hempstead, the student who had helped Professor Fred Nickerson with Lobzilla.

"Isobel. I didn't do anything. I promise you. I didn't!"

"I thought you cared about me." She choked on a sob. "Now I know it was just an excuse—" She froze, aware of me for the first time.

I looked down at my phone and kept my body as still and casual as possible, walking across the street toward Aunt Gully's van, watching them from the corner of my eye. Everyone seemed to think that if someone was looking at a phone, they weren't aware of what was going on around them. In many cases that was true but I wasn't sure what was happening with these two, or if their argument would turn physical again.

The girl named Isobel ran away from Max, darting across a wide paved courtyard toward the college green. Max watched her go, then stuffed his hands in his pockets and stalked down the sidewalk, through a circle of streetlight into shadow.

Chapter 6

I parked Aunt Gully's van by the shed at the Mermaid. It was seven o'clock—after the dinner rush but still many cars were crammed in our small parking lot. I got out and leaned against the van.

The night air was soft and cool, just right weather for a light sweater. Diners enjoyed their lobster rolls while sitting at picnic tables and on the Adirondack chairs under gently swaying multicolored fairy lights.

Their view was one of my favorites. A crescent moon hung low in the sky, its light creating a shining path across the Micasset River that sparkled at the end of our pier. When I was a little girl I imagined that I could follow that path right across the top of the waves to the moon.

Several sailboat charters from the Town Pier ran moonlight sailing trips and the boats slid by our dock on their way back home. The diners hushed as one sailboat, *Charlotte,* swept by, her rigging and sails silhouetted against the golden crescent moon. She was a ghost ship, a dream. Several customers applauded. From that magical view, I turned back to the Mermaid.

I'd seen Aunt Gully's Halloween decorations in the daylight, but now, in the dark, I got the full nighttime effect of her handiwork, which could only be described as Hansel and Gretel in Vegas. Transformed into a Halloween gingerbread house, the shack was draped—no, drenched—in orange fairy lights, flashing light-up plastic skulls, and glittery glow-in-the-dark pumpkins. Two jack-o'-lanterns nestled in the half barrels among yellow and purple mums. She'd even tucked a witch's legs under the porch, her homage to *The Wizard of Oz.* I shook my head. The woman's design aesthetic was More Is More.

Aunt Gully had even strung skeletons along the roofline of the lobster shed. Too bad our own monster lobster had been kidnapped—he would have been perfect for Halloween.

Who would want a giant lobster? What on earth would you do with it? I pictured someone trying to cook the monster crustacean and shook my head. What a waste. Poor old Lobzilla.

Great. Even I was calling it Lobzilla.

Warm light and music streamed out of the kitchen. Aunt Gully was singing, well, warbling along to a Broadway show tune. She always sang as she cooked, convinced that the music soothed the lobsters as they prepared to make the ultimate sacrifice for her hungry customers.

The sound of crunching gravel behind the shack caught my attention as I headed toward the kitchen door. I stopped. The crunching stopped. My skin prickled.

There were no lights in this area of the Mermaid. The back wall of the shack faced a narrow alley that ran from the parking lot to the sidewalk on Pearl Street. This was where we kept a Dumpster, stacks of crates, and recycling bins. The special Dumpster for lobster shells was at the back of the property, far away because of the odor.

I stepped toward the alley, placing my feet carefully so I wouldn't make any sound on the shifting gravel.

Movement, just past a stack of crates, caught my eye. A shadow? I gasped. No, someone—wearing dark clothes—was standing on top of a crate, peering in the kitchen window. Broad shoulders. A man? As my eyes adjusted to the dark, I saw that the figure was holding a phone up to the window. Taking a photo?

A Peeping Tom?

"Hey!" I darted toward him.

Startled, he turned and dashed toward the street. I ran after him.

In the dark behind the shack, I blindly followed the sound of his footsteps on gravel. As he reached Pearl Street, he cut right and pounded down the sidewalk toward the Town Pier. Cars lined the narrow street. Crowds gathered around the door to the Tick Tock Coffee Shop, which also sold ice cream. My prey dived into the crowd and barreled through.

"Hey!" "Watch it, buddy!" "What the—"

I slowed as I reached the crowd. "That your boyfriend?" One guy waved his ice-cream cone. "He's getting away."

I caught my breath. The sound of the guy's running footsteps faded as I watched his shadow flit around the corner. He was fast. I'd never catch him now.

I walked back to the Mermaid, unsettled, peering into the shadows outside every pool of streetlight.

When I pushed through the screen door, Aunt Gully was at the stove, hitting, well, missing a high note on her current favorite, a song from *Hamilton,* and stirring a huge pot of her chowder. Hector looked up from wiping down the big stainless-steel worktable in the center of the room.

"You're all pink!" Aunt Gully said. "Tough class?"

"You're not going to believe this." I pointed at the window, which I realized was directly over the stove where Aunt Gully was working. "There was a guy looking in the window! Right there!"

"Just now?" Hector headed toward the door. Hector was six four, with a bald head and biceps that bulged with muscle and tattoos he'd gotten when he was in the navy. Now I wish I'd called for help instead of chasing the shadowy figure myself.

"He's gone now." I explained what I'd seen.

"That's very odd." Aunt Gully put down her wooden spoon. "Who would want to watch me cook?"

"Did you recognize him? What did he look like?" Hector asked.

I shrugged. "It was dark and he took off as soon as he saw me. He was standing on an overturned crate. He wore dark clothes. Black ski cap." I considered. He'd moved fast, his jump off the crate into a full sprint had been effortless. "He's very athletic. He sure ran fast."

Aunt Gully gave me a hug. "Well, you scared him off."

Looking down at my yoga pants and Lazy Mermaid T-shirt printed with its strategically placed clamshells, I laughed. "Pretty scary."

"What happened in Boston?" Hector asked.

I gave them the upbeat version, emphasizing Serge's new dance for me.

"We'll be in the front row." Hector hugged me. Aunt Gully gave me a hug too, but the woman can read me like a book. She knew I was still disappointed.

I grabbed a broom and headed into the dining area. It was empty, thank goodness. Sometimes in the summer customers wanted to linger. Aunt Gully didn't mind if they lingered but I was glad tonight's magical moonlight had lured customers outside so I could get a head start on closing.

As I swept, I shook my head at the flimsy hook and eye that secured the front screen door. I closed the wooden, inside door and threw the bolt home. I peered out into the parking lot. Only a couple of cars were left; most diners were heading home. How I wish Aunt Gully had security. The thought of people coming here late at night, looking in the windows, and messing around with silly pranks made me furious.

I straightened chairs by the window. As I did, I caught sight of a small brown object on the windowsill. I picked up a small bundle of twigs, tied with wax-covered twine. I sniffed—the scent was sweet and reminded me of something I couldn't quite identify. Cough syrup?

I brought the bundle into the kitchen. "Aunt Gully, did you lose some cooking spice?"

Aunt Gully took it from me and sniffed. "Ah. At first, I thought it looked like cinnamon sticks. It's licorice. Some customer must have left it." She put it on a shelf and grabbed her bright red tote bag. "Maybe they'll come back for it." We stepped outside and Aunt Gully tugged the door closed behind her.

"Good night, ladies," Hector sang as he watched us get into the van. Then he turned toward Pearl Street. He and Hilda lived in an apartment over the Sirius Pet Grooming Studio a few blocks down the street.

It was a short drive to Aunt Gully's cozy cedar-shingled Cape, Gull's Nest. More and more of our neighbors had decorated for Halloween—several houses had hung small white ghosts from the spreading branches of an oak or maple in their yards. Our neighborhood of small cottages was a short walk from the beach. Tonight the sound of the waves washing onto the sand carried on a soft breeze that made the small white ghosts spin.

Aunt Gully had been busy decorating Gull's Nest, too. Jack-o'-lanterns flanked the front door, where she'd hung a black feather wreath decorated with a big purple bow. More orange fairy lights sparkled from the eaves and several scarecrows lounged on bales of hay. One wore a tutu.

"Is that for me?" We laughed and went in through the breezeway between the garage and kitchen.

Aunt Gully opened the kitchen door and flicked on the light. "Oh!" She stopped short at the threshold.

"What is it?" I moved past her into the kitchen.

Aunt Gully's kitchen usually looked like a pristine set from a sixties sitcom—pink Formica countertops, gleaming black-and-white checkerboard tile floor, cheerful gingham curtains, with a cookie jar shaped like a pink Cadillac parked on the counter.

Now a dozen cookbooks, tossed from their usual location on the counter near the stove, were scattered on the floor. Recipe cards from an old metal box were strewn on the table. Drawers had been pulled out and cabinet doors gaped open.

For a moment, we stood in shocked silence, a silence that told me there was no one else in the house.

"We should call the police—"

Aunt Gully may be only five two but when something sets her off, watch out.

"God bless America!" She steamrolled through the living room and down the hall to her bedroom. Doors opened and closed. "Nobody here and nothing's been touched," she called.

Adrenaline surged through me as I ran into the bathroom and flung aside the shower curtain. Then I raced to the upstairs bath and did the same, then the bedrooms, throwing myself to the floor to peer under the beds—but nothing appeared to have been touched there, either.

Strange.

I ran back downstairs. Aunt Gully was putting the kettle on. "I checked the basement," she said. "No one there."

I ran out to the backyard patio, flipping on the flood-lights as I did. The yard was as tranquil as ever—Aunt Gully's plants and garden looked the same as always, lush—but when the wind stirred the fairy lights strung overhead and leaves swirled across the slate patio and over my shoes, I jumped. But no one was in the yard. Nothing stirred. I didn't feel watched, which was an aty-pical feeling. Aunt Gully's friend and neighbor, Aggie Weatherburn, could see our backyard from her kitchen window and was generally there whipping up her divine coffeecake. Her window was dark.

When I returned to the kitchen, I locked the door behind me.

"Aunt Gully, did you lock the door this morning?"

Her silence told me she hadn't.

"These locks are so flimsy! A thief could break in with a bobby pin. Let's call the police. We should have called the police right away."

Aunt Gully gathered the recipe cards. "I'll call in the morning. I don't know what they can do now and I'd rather get a good night's sleep. I'll ask Aggie tomorrow if she saw anything. She goes to bed early and I don't want to wake her."

I took the cards from her hands. "I'll take care of these." I put them in alphabetical order, noting all the different handwritten cards, as she readied the tea. The cards were from her friends—Aunt Gully kept them as tokens of friendship. The woman never followed recipes.

Aunt Gully poured steaming water into two mugs, the scent of her herbal good-night tea calming. She shook her head and handed me a mug. "Who would do this? Who would want to ransack my kitchen?"

"Aunt Gully, Officer Petrie said you should get security cameras for the shack. Maybe we should get them for here, too."

Aunt Gully went into the living room and sank into Uncle Rocco's old recliner. She popped up the footrest and sighed. "Allie, I have nothing to steal. Whoever broke in surely realized that. And the shack . . . well, I feel terrible about Fred's lobster, but I don't want to live in a fortress, or work in one."

"What about the beer bottles at the shack? Officer Petrie said he'd do more stops there until they get a handle on who's doing it but that may not be enough."

Aunt Gully set down her mug and ran her hands along the armrests. "Strange goings-on, that's for sure, Allie. I'd say it's the full moon—it brings out the crazies—but it won't be full for another week or so."

That reminded me. "Speaking of crazies, what does Beltane want?"

To my surprise, Aunt Gully chuckled. "She's a character, all right." She picked up her mug and sipped again. "Beltane Kowalski used to be Jennifer Kowalski. Poor thing went off the rails a few years ago. After"—she gave me a look—"an affair with the president of the board of the historical society went badly. Almost lost her job, but everyone moved past it.

"But soon after, Jennifer, ah Beltane, took a bus trip to Salem with the Women's Club and next thing you know she's dyeing her hair, dressing all in black, and hanging pentangles in the trees around her house."

"Is she a witch?"

Aunt Gully eyes twinkled. "She thinks she is."

"And what does she want from you?"

"She wants me to, oh, it's ridiculous, Allie. She wants me to join her club."

"Witch club?"

"They're called covens, dear."

I choked with laughter, tea spurting out my nose. Aunt Gully, on the board of the Ladies Guild at St. Peter's, in a coven. I wiped my eyes. "Do you want to join Beltane's Wiccans, Aunt Gully?"

"Black's not my color," she said. "Besides, she's not a Wiccan, Allie. They meet at the Psychic Shop above the Tick Tock Coffee Shop. No . . ." Aunt Gully put down her mug. "Beltane came back from Salem with all these ideas. She was extreme. The group at the Psychic Shop kicked her out."

"Whoa." *What was so bad that a bunch of witches would kick out another witch?*

"Want a cookie? I made oatmeal raisin this morning." Aunt Gully started to get up.

"I've got it." A cookie would hit the spot. I went into the kitchen and lifted the lid on Aunt Gully's pink Cadillac-shaped cookie jar. Except for a few crumbs, it was empty. "Aunt Gully! The thief stole your cookies!"

Aunt Gully steamrolled into the kitchen, hands on her hips. "That's it. I'm calling the locksmith for new locks in the morning."

Chapter 7

The next morning, Aunt Gully called our neighbor Aggie Weatherburn. Unfortunately, Aggie hadn't seen anything unusual at Gull's Nest the night before.

As I packed fresh aprons in Aunt Gully's tote bag, she bustled into the kitchen, carrying a black dress over her arm.

I took it from her and held it at arm's length. It had a matching apron and cap, made of a coarse, scratchy homespun fabric. "I'm confused. You're going to be a Pilgrim for Halloween?"

Aunt Gully shook her head as she went to the coat closet by the back door. She opened the door and shimmering pink tulle spilled out. She held up a gown with a frothy pink skirt, fuller than any tutu I'd ever worn. She waved a gold wand.

"Glinda!"

She spun. "You know me. The good witch!"

I pointed at the plain dress. "So what's this?"

"I'm making my Noank chowder for the historical society's commemoration. They want us all to look historically accurate." She stuffed the poufy pink dress back into the closet.

"Yum." Noank style was my favorite. It's different from creamy white New England clam chowder, which is what we served at the shack. Noank, or Rhode Island, chowder is clear, so nothing gets in the way of the briny tang of the sea and the sweet flavor of the clams. Many folks think it's plain but to me the flavors are even more distinct and delicious.

"The Parishes are still calling it a commemoration instead of a birthday?" Otis Parish, the founder of Mystic Bay, had been born on October 31. This had always been a thorn in the side of his stuffy descendants.

Aunt Gully tied a knot in an orange and black pumpkin-print scarf. Tiny skeleton earrings danced as she turned her head. "Royal Parish takes his family history seriously. And they're doing a grant presentation, too."

"Grant presentation?" I'd heard Madame Monachova talking about a grant at the studio.

"The Parish family gives a big grant once a year to a history or art organization," Aunt Gully said.

Maybe this was the grant Madame applied for. For years, she'd talked about creating her own ballet. Why hadn't she mentioned it? Maybe she didn't want to jinx herself?

Aunt Gully gathered her black dress. "You and Verity are going to a party tonight, right?"

"Yes, one of her customers invited her. She's been vague about it—said she wants to surprise me. I'm going to pick up my costume at her shop this afternoon." My best friend, Verity Brooks, owned a vintage clothing shop. I couldn't wait to see what she came up with for tonight's Halloween party.

"Oh, don't let me forget the candy to hand out at the Mermaid!"

Mystic Bay merchants gave candy to kids who came in costume on Halloween. I loaded two cartons of candy bars into the van.

As we left the house, Aunt Gully pulled the kitchen door shut firmly. "Locked."

At the Mermaid, we spoke to Officer Petrie about the break-in at Gull's Nest and the Peeping Tom at the shack. "Thank goodness you scared the thief off before he got past the kitchen." He shook his head. "Locks, Gully. They only work when they're used. Look at Royal Parish out on Rabb's Point. He must have a very expensive security system and still burglars got in."

I put Aunt Gully's oversized cooking pot into the van. It was a bright blue-sky day and tourists plus local kids in Halloween costumes were already crowding the narrow brick sidewalks of Pearl Street.

"Why don't you and Verity stop by the commemoration?" Aunt Gully said. "I'll make sure to put some chowder aside for you."

A historical society event normally wouldn't interest me, but now that I knew Madame Monachova might be there, possibly getting a grant for her new work, I wanted to go. Plus, Aunt Gully's chowder was a powerful lure. "Sure."

Aunt Gully got into her van and started the engine. The van shook and belched a cloud of gray smoke.

"I thought you were going to look at a new van," I said, coughing.

Aunt Gully slid on her sunglasses, a bright red that matched her lipstick. "Yes, when I have time. Tootles!"

I shook my head. Aunt Gully would get a new van when this one fell apart around her.

As I went into the shack, the American flag by the door fluttered. Aunt Gully's remembrance for Uncle Rocco. I wondered if Aunt Gully didn't want to replace the van because it reminded her of him.

My reverie was interrupted by the rumble of an SUV emblazoned with WWMB NEWS. It rolled up to the front door of the shack.

Leo Rodriguez waved and jumped out of the SUV, smoothing back his thick black hair. I tried to flag down Aunt Gully, but she'd already turned onto Pearl Street. Either she didn't see me or she decided to let me handle Leo as a growth opportunity. She was big on those.

I have nothing against the news, but over the past summer, every time something terrible happened in Mystic Bay, this same reporter was on scene, and here he was again.

He'd seen me. I couldn't run and hide, no matter how much I wanted to. I looked down and sighed. Why was it that every time I saw him, I was wearing a clamshell bikini T-shirt?

Leo jogged up to me with hand outstretched. His camera crew got out of the SUV and started setting up equipment.

Just then, Fred Nickerson's blue station wagon pulled into the parking lot. I relaxed. With Fred, the real heart of the Lobzilla story here, Leo would lose interest in talking to me.

My smile was genuine as I shook hands with Leo.

"Allie, how are you?"

"Fine, Leo, and you?"

"Can't complain." His smile was megawatt, movie-star brilliant and his eyes held genuine warmth.

I felt myself melt a bit. *Don't get distracted, Allie!* "You're here about Lobzilla?"

"He's big news." He chuckled. "I love what you guys are doing to help find him."

I blinked.

"Maybe it's your sister, Lorel?" He slid his phone from the pocket of his navy blue blazer and turned the screen so I could see it.

On the Lazy Mermaid Facebook page, a cartoon Lobzilla waved a claw. "REWARD. Dinner for two at the Lazy Mermaid for the return of one Lobzilla."

The post had over one thousand likes.

Leo smiled and slid the phone back in his pocket. "Your sister's on top of things."

"Am I the only one who thinks it's odd that the prize for returning a lobster is a lobster dinner?" I said.

Leo threw his head back and laughed. I almost liked him then.

"So, what's the news on Lobzilla?" Leo said.

I waved at Fred to come over. "Oh, look, here's Professor Nickerson now!" A short, broad-shouldered woman trailed him, walking with her hands on her hips.

Fred hung back but I took his arm and steered him toward Leo. The woman narrowed her eyes at me. "Leo Rodriguez, this is Professor Nickerson from Graystone College and . . ." I turned to the woman.

Fred shook hands with Leo. "This is Gladys Burley, my neighbor."

"How do you do?" Leo stretched out his hand but Gladys didn't take it. He smoothed his hair and turned back to Fred.

"Well, I've got to get cooking. See you!" I hurried away, feeling waves of animosity emanate from Gladys. *What is going on with Gladys?*

"Allie, we'll talk later," Leo called.

I waved. I planned to be too busy.

I squeezed past some Gully's Gals who were snapping photos from the kitchen door. "Leo Rodriguez! He's even more handsome in real life!"

I washed my hands and caught Hector's eye. He knew how I felt about Leo Rodriguez.

Hilda bustled into the kitchen and stopped short. "What's this?" She pointed at the tiny bundle of sticks I'd found at closing time the night before.

"Aunt Gully says it's licorice root. I found it in the dining room, by the window, last night."

Hilda's eyes went wide. She pinched the bundle between two fingers and dropped it into the trash.

"What's wrong, Hilda?"

"Bad juju." She shook her head. "I had a friend who got into some weird stuff when she was younger. Casting spells and nonsense like that."

With a shock I remembered who'd been sitting near the window yesterday. "Beltane was sitting by that window."

Hilda frowned, her big dark eyes troubled. "I know she's been after your aunt to join her—" She hesitated then said, "Club," at the same time Hector said, "Coven."

I spread butter on some hot dog rolls and put them on Aunt Gully's specially built grill to toast. "I wondered why she's been coming in for the last few weeks."

Hector grinned. "It's not the delicious lobster rolls made by the devastatingly handsome captain of *Happy Place*?" *Happy Place* was Hector and Hilda's boat.

I nudged Hector with my hip. "Would you want Beltane coming in for that reason?"

Hector shuddered and took a lobster out of the steamer. "God, no."

"Incoming!" a Gal called, using code for *tour bus*.

I ran to the front window. A huge bus nudged into the

parking lot, but there was no place to park. The driver just stopped and opened the bus door. Passengers streamed out. We kicked into high gear, ferrying live lobsters from the shed to the steamer, from the steamer to the stainless-steel table, where we picked the meat from the steaming shells and layered it into the toasted rolls. The cool fall weather enticed a fair number of diners to try the chowder. Every time I went past the window I looked out, watching Leo interview first Fred, then a couple of tourists, about the disappearance of our celebrity crustacean.

I went back into the kitchen just as a deliveryman knocked on the screen door. I signed for a large, flat package.

As I opened it, Bit Markey hung his backpack on a peg by the back door. "Avast, ye swabs." He was dressed in a striped T-shirt and baggy pants cut off to shin length. His glossy dark hair curled under a bandanna tied around his head and an oversized fake beard hung from his ears.

"Blackbeard, reporting for duty." He and Hector fist-bumped.

"You look great, Bit."

He stood by me as I pulled a poster out of the box. It was the Lobzilla Wanted poster Lorel had designed.

"Cool!" Bit said.

I tried not to roll my eyes. I wondered if I could toss it out without anyone noticing.

"Oh, that's so cute!" The Gals gathered around and next thing I knew I was hanging the poster by the front door between the mermaid figurehead and one of Aunt Gully's scarecrows. Within moments, tourists were taking selfies with it. The poster was a good idea, I had to admit.

A woman pushed past me into the shack. "Well, if they'd had a security system, the giant lobster wouldn't have gotten stolen in the first place," she said to her friend.

Johnny Sabino from the *Mystic Bay Mariner* parked on the street as the bus backed out, setting off honking from drivers trying to enter the parking lot from Pearl Street. He greeted Leo and Leo's tech crew, who now enjoyed lobster rolls on the Adirondack chairs. I envied them having the time to relax.

I hauled a bucket to the shed to collect more lobsters for the steamer. Fred and Gladys sat at the rickety picnic table we sometimes used for meetings.

"Fred, how are you doing?" I said.

Gladys glared at me. I angled the bucket between us. *Whoa, lady, I'm not after your man.*

Fred's thin shoulders rose and fell with a sigh. An untouched lobster roll sat in front of him.

"You have to eat, Fred." Gladys's soft, high-pitched voice was at odds with her gruff demeanor.

Fred pushed his glasses up his nose. "If only I'd taken Lobzilla to the lab on Thursday. But I needed a bigger tank, I thought it would be less stressful, and your tanks were fine, so . . ."

I reached out to pat Fred's shoulder, but at Gladys's look I jerked back my hand. "It's not your fault. Really. Who could know that someone would steal Lobzilla? Who knew we had him at that point?" I could have bitten my tongue. Johnny had been on scene from the beginning plus everyone on the school field trip and all their friends on social media. But the question remained:

Who wanted a three-foot-long lobster?

"I'm sure they'll find him soon. My sister's offering a reward."

"That's a wonderful idea." Fred straightened his shoulders and bit into his lobster roll.

"Your sister?" Gladys said. This woman's hackles were up because my sister made a poster of a lobster?

"Oh, I have to go." *Good grief, what is up with Gladys?*

When I went back to the kitchen, I called over one of the Gals. "Could you take a look at the woman with Fred Nickerson?"

The Gals at the table exchanged glances. "Woman with Fred Nickerson? We don't even have to look." They laughed, but one went to the window. "Yep, that's Gladys Burley. They live next to each other on Seabright Road. His guard dog. She takes care of him—cooks, cleans. Once, I even saw her cleaning his gutters."

"Cleaning his gutters?" *That's love.*

She ladled some of Aunt Gully's chowder into a bowl. "Mmm. That smells good. Not that he notices what Gladys does. The only thing he loves is fish. Gladys took him under her wing."

Like the wing of a hawk. I shuddered. This talk of birds made me think of Beltane's glittering black eyes.

As the Gals chatted, I went to the trash can. The bundle of sticks Hilda had thrown away sat on top of a discarded hair net. I hesitated, then slipped the bundle into my pocket. I wanted to know what Beltane was up to and I knew just the person to ask.

Chapter 8

I hurried from the shack, heading up Pearl Street.

Afternoon was flowing into evening, sunset's fingers of pink and flame reached upriver from the Sound. Clouds tinged with red scuttled in the light breeze. If this weather held, it would be perfect for Halloween trick-or-treating tonight.

The shops on Pearl Street were decked out with fall colors, carved pumpkins, masses of mums, and big purple and green cabbages. Banners with cornucopia, pumpkins, and scarecrows fluttered from shopfronts. Most businesses were handing out Halloween candy. Little kids in costumes—mermaids, cowboys, superheroes—ran from door to door with plastic pumpkins and bulging pillowcases, shrieking with excitement and an early sugar high.

I stopped at a door painted lilac, sandwiched between the Tick Tock Coffee Shop and Mystic Yarns. A neon light blazed in the second-story window: PSYCHIC. This psychic had moved in a few years ago. What was her name? Deena? Daphne? I wasn't sure I believed in psychics, but the little bundle in my pocket radiated with menace that set me on edge and made me want answers.

A tiny white terrier sniffed my ankles as I passed a woman enjoying a cup of tea at a café table on the sidewalk. I bent to stroke his soft fur. He licked my hand, his warmth reassuring, grounding. I pushed open the door and went in.

I closed the door, shutting out the street noise. I stood in a dimly lit vestibule. A sign at the foot of the stairs read PSYCHIC READINGS BY DELILAH BALL. *Delilah, that was it.* I started up the staircase.

The walls were painted black, decorated with symbols—stars, astrological signs, runes—in shiny silver paint. Dozens of mirrors, none the same, lined the steps, with the disorienting effect that dozens of redheaded Allies climbed the stairs. The scent of incense—was it sandalwood? frankincense? and something else I couldn't identify—grew stronger as I reached the top step. Water trickled somewhere, a peaceful sound, but a shiver passed through me, as if a cold finger traced the nape of my neck.

Shake it off, drama queen.

At the top was an open door leading into an overstuffed waiting room. I stepped inside. No, it was a parlor. Old-fashioned Victorian couches upholstered in ruby velvet, windows swagged with the same heavy fabric and tied back with black tassels—the room looked like a bordello in an old western movie. The heavy drapes blocked noise from the street below so well that I could hear the gentle ticktock of a tall grandfather clock in the corner of the room.

Words were written in Latin on the wall over a heavily carved desk. With a shudder I turned to face a wall of stuffed and mounted animal heads—a goat with magnificently curled horns, a deer, and a bear.

"Good evening."

I jumped and turned. Delilah had come out of a door by the clock. It started a low, mellow bonging.

"Don't you love that sound?" She approached and took my hand. Her hands were cool and soft. "Allie, right? From the shack. And I saw you in *Ondine* this past summer. Amazing performance."

"Thank you."

Delilah was a short, curvy woman draped in multiple rainbow-hued scarves and heavy gold necklaces. An onyx pendant of the Egyptian cat god, Bastet, nestled in the scarves. She'd swathed her head in a dark blue velvet turban, but tendrils escaped, tendrils the same deep red as the leaves of the sugar maples on Old Farms Road.

Delilah patted the couch. I lowered myself onto cushions that were so deep I wondered if I could get out. *Get out! You can never leave!*

A giggle rose in my throat. I coughed to hide it.

"Social call or business? I have an appointment in fifteen minutes, so I don't really have time for a full session. Halloween, you know? I'm booked."

"I'd be happy to pay, because it's not really just a social call." I reached into my bag.

She waved it away. "How about a free bowl of your aunt's chowder next time I'm in."

"That's great."

Delilah leaned toward me. "What is it, honey? I sense you're upset?"

She probably said this to everyone. Everyone's upset about something.

The expression in her deep blue eyes was warm but

something about her made me uneasy. Or maybe it was the statue of a prancing naked demon on the bookcase behind her.

I pulled the bundle of sticks from my pocket. "What is this? Aunt Gully says it's licorice."

She had pince-nez on a jeweled lanyard around her neck. She took the bundle from my hand. "Root. Licorice root. I don't even need my glasses. It has a nice scent, doesn't it? I add it to a lot of herbal remedies—it adds sweetness to the herbs, which can sometimes be bitter." She hesitated. "Where did you get it?" She kept her voice light, but glanced away, her body stiff.

My guard went up. "Someone left it at the shack."

"Just left it? With nothing else?"

"Yes, I think so." Suddenly, I felt foolish. The bundle probably fell out of Beltane's pocket or bag. Delilah tilted her head as she gave the licorice back to me, the look of a woman who knows more than she's letting on. I wondered if she'd read my mind and knew I was talking about Beltane.

"Licorice root is used in spells," she said. "Usually cast at the half-moon—the light and the dark represent two spirits. The practitioner will circle the root with eight candles and in the center is something belonging to the one the practitioner wants to gain power over."

Gain power over? To my shocked expression she said, "Or sometimes it's just to change someone's mind."

She reached out for the bundle again, but then jerked her hand back, as if she'd touched a hot stove. "Beltane," she said.

I nodded, spooked. Suddenly, the room was suffocating and I couldn't wait to get out. Plus the sound of water made me realize I really wanted to go to the restroom. "I'm sorry, could I use your . . . ?"

"Of course. Down the hall on the left."

I hurried down the hallway. The bathroom had deep violet walls and the toilet was topped with one of those fussy little dolls whose long crocheted skirt covered an extra roll of toilet paper. The doll was dressed as a witch. On the back of the door was a sign: IF YOU SPRINKLE WHEN YOU TINKLE, PLEASE BE SWEET AND WIPE THE SEAT.

I snorted. *Witches: they're just like the rest of us.*

When I finished washing my hands, I opened the door and noticed a room across the hall, the doorway covered with a beaded curtain. I made sure Delilah wasn't watching and pulled them aside. Shelves lined the walls of the room, shelf after shelf lined with glass jars, each full of herbs, leaves, powders, and other things I couldn't identify. I let the beaded curtain fall closed as quietly as I could and headed back to the parlor.

Footsteps thudded up the stairs. A couple walked slowly into the parlor, their eyes wide.

"Thank you, Delilah," I said on my way out. As I walked through the doorway, I caught sight of my reflection in a mirror. In it, Delilah gave me an appraising glance. I rushed down the stairs.

I walked to the center of town, laughing at myself. The psychic's front window faced Pearl Street. She probably saw Beltane go to the Mermaid. You couldn't miss her. Of course, Delilah knew Beltane. How many witches were in Mystic Bay anyway? Beltane probably bought the licorice root right upstairs at the psychic supermarket.

A thought gave me pause: Could Delilah and Beltane have been working together?

The everyday sights of Mystic Bay cleared the cobwebs of the supernatural that clung to me after leaving the psychic. Sure, plenty of kids were dressed as witches, but the happy Halloween vibe wiped away my unease.

I passed the lime-green sign of ultraexpensive boutique Fashions by Franque and entered the door under the carved neon-pink sign of Verity's Vintage.

Verity's been my best friend since preschool. She stood behind a glass showcase wearing a fur stole and a flapper's jeweled headband. The headband sparkled in Verity's smooth black curls and the white mink stole set off her caramel-colored skin.

"You look perfect!" I said. "Is that your Halloween costume?"

She admired herself in a mirror. "I wish. Too bad tonight's not a Gatsby party."

"Thank goodness we don't have to wear the dowdy Pilgrim dresses that Aunt Gully's wearing at the historical society event."

Verity shuddered. "Don't get me started. Have you seen what women in Mystic Bay had to wear in the 1700s? Unless you were royalty you were just, ugh, a peasant in a linen bag. But the party tonight will be a real party. Isobel Parish told me herself."

"We're going to a party thrown by one of the Parishes?" This was an exciting development. The Parishes were the founders of Mystic Bay and were still one of the wealthiest families here. This would be some party.

"Isobel's a customer. She told me that she's thrilled that we're friends because she wants to meet you. She likes ballet. Go figure."

Verity led me to the dressing room at the back of the shop. "She's a freshman at Graystone College and wanted to invite her friends. So after the historical ceremony thingie there will be a real Halloween party at the fabulous Parish home."

Excitement kindled in me. "I can't wait to see my costume. Is there a theme?" I remembered Delilah and Beltane. "Not witches, I hope."

Verity cocked her head as she lifted two hangers from a rack. "I'm sure you have a story for me. Drumroll, please—the theme is pirates! I knocked together two costumes. And look at this!" She lifted a huge black velvet hat draped with a black ostrich feather. "My hat. I don't want to cover your pirate-wench hair."

She gave me a hanger with a pair of black breeches, an oversized white poet's shirt, and a ruby-red velvet vest. "And wait for it." She handed me a pair of knee-high black leather boots.

Boots are my absolute weakness. I ran my hands over the supple leather. I peeked inside. "And they're my size!"

"It was meant to be." She pointed to two black velvet cloaks. "We even have these. I got them from a Broadway by the Bay actor's house when he retired to Florida."

I swung the cloak over my shoulders and struck a pose in Verity's full-length mirror. "You've outdone yourself, Verity."

"This will be a party to remember."

Chapter 9

The late afternoon sunlight was golden and surprisingly warm for late October. Verity and I drove into Rabb's Point, a waterfront enclave not far from the Mermaid. Verity's '62 DeSoto, which we called the Tank, rolled past tiny antique fisherman's cottages that in recent years had been expanded with huge additions. Modern life just didn't fit inside tiny old houses. Though the additions were tasteful, the original houses looked dwarfed and sad.

We turned onto a narrow lane canopied with old oaks and lined with gray stone walls. There weren't many houses on this almost mile-long road. We passed the yacht club, then a couple of narrow gated driveways leading to private estates.

The road forked.

"That road to the right goes to Isobel Parish's house. Where the real Halloween party will be tonight," Verity said.

We turned left into a parking lot by a sign on a black wrought-iron post: OTIS PARISH HOUSE. HOME OF THE MYSTIC BAY HISTORICAL SOCIETY.

The Otis Parish House was a large brown saltbox. *Saltbox* meant the back roof of the building sloped down at a steep angle, so the snow wouldn't accumulate and that you'd better watch your head because of the low ceilings. Brooding and brown, with tiny slits for windows, it was a most unwelcoming house.

To say the Parish family was influential was an understatement. Otis Parish was the founder of Mystic Bay. Parish Farms was the name of a neighborhood development. Mystic Bay kids skated on Parish Pond in Parish Park, which was near the Parish shipyard. Parishes had been senators, selectmen, mayors, judges, bankers. If there was money or power, there were Parishes.

Every third-grader in Mystic Bay took a field trip to the home, churned butter in the kitchen garden, watched the spinning wheel and sheep shearing demonstrations, and walked the hallway under the gimlet eyes of the Parish ancestors whose portraits lined the walls. I still had nightmares of the portrait of Otis Parish. The stern-faced governor of the colony looked down his long nose from his portrait above the hearth.

We found a parking space by a small red barn behind the house. A sign reading ANNEX hung by the worn brick path leading to it.

Verity and I followed the path to a kitchen garden on the south side of the house.

There a docent dressed in a plain gray homespun dress, white apron, and simple linen cap led a tour group. Dozens of visitors thronged the grounds, some dressed in historically accurate garb, some in Halloween costumes. There was a festive feel in the air, no doubt due to the unseasonably warm, sunny day. A dreary, wet October day would have been much more fitting for the dour Parish ancestors.

We skirted the tour group and went in the kitchen door.

Aunt Gully was stirring a huge pot of her chowder over a fire in the open hearth. The hearth ran the entire side of the room and was so big that Aunt Gully fit inside. The heat made her cheeks even pinker than usual. She now wore her homespun costume with a white linen apron and bonnet. She spun and did her Marilyn Monroe pose, one arm held high, hand on her hip, her shoulder forward. "I feel like an extra in *The Crucible!*"

Verity tapped Aunt Gully's swinging skeleton earrings. "These are great!"

"Oops, I forgot." Aunt Gully tucked them in her pocket.

I nodded to the other kitchen helpers. "If those dresses were red they all could be extras in *The Handmaid's Tale,*" I whispered to Verity.

Aunt Gully stirred her chowder. "I was hoping I'd see you in your costumes."

"They're in the car. Can we change in here later?"

Aunt Gully nodded toward the far end of the kitchen. "Yes, in the office. Oh, Allie, I saw Madame Monachova."

"She must have applied for a grant," I said to Verity.

"Fingers crossed for her!"

"I'm glad you girls stopped by. So many people are here, almost double what we had last year. I've been cooking up a storm," Aunt Gully said.

"How can we help?"

"Allie, will you go into the garden and pick me some more thyme? It's by the trellis. And Verity, will you slice these loaves of bread, please?"

I was grateful to escape the kitchen's heat. The tour

group streamed from the garden into the Annex building as I stepped outside.

A single bee buzzed over late-blooming herbs. I crouched and ran the leaves through my fingers, releasing the fragrant oils. As I gathered some thyme, movement by the back gate caught my eye.

Beltane stood outside the garden gate like a wraith, dressed in the same simple dress as Aunt Gully, except hers was black and she'd topped it with a magnificent flowing cape. She hadn't covered her hair, but wore it thickly gathered at her neck.

She kept popping up. Was she stalking Aunt Gully? I knew she worked at the historical society but now I suspected that she'd asked Aunt Gully to be part of the celebration in order to get closer to her. *What a witch.*

Whatever else you could say about Beltane, the woman had magnificent posture. She stood like a queen, her head high, her shoulders back, her chin lifted. There was something powerful about her. Beltane had stage presence.

A man joined her and I had the sensation that I'd traveled back in time. He was dressed in colonial garb, with a long linen overshirt, breeches, and leather boots with a buckle, all topped with a long black cape that flowed in the wind.

The man had sandy-brown hair and his hairline was high; the breeze lifted a slight comb-over. Wide-set eyes and a full beard flecked with gray. Handsome. The only discordant note was the stylish black-rimmed glasses, but that was the only discordant note. I could have been back in the 1700s.

Beltane's expression hardened.

I stayed crouched. I didn't want her to see me.

"Did you have a chance to get those loans together for the history department?" The man spoke easily, not cowed by the anger radiating off her.

Beltane's voice was a hiss. "As if I don't have enough to do with last-minute requests like that! I had to arrange this whole celebration—"

"Royal wanted to move on that."

"Of course I did the loans! The box is in the office in the Annex." Beltane spun away from him and stormed down the path into the house, inches from me. I turned my head away, hoping that she hadn't recognized me. When I turned back, the man was still looking toward the path Beltane had taken, a bemused smile on his lips.

"Lyman." Another man in colonial costume hailed him.

Beltane's companion's smile widened. "Royal!"

I stood and scooted behind the trellis to get a better look. I'd never seen this scion of the influential Parish family.

Royal, tall and broad shouldered, wore the same flowing cape over colonial clothes as the man named Lyman, but also wore a tall hat that made me think of pilgrims. Again I had the feeling of being lost in time, but the effect was ruined when a woman came up to Royal, fluttering a fan, her dark hair swept back into place with a white rose. She was dressed in something Martha Washington would have worn, a frothy ball gown printed with pink and blue flowers, with lace at the low neckline. Royal took her arm as if trying to keep her from making any further mistakes. When she faced me I realized it was the woman I'd seen talking to Madame Monachova in the college dance studio.

I felt something touch my hair and then yank.

"Ouch!"

I turned. A woman in a colonial dress stood behind me, a baby girl strapped to her in a backpacklike carrier. The little girl reached out again and her mother took her hand.

"Oh, I'm so sorry! Prudie, stop that!"

I disentangled my hair from Prudie's chubby, sticky fingers. Prudie wore a little white linen bonnet just like the one her mother wore with her simple colonial dress.

"It's okay." I laughed. "She looks very historically accurate."

"I try." The woman smiled. She looked about thirty, with a round face sprinkled with freckles and oversized tortoiseshell glasses. "I'm Fern Doucette. I volunteer here on weekends. I'm coordinating the volunteers from the college. Sorry, don't think we've met. Thank you for helping."

"Oh, I'm not with the college. I'm Allie Larkin. My aunt Gully is cooking the chowder."

"Oh, sorry, I just assumed. We have so many volunteers from the college today. I love Gully! She's such a dear to help us out. Actually she asked me to see where you were—she just said 'Find Allie the redhead.'"

The thyme! "I got distracted!" I hurried inside and gave the herbs to Aunt Gully.

Aunt Gully laughed. "Be sure you get a bite to eat before the ceremony's over. We have a lot of people today."

I poked my head into the dining room where a long buffet table had been set up. Verity stood at one end, arranging napkins that didn't need arranging while chatting with a guy in a Graystone College T-shirt. He was cute. I met her eye and gave her a smile, then returned to the garden, snagging two mugs of chowder on the way.

Fern and Prudie were still at the trellis. Fern had taken off her bonnet and fanned herself with it.

"Chowder?" I offered her a mug.

"Oh, thank you!" The toddler pulled on a strand of Fern's coarse, dishwater-blond hair. Fern winced.

I nodded toward a bench under a tree on the front lawn of the house. "Let's go there."

We passed a few teens in Halloween costumes, whooping on the front lawn.

We settled on the bench. Fern took Prudie out of the carrier.

"There are so many irreplaceable artifacts and antiques that Prudie could get her hands on inside the house. And I couldn't get a baby sitter so we'll have to stay outside." Fern blew on a spoonful of chowder and gave Prudie a taste. Prudie spit it out. I laughed. Fern gave Prudie a cracker.

"I could watch her for you," I said. "If you want to go inside for a while."

Fern shook her head. "I'll listen from outside the window. I want to hear Royal Parish announce the Parish Grant. Twenty-five thousand dollars for the lucky winner."

"Did you say you were at the college?"

Fern shook her head. "I got my grad degree from Graystone a year ago—I did anthropology, history, and women's studies."

Triple major. Impressive.

"Plus Prudie," I said.

Fern smiled. "She was a nice surprise. I'm, I was, a part-time teaching assistant for Lyman Smith in the history department." *Lyman Smith.* That must be the name of the man who'd spoken so imperiously to Beltane. Not that many people could be named Lyman.

Fern continued, "I'll be going back to work for him soon. I just had to arrange child care."

Johnny Sabino set up a camera tripod just a few feet

in front of us. "All the folks who are in the running for the Parish Grant, gather here for a photo, please." He beckoned.

Almost two dozen people milled uncertainly by the front door. Most wore business dress or New England "school clothes"—wool skirts and cardigans on the women, button-down plaid shirts, sweater vests, and corduroy or chino slacks on the men—but a few were in historical costume.

Madame Monachova stepped out the front door. She wore a pale blue colonial dress topped with a black cloak, which fell elegantly from her shoulders. Johnny waved her to the front of the group.

The man I'd seen talking with Beltane and Royal Parish stood next to Madame, a satisfied smile on his face.

"That's Professor Smith." Fern jutted her chin toward him.

He looked like he knew he'd already won.

The woman in the Martha Washington dress hovered by Johnny, blocking our view with her elaborate, broad skirt.

"That's not really colonial clothing, is it?" I whispered to Fern.

"Off by a hundred years, and Virginia colonial rather than New England colonial."

"Maybe she didn't know."

"That's Kathleen Parish, the wife of Royal Parish. Of course she knows," Fern scoffed.

Looking at Fern's accurate but drab dress and cap, I could hardly blame Mrs. Parish for her little rebellion.

Fern shook her head. "Remember, *colonial* means more than just the Revolutionary War period. In this area, colonists arrived to settle from Massachusetts in the 1600s, so the clothing style is not what you think, with the tricorn hats and cutaway coats. They were Puritans, so you do have a bit of that pilgrim-hat thing. And soldiers of the time would have used those muskets and also those pikes." She pointed at two guys who carried long poles topped with mean-looking, pointed, leaf-shaped blades. They flanked the grant hopefuls.

"Whoa. They look dangerous."

Fern nodded. "The most famous weapon here is the Parish sword that hangs over the fireplace. Well, that's a reproduction. The real one is in Royal Parish's home office."

"'The Parish sword, given to Otis Parish for his service to the Crown,'" I recited from memory.

Fern laughed. "That's right, you're from Mystic Bay. So you know about the Parish burying ground and all the stories about Otis and his son Uriah."

Along with ringing the doorbell at the haunted Wells House, the other big dare for kids in Mystic Bay was to visit the grave of Otis Parish on Halloween. His grave wasn't far from an unusual structure some called Witch's Rock. It looked like an altar—a large stone slab set across two large boulders. Everyone said that if the ghost of Otis Parish caught you, you would be murdered on the altar.

The group of grant hopefuls dispersed. Lyman Smith left the group and chatted with Johnny Sabino. Verity ran over to us from the kitchen garden.

I introduced her to Fern. Verity cooed over Prudie.

"We were just talking about visiting the grave of Otis Parish," I said.

"An interesting family." Fern's eyes gleamed. "Professor Smith has been working with the Parish family to document their old cemetery, including the grave of Uriah Parish."

"Don't you mean Otis?" I said.

"Uriah was Otis's son. I've done my own research and have made some important discoveries in an old diary. The story—"

Lyman Smith joined us, shaking his finger. "Loose lips, Fern."

Fern's cheeks flamed. "Oh, hi, this is the professor I told you about. Lyman Smith, this is Allie Larkin and Verity Brooks."

He gave us a curt nod. Prudie threw her half-gummed cracker at him. He stepped away from her with exaggerated care. "Fern, is the plaque for the Parish display at the college museum ready?"

She bowed her head. "It's in the annex. I'll get it." Fern had seemed excited about returning to work for this guy, but as she spoke to him her shoulders curled. From what little I'd seen, he'd be a difficult person to work for.

"Excuse me." Professor Smith went back to the house.

Verity and I shared an uncomfortable glance. *What a pompous jerk.*

"I'd better go. Nice to meet you guys." Fern hurriedly put Prudie in her pack and gathered her things. Prudie gurgled and reached out her hands to me as they left.

"Let's go see the grant presentation. Oh, I hope Madame Monachova wins!"

Verity said, "Fingers crossed."

Chapter 10

Verity and I went inside and found a spot at the back of the crowded front room. We wedged ourselves into a corner next to a showcase full of colonial-era sailor's equipment: knives, hooks, and marlinspikes. Marlinspikes were metal tools, with long cone shapes that tapered to a point. Sailors used them to untie knots or splice line. My dad carried one on his lobster boat, but these were made to work the huge ropes on old whaling vessels.

There were several empty spaces filled with little white cards that read either *On loan to Graystone College* or *On loan to Mystic Marine Museum*.

Someone had left a program on top of the glass. I skimmed the list of people who had applied for the grant money. Three names jumped out at me:

Madame Svetlana Monachova for the creation and choreography of a new work in celebration of Graystone College's one hundredth anniversary. She'd talked about this for years. *Please let her win.*

Professor Lyman Smith, for work to catalogue and maintain the historic stones of the Parish Burying Ground. *Wasn't that a bit self-serving?*

Professor Fred Nickerson, for the maintenance and up-keep of the research vessel, *Sparhawk*.

A portrait of Otis Parish as well as the famed Parish sword were hung over the fireplace at the end of the room. Four college-age guys marched in and flanked the fireplace, two with muskets, and two with the pikes. They were backdrop, almost literally spear carriers in this little historical reenactment drama.

One student was dressed more elaborately than the others. He had the same type of breeches and shirt, but also wore a cloak and hat almost identical to the ones worn by Royal Parish. With the crowd in the room and the heavy cloak, his face was red and sweat shone on his upper lip. Like the other guys, his running shoes were an unintended comic touch.

With surprise, I realized I'd seen him before. He was the guy who'd helped Fred Nickerson with Lobzilla and who had argued with the girl from the fencing class. Max Hempstead.

I told this to Verity in a whisper.

"Busy kid," she replied. "Teacher's pet. Hey, isn't that Fred over there?"

Wedged in the corner across from us, Fred Nickerson stood with his guard dog, Gladys Burley. She caught my eye.

"Why is she looking at you like that? What did you do to her?" Verity whispered.

"Nothing! I swear!"

Royal and Kathleen Parish entered, her broad skirts sweeping the floor. Cameras were raised and the crowd applauded. Johnny Sabino crouched at the front of the room with his camera.

Royal Parish basked in the attention. I've seen a lot of people who like the limelight—I am a dancer, after all, and love curtain calls as much as the next performer—and Royal Parish did. More than that, he took it as his due. Since he was funding the grant, I guess it was. His wife had smiled, but as she turned from the college kids to face the room, her smile disappeared and she lowered her eyes. This struck me as odd—she'd dressed for attention and now she looked uncomfortable.

I looked around at the crowd of hopeful faces. The term *vassals* came to mind. Also *supplicants*. *Beggars*.

"Welcome to the celebration of the birth of our town's founder, Otis Parish," Royal said. He gestured to a portrait on the wall behind him. "He's looking good for 364 years old!" The crowd laughed. Verity rolled her eyes. Every art and history organization was on a shoestring budget. Everyone was willing to laugh at whatever lame joke Royal made to get money for their group. No matter what happened, they'd want to stay in Royal's good graces.

Royal spoke about his family history, in excruciating detail, for almost twenty minutes. The room grew stuffier. My mind wandered. Verity stifled a yawn and whispered, "This is actually making me wish I was scrubbing out pots in the kitchen."

"And so, it's time to announce the annual Parish Family Grant, to support history and the arts in our little part of the world." Royal pulled a card from somewhere under his cape.

The crowd stirred.

Please let it be Madame Monachova.

"The Parish Family Foundation will grant $25,000 to the history department at Graystone College!"

The air was momentarily sucked out of the room, but everyone collected themselves and applauded. Lyman Smith raised his clasped hands over his head, like a champion boxer. He'd donned his long cloak. On his tall frame it looked handsome, dashing even. Some men can carry off a cloak.

Fred Nickerson's shoulders slumped, well, slumped even more than usual. His spine curled like a question mark. Gladys glared at Royal.

Verity jutted her chin and whispered, "If looks could kill, Royal would be dead."

"Didn't Fern say that the history department was documenting Royal Parish's graveyard? Isn't that like paying yourself?" I muttered. Maybe I was just disappointed for Madame Monachova but it seemed so unfair. I craned to spot her in the crowd but didn't see her.

Royal and Kathleen flanked Lyman as he held a plaque, and they in turn were flanked by the role-playing soldiers from the college.

They all smiled for Johnny Sabino's camera. Then Royal raised his hand. Chatter subsided. "Everyone's welcome to join us at the party up at the other Parish House." He chuckled but no one laughed at his lame joke.

The crowd streamed toward the buffet in the dining room, disappointed murmuring barely restrained. Fred and Gladys joined me and Verity.

"Allie." Fred ran his hand through his hair, making it stick up straight. Gladys gripped his upper arm as if afraid he'd get lost in the crowd. "Any news about Lobzilla?"

"No, sorry, Fred. I was hoping you'd heard something."

He shook his head. "Nah, now this." He pushed his glasses, which had been taped together with masking tape, up his nose as he looked at Royal surrounded by his court. "I'd hoped to get the grant to do some repairs to *Sparhawk*. I guess that'll have to wait."

"I'm sorry."

Gladys turned her glare from me toward Royal.

"Well, that's life," Fred said.

"Are you going to the Halloween party?" Verity asked.

"We're invited." Fred made it sound like the invitation to his own hanging. He and Gladys joined the throng heading for the buffet.

"I feel bad for him. If he had Lobzilla, he could turn him into a media star, you know, maybe sell Lobzilla-themed T-shirts to make money for his repairs," said Verity.

"Have you been hanging out with Lorel?" I considered. "Though that's not a bad idea."

As I scanned the crowd, looking for Madame Monachova, I saw Royal put an arm around the history professor. "These kids look great, Lyman. Bang-up job! Great idea of yours to have them here. Last-minute, but you made it work."

"The Royal court," I muttered.

"You all look so wonderful in those uniforms," Kathleen said. "Great job, Lyman."

Finally, I spotted Madame Monachova by the front door. She was so short she got lost easily in the crowd.

Kathleen spoke quickly to the young men surrounding Royal. "Thank you. You're all from Royal's fraternity, right? See you at the party." She then swept to the door where she touched Madame Monachova's arm. With that gesture I was certain she was the woman I'd seen speaking to Madame at the dance studio. She put her arm around Madame and the two left together.

I started after them, but Verity pulled me back. "Time to get dressed for the Halloween party."

We grabbed our costumes from the car, ran into the office, and changed into our pirate garb.

"The finishing touch." Verity handed me a huge gold hoop earring. She wore the other. "Two together would be too much."

As we emerged from the office, several volunteers clapped and whistled.

"You girls look great!" Aunt Gully tucked a dishcloth into the plastic laundry basket she used to carry her cooking equipment. "Now I'm off to see the wizard!"

"I've got it." I picked up the basket as Aunt Gully said good night to her helpers.

"I wish you were going to the big Halloween party, Aunt Gully," Verity said. "It's going to be good."

"Oh, Kathleen Parish sent me an invitation but I love the trick-or-treaters," Aunt Gully said. "I can't wait to go home and get into my Glinda costume."

We stepped out the kitchen door into the cooler, fragrant air of the garden. "Glinda is perfect for your aunt," Verity whispered to me.

Traffic clogged the entrance to the parking lot. Cars streamed up the right fork of the road to the Parish mansion but just as many came back down the same way. People parked along the side of the road and walked back toward the mansion.

"No room left to park by the house," Aunt Gully said. "You girls may as well walk. I've been to receptions at the big house. It's so close you can actually see the historical society's kitchen garden and lawn from the mansion."

I put the basket in the van as Aunt Gully got in the driver's seat.

"Oh, wait!" She rummaged in her glove compartment. "Take this. It's some newfangled flashlight Hilda gave me. This way people can see you in the dark when you leave the party."

I took the flashlight. It was no larger than a pencil and would fit in the pocket of my pants, or—I experimented—I could tuck it into the top of my boot.

"Have fun, Aunt Gully!"

We waved as she joined the line of cars waiting to exit.

"I hope your aunt saves me some candy bars."

"She'll stash some away for us." She always did.

Chapter 11

We joined the stream of revelers walking up the road to the house. Although we'd just left the original Parish House, there was a small carved wooden sign that read PARISH HOUSE halfway up the drive. Unlike the Parish House of 1654, Royal Parish and his family lived in a sprawling modern home, imposing and gray shingled, set on a point that jutted into the bay. The evening breeze carried the scent of salt water—we were close to the shore. Multicolored spotlights lit up the front of the house and as we approached I heard dance music thumping.

"Otis Parish must be spinning in his grave," Verity said.

"If Otis is in his grave," I said. Verity screamed and punched my arm as we entered.

Inside the front door, Verity and I stopped to stare. The entry was a vast two-story foyer, which had been strung with ship's rigging. "I just know some guys will be climbing that by the end of the night," Verity said.

"I might be," I breathed.

A few older folks from the grant presentation passed us, their eyes wide, their smiles unsure.

A woman in a gray maid's uniform offered to take our hats and capes. The night was unseasonably warm and I knew I'd be dancing so I handed my cape to her. Some guys didn't wait in line; they ran into the coat room, threw their capes on a table, then dashed across the foyer into a hallway—probably looking for the keg.

"No, I need my cape for my costume." Verity swished hers. "I look too good to take this off."

"Verity!"

We turned and I almost gasped with surprise. There stood the girl from the fencing class, the girl I'd seen fighting with Max.

But tonight Isobel Parish was beaming in a pirate costume that put ours to shame. She wore a flowing white poet's shirt with bell sleeves, topped by a blue velvet vest embroidered with gold thread. A paisley scarf was wrapped around her head, her gold hair curling on her shoulders. Her long legs were encased in brown tights with brown leather boots with a full cuff and buckles. The most spectacular part of her outfit was a sword scabbard that hung on a jeweled belt.

"That's what I call a costume," Verity said.

Isobel Parish looked every inch a pirate queen.

"Isobel, this is my friend—" Verity began.

Isobel grabbed my hand in hers, her hand callused, her grip crushingly strong. "Allegra Larkin!"

If she recognized me from that night I saw her fight with Max Hempstead, she didn't show it. "Oh my God! Let me get a pic." She held out her arm to do a selfie. "I'm a huge fan!"

Her enthusiasm overwhelmed me. We all smiled for the photo.

"I heard that you're working at the college with Madame Monachova," she said.

"Do you know Madame?" I said.

"My mom was one of her students years ago," Isobel said. *Ah, now the way Kathleen Parish rushed to Madame after the grant presentation made sense. She must have known how much Madame wanted the grant.*

Some guys stumbled up to us, drunk already, beer slopping from red plastic cups onto the gleaming marble floor. One leered. "You girls want to climb my rigging?"

"Frat boys!" Isobel snorted. "Come on."

We turned on our heels and followed Isobel down a hallway. As we left the foyer, the lights dimmed and multicolored disco lights flashed round the walls and ceiling. Tendrils of white mist swirled in front of us; there must be a fog machine somewhere.

In the hallway, several portraits of the Parishes looked down their noses at us. Isobel ignored them. She walked with a long-legged stride, a swagger, her head held high, her chin the same prominent one as her forebears. The sword belt she wore rode low on her hips. The scabbard that hung from it didn't look like a costume.

"Is your sword real?"

Isobel unsheathed her sword. "This is an épée." She made a slashing movement with the narrow, flexible blade.

"Like Zorro," a voice behind us slurred.

The frat guys had followed us. Isobel raised the blade and advanced on them.

"En garde!" Blade slashing, she ran at them with the same quick advancing steps I'd seen her use on her unfortunate fencing partner. The boys stumbled backward toward the foyer. She whacked one on the bottom as they turned and ran.

Verity and I laughed and high-fived her. She sheathed her sword. "Come on, I want to show you something."

We followed her upstairs through a back staircase near the kitchen, then along a hallway carpeted with oriental rugs so deep our footsteps made no sound. She keyed in a passcode on a heavy wooden door, then pushed it open.

"The library," she said.

"Mrs. White in the library with a candlestick," Verity whispered.

"My dad uses it as an office. His inner sanctum." The bitterness in Isobel's words surprised me.

The walls were lined with matching sets of law books. Shelves that didn't hold books had sailing trophies and photos of Royal and other men with the Parish chin. I didn't see any photos of Isobel.

The large room was dominated by a bay window that drew me, Isobel, and Verity. As I crossed the room, I remembered that there had been a break-in here. How on earth had someone gotten into this house? The security system must have cost a fortune.

A pool and broad patio spread underneath us, lit with torches and dozens of jack-o'-lanterns. Isobel pointed north. "Just down there is the old Parish House." She pointed at the dark tree line that bordered the broad lawn. "There's a path that goes just past the stable all the way to Old Farms Road. But it's shorter to cut across the lawn. Some of our neighbors do it all the time."

Verity shuddered. "That path leads to the cemetery, doesn't it?"

"Don't worry, Uriah doesn't bother us." Isobel laughed.

"Don't you mean Otis?" I said.

Isobel snorted. "Otis, Uriah, who cares?" She turned

back to the window. "And the south side of the house faces the water."

I oriented myself—the scent and sound of the ocean flowed in an open window across the room where green plants topped mahogany filing cabinets.

Isobel leaned against a heavy mahogany desk, the top clear except for a blotter, a silver laptop, and a lamp.

She nodded toward the fireplace. "That's our family heirloom. *The* family heirloom."

I expected another portrait but over the fireplace hung a sword. "The sword? The Parish sword?"

In one step Isobel was at the mantel, reaching up and taking down the family heirloom. She weighed it in her hand. "The real one. The one at the historical society is a repro. You wouldn't believe how many museums have offered to buy this. Oh, and the collectors. They're the worst. They'd pay a fortune to hang it over their own fireplace mantel."

"It looks like something George Washington would have carried," I said.

She held the sword out to me. I hesitated, then took it. It was a long sword, with a thicker blade than the narrow épée at Isobel's side.

"It's lighter than I expected," I said.

"It's got good balance." Isobel's eyes gleamed. I didn't want to say anything to upset her, but weapons were not my thing. To me, the sword vibrated with memories of blood and violence.

Get a grip, Allie. It's a party. And it's just a sword.

I struck the same pose I'd seen her do in class and downstairs then advanced on her. Lightning-fast, she whipped out her sword and countered me, her steel ringing on my blade and forcing mine to the floor. "You know, you'd make a good swordswoman. You've got the footwork down already."

"I'm a lover, not a fighter." I handed back the sword. She held it out to Verity.

Verity took it in both hands. "Whoa. This is really old, isn't it?"

"Yes. In my family for hundreds of years. I think if there were a fire, my dad would grab this before he'd grab me." She said it like a fact, not a joke. "And that portrait." She nodded toward a portrait on the wood-paneled wall next to the fireplace. The man pictured looked uncannily like her father—same prominent chin and eyebrows, a long thin nose with deep-set eyes, wearing a long black cape—stood at a table, his finger pointing to a spot on a map, probably Mystic Bay. The gesture said, *I own this.*

"That looks like your dad."

"Yep. He used it to create his costume, so did his friend Professor Smith. But enough of a history lesson." She returned the sword to its place. "Let's get back to the party."

We followed her from the quiet room into the buzz of music and laughing voices. I looked down the hallway and saw a hooded figure in a black cape disappear around a corner. Isobel pulled the door closed and we went downstairs.

At the foot of the stairs, a tall guy with dreads grabbed Isobel's hand and tugged her onto the dance floor. Shouting led us outside, where floodlights illuminated the broad patio and lawn.

Isobel had strung doughnuts from the branches of trees. "I haven't seen this since fifth grade!" I said. Partygoers held their hands behind their backs and raced to see who could eat a doughnut fastest.

Verity and I went straight for the doughnuts, skirting the huge swimming pool lined with kegs.

Some guys barreled into the pool, splashing everyone. I wiped water from my lips. "Saltwater pool." I grimaced. "I think there's beer in there, too."

Verity and I simply tugged down our doughnuts, then walked back into the house, munching. Maybe it was sad that I thought of it this way, but the college-age kids— and I wasn't much older—well, I thought of them as kids. The two boys who'd been scared off by Isobel earlier tailed me and Verity.

"We have stalkers." I sighed.

"We'll lose them. I need the restroom."

Down a quiet hallway, we found the powder room, which had marble floors and white velvet couches. "Of course, everyone has four stalls in their powder room," Verity said.

When we finished, we stepped into the hall. Just a few feet from us Royal Parish grabbed Isobel's arm and yanked her into an alcove. Verity and I stopped short, afraid to move. We couldn't see Isobel and her father, but their voices carried.

"Enough!" Royal shouted. "You've had enough to drink!"

"Dad, for heaven's sake, shut up."

Despite the party music that thumped in the background, we could still hear them.

"Who's that boy? How many are you juggling this week?" Royal Parish's voice shook with barely restrained fury.

Isobel shouted, "None of your business, Dad. I know what I'm doing."

"Clearly you don't. Isobel, you embarrass yourself,

you embarrass our family! You've already dragged our family name, our family honor, in the mud enough."

"Funny you should mention mud, Dad. After what you did in the cemetery."

Isobel shot out of the alcove and ran down the hallway. Royal stalked after her, his cape flowing behind him.

Neither had looked our way. *Thank goodness.* Verity and I exchanged glances.

"Family honor?" I said. "Who talks like that?"

"I feel for her," Verity said. "Her dad's unhinged."

My upbeat party mood disappeared. I was uneasy now, keeping watch for Isobel and Royal.

Now it struck me that the crowd was such an odd mix. A few guests from the earlier grant ceremony stood stiffly as frat boys stumbled by spilling beer from red plastic cups. One of them handed us drinks.

"There's Isobel." Verity jutted her chin.

Isobel and a different guy, this one with a full beard dressed in a black robe, danced close, then she pulled him through the patio doors and they melted into the shadows of the garden. Clearly Isobel had no interest in heeding her father's warning.

"Look, there's Fred and Gladys." Across the patio, Fred looked uncertainly at a doughnut on a string. Gladys fished in her pocket and took out what looked like a switchblade. She slashed the string and handed Fred the doughnut.

"Gladys takes care of business," Verity said.

"Fred's so much better on the water than on dry land," I said. "He knows what he's doing on a boat."

Verity frowned at her red plastic cup of beer. "I don't want to waste calories on beer."

"Agreed. I'd rather have a margarita. Or really, anything else. Let's check out the bar."

We danced back to the other side of the ballroom. The older crowd had taken over a small room off the ballroom. I nudged Verity. "In here."

The room was wood paneled and clubby. A small bar staffed by two bartenders was surrounded by older folks escaping from the pirate bacchanal in the other rooms. A waiter circulated with a tray of champagne.

A group by a fireplace surrounded Royal. I recognized people from the grant ceremony. Professor Smith was flushed, beaming. Royal still wore his splendid cape and there was no sign of his argument with Isobel on his haughty face. He held a tumbler of what was probably very good Scotch and made a toasting gesture toward the portrait over the fireplace. He did look royal, I thought, and the others were his court. They posed for a photo.

Verity and I snagged champagne flutes and clinked glasses. "Let's get out of here before anyone tries to give us another history lesson," I said.

We followed the crowd to the dining room.

The dining room was huge, almost forty feet long, wood paneled and formal. Orange and white twinkle lights crisscrossed the ceiling along with white, yellow, black, and orange balloons. A buffet was spread underneath with dozens of dishes, a carving station for roast beef, a hibachi with Korean BBQ, fish tacos, lamb kebabs, and falafel wraps from Montauk House, my favorite café in nearby New London. We filled our plates and took them outside.

"No lobster," Verity said.

"I'm actually okay with that." I nibbled a lamb kebab.

We found two chairs on the patio, and Verity and I dug in. The food was amazing, the setting gorgeous. I felt my muscles relax. When I finished eating, I set aside my plate and sipped my champagne.

The two college freshmen who'd been tailing us returned and sat on the slate patio at our feet. "Who's Otis Parish? I just heard Professor Smith telling the guys by the keg that he walks on Halloween night."

Across the pool I could see a crowd gathering by the row of kegs. Laughter subsided and I could make out the undercurrent of a warm, deep voice. Professor Smith seemed like a jerk but evidently he was a good storyteller. Music from the house obscured the words, but I could tell that the crowd was hanging on every word.

I considered the crowd. I hadn't recognized any of the partygoers. I'd heard Kathleen Parish mention the fraternity. Many of these students probably weren't local. They'd never heard the legend of Otis Parish.

Verity and I looked at each other.

"Let's take pity on them. They're kind of cute," she said.

"Like puppies," I said.

Verity took a deep breath. "When Mystic Bay was first founded in the late 1600s—"

"The British Crown gave land to a worthy gentlemen, Otis—"

"Get to the dramatic stuff," Verity said.

"Right." I considered. "People don't mention this about the founding of our town, but at one point, the Parishes led the slaughter of the native village. Chased the survivors off of their own land. As he died, the tribe's chief put a curse on Otis Parish, the founder of Mystic Bay." I sipped my drink.

"There's an altar in the woods that was used by the native people for centuries," Verity said. "That's where Otis's ghost will chop off your head and hands if he catches you on Halloween night."

I choked on my champagne. Verity was embroidering the tale. Well, everyone did.

I coughed and took a tiny sip. Much better. "Now the neighborhood witches use it."

One guy said, "I've got to see this!"

"They say that Otis rests uneasily in his grave, because of the guilt. And that on his birthday, October thirty-first, he is cursed to walk. So that's why people put stones on his grave, so he can't get out." I considered. If Otis hadn't had a Halloween birthday, probably nobody would have paid him a bit of attention.

Verity leaned forward. "And the curse? The curse took effect years later. The town was struck by a terrible disease. We do know that his favorite son, Uriah, was killed and became a vampire. But that part is murky."

I was waiting for the history professor to step forward and correct us for spreading old stories.

"Did it work?" one of the guys asked. "Do the rocks keep him in?"

Shrieks and laughter burst from the group surrounding the professor.

"Nope."

"I thought someone said Otis was a vampire?" one of the guys said.

Murmurs from the group by the kegs grew louder. Some of that crowd started moving across the patio to the lawn.

"I heard they're both vampires, Otis and Uriah," Verity said.

"I think the story got scrambled." I thought the vampire bit was exaggeration by high school kids to scare the younger kids. "Putting the rocks on the grave became a fun thing to do and that's why everyone talks about

Otis and not Uriah. But somehow it all got turned into Otis walks and we have to keep him in his grave on Halloween night."

"Let's go see Otis." The two guys leaped to their feet.

I shrugged. "Why not? Let's go."

Everyone else had the same idea. Laughter and whispers in the darkness surrounded us as guests streamed across the lawn into the woods behind the Parish home. Everyone turned on their phone's flashlight. We followed bouncing paths of light across the velvet-soft grass and onto a rough path through woods.

Chapter 12

As we pushed through thicker vegetation to the grave-yard, the laughter and chatter tapered off. I held onto Verity's arm, cursing my champagne-fueled decision. One trip over a root or headstone and I'd mess up my ankle again.

Just two minutes later a guy in a Dracula cape stopped short in front of me. "We're here," he whispered. I was surprised at how close the graveyard was to both the new Parish House and the historic Parish House.

A voice behind me called. "Does anyone have a decent flashlight?"

I remembered Hilda's flashlight. I pulled it out of my boot and turned it on. Its very bright beam sliced through the darkness.

Headstones of deteriorated granite loomed out of the dark earth. All that remained of many was the thinnest sliver of gray stone mottled with lichen. I couldn't help thinking of teeth, that we were standing over a mouth waiting to devour us.

Others aimed their flashlights toward the grave, and I lowered my flashlight so I could see the ground. Now all

I wanted was to get out of here without tripping. A name from a headstone became visible in my beam. *Mercy Parish.* I shivered. Some long-ago relative of today's Isobel Parish, who was probably too sensible to join in this escapade.

Someone laughed. "Hey, leave a stone for Otis. Which grave is it?"

"The one with the pile of stones, you moron. Over there." Someone else's flashlight drew a path across the cemetery to a low pile of stones. The beam swung wide, illuminating a space next to Otis's grave where some wooden stakes had been driven into the ground and white string connected them. Just what I needed— more obstacles to avoid in the dark.

A guy behind me dressed in a black robe slipped an arm around me. "Don't worry." A cloud of beer breath surrounded me as he whispered in my ear. "I've got you, pirate wench." His hand started to travel from my waist to my bottom. *Creep.* I hip-checked him and he stumbled and fell over a low stone.

The soil under my feet turned soft and the scent of newly turned earth was strong. I prayed I wasn't stepping onto a recently dug grave, ready to give way beneath my feet.

"Which way to the grave?" a girl shrieked.

Some people started chanting, "Otis! Otis!"

More drunken laughter rang out in the dark.

"Hey, somebody lost a hat."

I flicked up my light as a guy picked up a hat and put it on.

Where have I seen that hat? It looked like the tall Pilgrim hat some of the men had worn at the historical society: Royal Parish, Lyman Smith, and Max Hempstead.

"Let's get a selfie with Otis's grave, okay?" a guy shouted. "Who has that bright light? Spotlight me!"

I turned my flashlight beam toward the front of the group, spotlighting two guys in pirate outfits. They trampled the white string surrounding a large pile of stones, clambered on top, and struck poses.

"You're knocking off the stones! They keep him inside!" someone yelled.

"That pile of rocks is smaller than I remember," Verity whispered.

A gust of wind stirred the dry leaves on the ground, sending them swirling around our ankles as several people snapped pictures.

One of the guys posing on the grave swore and pushed his friend away, rocks rattling to the ground as he struggled to maintain his balance. "Wait a sec. There's a dude back here. Passed out."

"Who is it?" Another guy, dressed in a toga, pushed to the front and circled behind the guys standing atop the stones. He disappeared behind the headstone as he dropped to his knees. I tried to keep my flashlight beam on him so I could see what he was doing. I moved closer, threading through the crowd.

One of the pirates standing on the pile of rocks slipped and shouted, "That's blood! On his shirt!"

Screams rang out. People pushed, some to get closer to the grave, some to get away. Verity and I moved closer to each other.

Blood. My heart thudded.

"Somebody call 911," the guy in the toga called.

"What do I say, where are we?" a girl's voice said.

The screams cleared my head.

"The Parish graveyard off Old Farms Road," I said.

"Right." The girl dialed.

"Something's on the ground next to him. It's moving! An animal!"

The guy behind the grave yelled, "I need more light!"

More screams cut the air and now everyone was pushing and running back toward the house. Verity and I clung to each other to remain upright. Then I hurried to the guy behind the grave, following my flashlight beam as I clambered over the rocks strewn around the grave.

The powerful beam spotlighted a man's body splayed on the weeds behind Otis Parish's headstone. I traced the light from his sneakers, breeches, and shirt, gasping as I saw the dark stain at his stomach and neck. The guy's eyes were closed, his mouth slack, but still I recognized him.

"Max," I said. Max Hempstead, the guy who helped Professor Nickerson with Lobzilla. The guy who had fought with Isobel Parish. The guy who'd been one of the colonial spear carriers for Royal Parish at the grant ceremony.

The pirates who had posed atop Otis Parish's grave, so bold a moment before, melted back, pushing each other in their haste to get away from the body.

The guy in the toga ripped his costume from his shoulders and pressed the cloth against Max's wounds.

"Allie!" Verity moaned. "Is he—dead?"

Another gust of wind loosened a shower of leaves and tossed my hair around my face. I shifted away from Max's body as two other students gathered to help. A white scrap of paper fluttered in the vines by Max's feet. I feared it would blow away. *Could it be important?* I picked it up and tucked it into the top of my boot. My hand shook as I again moved the beam up toward Max's face.

"My God, his neck," I whispered. I had to look away.

Verity moaned.

A mottled shadow writhed on the ground next to him. It made a small whispering noise, a scraping in the dirt. A familiar odor rose.

"That's—" I moved my flashlight, the beam shining on mottled shell and antennae.

The young man kneeling next to the body, now dressed only in shorts, looked up at me as he held the white costume against Max's wounds. "It's a freaking giant lobster."

"That's not any lobster," Verity said. "That's Lobzilla!"

Verity grabbed my arm and yanked me to my feet so violently I dropped the flashlight. The next thing I knew she was dragging me into the trees. I lifted my knees high. I was terrified to trip over a tree root or headstone or rock and reinjure my ankle.

"Verity, stop! Why are we running?"

Verity bent over, panting. "I don't know, I just panicked. Allie, what was that lobster doing next to that guy? And"—she looked around—"where are we?"

I grabbed her arm. We'd gotten disoriented and had run into a small clearing in the woods. The cloud-covered moon gave stingy light as our footsteps whispered through a soft carpet of fallen leaves.

A large, flat stone, as big and long as a mattress, sat on top of several other large stones, leaving an open space underneath.

"Witch's Rock," Verity whispered. She played her cell-phone light on top.

White candle stubs formed a circle on the altar's surface. I reached out. All thought of Lobzilla and Max disappeared as I remembered Delilah's words. The stone was cool and rough except for spots where lichen grew. I counted the candles, suspicion and horror growing.

"Eight candles." Verity aimed her light into the center of the circle. It spotlighted a wooden spoon.

"What the heck?" I whispered. A wooden spoon just like Aunt Gully always used. "Aunt Gully's spoon."

"Why is Aunt Gully's spoon on the Witch's Rock?" Verity whispered.

I knew why. Someone was trying to put a spell on her.

A gust of wind rushed into the clearing, stirring up a whirlwind of leaves.

"Allie, let's get out of here!" Verity cried.

We ran out of the circle. "Where are we going?" Verity said.

Dance music from the party carried on the breeze. "Follow the sound of the music!"

Chapter 13

A few guests pushed past us toward the graveyard as we ran back to the party. The group that had been at the grave stampeded, screaming, toward the house. Verity and I burst from the woods and cut across the lawn, our footsteps pounding onto the grass like a drumbeat.

Just before I dragged myself up the steps onto the patio, a slight figure stepped out of the shadows in front of me.

I shrieked.

"Allie! It's me." Madame Monachova held a hand to her chest. "What is it? What happened? I was feeling tired and was going to go home but then I heard screaming."

Verity panted. "It's crazy. There's a dead guy down in the cemetery. I mean, he just died. He was killed."

Inside the house, the music stopped abruptly. A siren's wail grew loud in the night, along with shouts and urgent conversation.

I took a deep breath. "He was a student at the college. His name's Max Hempstead."

The siren cut, thank goodness, but flashing red lights flickered from the drive. The group that had gone to the graveyard was now sharing the news of what had happened with their friends. Several partygoers slid from the doors of the mansion, rushing back to the graveyard to see the body.

"Ghouls," Madame Monachova said. In the flickering torchlight, she led me to a bench and sat next to me. Verity sat on her other side. "Are you girls okay?" The lights in the ballroom flicked on. Dancers blinked in the light as EMTs with squawking radios hurried past them, through the patio doors and onto the lawn.

"The police are coming, yes?" Madame Monachova said. "Or is there another way to the cemetery?"

"Yes, Old Farms Road," I said. There were only a few houses on Old Farms Road. The narrow lane was barely wide enough for two cars to pass. Visitors to the Parish cemetery parked along its stone walls, where a towering old willow overhung the road.

Madame Monachova pressed her hand to her forehead. "What a night. I don't even know why I came to this party." She gave me a wan smile. "Especially when I didn't get the grant for my choreography project. I thought I should be, how do you say? A good sport. Come and thank my host."

Kathleen Parish ran up to us, her broad skirt silhouetted against the bright lights from the ballroom. "I cannot believe this!" She fumed. "What these kids get up to and now somebody gets hurt."

"Hurt?" Verity clutched her throat and looked at me, her eyes wide.

Kathleen doesn't know.

"Royal insists on inviting these boys from that frat. They're always in trouble, always need bailing out. And now this. Another prank gone wrong. Have you seen Isobel? Or Royal?"

Madame Monachova shook her head.

"Prank?" If this was a prank, it went beyond wrong. How could somebody accidentally—I clutched my throat—stab someone. "I don't see how this could be a prank."

"Some kids said there was a lobster on top of some drunk boy." Kathleen's voice trailed off.

"He's not drunk. He's dead," Verity said. "It's awful."

"It's Max Hempstead," I said.

Kathleen gaped at me, then Verity. She took a step backward, her face stricken. "Max Hempstead? Are you sure?" Kathleen's chest heaved. "Where's Isobel? And where the hell is Royal!"

"Kathleen!" Madame Monachova rushed to her. "What is it?"

"I have to find them." Kathleen ran to the lawn.

"Is she going to the cemetery?" I said.

"I must see what's wrong." Madame Monachova ran after her.

"Whoa, she's panicked! " Verity said.

"Let's go help." We rushed after them. Kathleen ran across the grass, her white sprigged dress glowing in the darkness. Madame Monachova darted after her. For a woman in her seventies, she ran easily, her long cape trailing in the grass behind her.

Two dark figures herded kids back toward the house—cops in the tan uniform of the Mystic Bay Police Department. One held up his hand to stop Kathleen. When she didn't stop running, he intercepted her and grabbed her arm. She twisted in his grip, shouting, her voice shrill.

Madame Monachova rushed up and spoke quietly to the police officer. Kathleen sobbed and covered her face with her hands, then headed back with Madame Monachova's arm around her waist.

"The police must have come in from Old Farms

Road." We ran over to Madame Monachova and Kathleen.

"Breathe, there, there," Madame murmured, her face drawn with concern.

"Mrs. Parish, please sit down." I took her elbow and helped Madame steer Kathleen to the bench where we'd been sitting earlier. A dark stain smeared the seat.

"Wait, something spilled there." I looked behind me, hoping my pants hadn't gotten stained.

Someone flipped on bright floodlights, dazzling us.

Verity gasped. "Your dress!" She pointed at Kathleen.

Kathleen looked down at her dress. A dark handprint smeared the waist. "What on earth," she said in a whisper.

Madame Monachova looked from the stained fabric to her hand. She cried out. Her hand was smeared with—blood.

"Oh my God," she said.

One of the cops came over. "Lady, you okay?"

Madame Monachova swayed. "I—I don't know."

I put my arm around her and led her to another bench. Distracted with worry, I accidentally stepped on the hem of her cape and stumbled, trying to make sense of what was happening. *Is Madame injured?*

"Allie, look!" Verity pointed.

Where I'd tripped I'd left a boot print in blood on the marble patio.

Hours later, after answering questions from the police and leaving our contact information, Verity and I went back to the Tank.

I slammed the door and held my hand to my pounding head. The police had taken Madame Monachova to the station for questioning. Her cape had been heavily stained with blood. It had transferred to Kathleen's beautiful dress and then to my boot when I tripped over her cape. I scrubbed the sole of my boot with bar towels in the Parish kitchen. I'd probably obliterated evidence.

I didn't care.

"This is the grossest night of my life," Verity said.

"Verity, how could the police think for a moment that Madame Monachova could kill somebody? And that way?"

Verity took a deep breath and turned the key. The engine roared but we sat there, staring at the trees illuminated by the headlights.

"You got me," Verity said. "Madame doesn't look like she could hurt a fly. Do you think she knew that guy, what's his name, Max? Did he take one of her dance classes?"

"He wasn't in the class I help her teach. I'd assumed he was a marine biology student. I saw him with Fred Nickerson when Bertha found Lobzilla."

"And why was Lobzilla there with Max?"

I shook my head. I'd told the police about the lobster as soon as I could. Fred had heard and when we'd left he was pleading to take the lobster away. I had no idea what the police would do. Was Lobzilla evidence?

"Why do you think Kathleen was so upset?" Verity said.

I thought back to the night I'd seen Max and Isobel. "The other night at the college, when I was leaving class, I saw Max and Isobel. They were fighting." What had she yelled at him? "She said something odd. 'Max, I hate you. I thought you liked me. Now I know it was just an excuse.'"

"An excuse to what?" Verity asked.

"I don't know. He said he didn't do it. Whatever it was." Suddenly I was exhausted. "Let's go home, Verity."

Chapter 14

The next morning, I slowly lowered myself into my chair at the kitchen table. Aunt Gully set a mug of tea in front of me and I wrapped my hands around it. Frothy pink tulle spilled from the coat closet by the kitchen door. "I wish I'd seen you in your Glinda costume."

Aunt Gully gave me a small worried smile as she set a plate of scrambled eggs and toast in front of me. To my surprise, I was ravenous.

When Verity had dropped me off, I'd told Aunt Gully about the terrible end to the party.

Just before I'd gone to bed, I'd received a call from Madame's sister, Yulia. The horror of discovering the blood on her cape and the stress of being questioned by police had been too much. Madame had collapsed. She'd been hospitalized and was stable but needed someone to feed her cats, Raisa and Rudi. Yulia gave me the security code to Madame's house and asked me to pick up a few things and bring them to the hospital. She didn't want to leave her sister alone. And would I cover a class for Madame that evening at the college?

I'd said, "Of course."

The news was on the little TV Aunt Gully had on her kitchen counter. Leo Rodriguez's face came on-screen. I hit the mute button, but could still read the words scrolling on the bottom: *"Student murdered at Halloween party . . . Bizarre twist, giant lobster left at scene . . . Campus thrown into mourning . . . Fraternity brothers to arrange special celebration-of-life service."*

My older sister, Lorel, entered the kitchen door from the breezeway, adjusting the belt on a dark blue sheath dress. "Morning. What's going on?"

"Lorel! What brings you home this early on a Sunday?" After the death of a longtime friend a couple of months ago, my sister had gone back to Boston, where she was vice president of the social media company where she worked. She hadn't been home since.

"I can't come home for a visit?" She gave Aunt Gully a kiss on the cheek and started the coffee maker.

I filled Lorel in on the previous night as she sipped her black coffee. "Sis, this is awful. Madame Monachova is no murderer. I can't believe anyone would think that," she said briskly, smoothing her glossy blond hair.

"And what on earth was Lobzilla doing there?" Aunt Gully said.

I shook my head. "No idea. I do know that Fred was talking to the police about taking him to the lab. Lobzilla was moving when I saw him." I didn't mention what a shock it had been to see that lobster by the body of Max Hempstead.

"I'll call Fred to find out," Aunt Gully said.

Lorel set down her coffee cup. "Did Aunt Gully tell you about the exciting development?"

"Exciting development?" I set down my fork.

Aunt Gully poured herself more tea and took a long sip.

"Allie, for the last month, a company in New Hampshire has been writing to Aunt Gully about her chowder. They're starting a franchise called Chowdaheads."

Aunt Gully caught my eye, eyebrow quirked.

Aunt Gully had mentioned the Chowdaheads offer, but she'd tossed the letters in the trash because she wasn't interested. I knew where this conversation was going.

Lorel plunged ahead. "Cute, right? Anyway, I ran into Don O'Neill, the president of Chowdaheads, at a conference. He wants to buy Aunt Gully's chowder recipe. Isn't that wonderful?"

I looked at Aunt Gully. "Is it?"

Aunt Gully took a deep breath. "It's a nice compliment. Oh, look at the time. I'm off to church."

"I'll go with you." Lorel put her mug in the sink. *She's going to church with Aunt Gully? Without complaining?* She really did want this deal to go through.

Aunt Gully had her Zen face on. She'd obviously told Lorel no a million times.

Lorel looked at me as Aunt Gully took her pink sweater from a peg. "Coming?"

I almost laughed. "I promised I'd bring some things to Madame Monachova this morning."

"Give her my best. You can always go to the five o'clock service later," Aunt Gully said.

I didn't want to lie. "See you later."

As I tidied the kitchen, my friend Bronwyn Denby texted. *Can you meet for coffee?*

I texted back that I was meeting Verity at one of our favorite coffee shops, Grounded, at eleven.

Bronwyn texted: *See you there.*

As I pulled the door closed and stepped into the breezeway, I noticed the boots I'd left outside.

The boots I'd worn to the Halloween party.

I'd worn them home, then taken them off as soon as I could. I didn't want to bring them into the house and I couldn't bear looking at them. I grabbed a shopping bag—I'd give them back to Verity and let her decide what to do with them.

As I put the boots in the bag, a crumpled scrap of paper fell to the floor.

I froze. I'd forgotten the scrap that I'd picked up next to the body. It was a clue, an important clue. I flattened it and read: "M—meet me at the grave. I'll bring the money."

M?

M must be Max.

I turned it over. The message was typewritten. The paper plain, like you'd find loaded into any printer.

I got an envelope from Aunt Gully's desk, berating myself as I slipped the paper into it. *How had I forgotten this? I should have given it to the police!*

I took a deep breath. My friend Bronwyn was studying criminal justice and worked as an intern for the Mystic Bay Police. Bronwyn would know what to do.

Bronwyn would kill me.

Chapter 15

Bronwyn, Verity, and I met at Grounded Coffee Shop not far from Verity's vintage clothing store. Verity lived in an apartment in a rundown, prerenovation house off a side street nearby—the only way she could afford three bedrooms with enough space to hold her stock. Bronwyn still lived at home, with her parents and four teenage brothers in a red Cape in the rolling hills north of Mystic Bay.

I handed Verity the shopping bag with the boots. She sighed and put them in the trunk of the Tank. "Sure you don't want them?"

"Not now."

We went in, ordered drinks, and found a comfortable spot on a pillow-covered divan in a corner of the café. There were lots of pillow-covered couches at Grounded and soft Spanish guitar music always played on the sound system. I exhaled as I relaxed against the soft cushions.

"You girls look like an ad in a fashion magazine," said the server as he dropped off our drinks. We laughed. Bronwyn was stocky and muscular, with brown tousled pixie-cut hair and serious gray eyes. Verity's mocha skin was from her African-American dad and her hazel eyes from her Irish-American mom. My red hair and blue eyes meant that I'd always have to worry about getting a sunburn.

I sipped my tea, considering when I'd tell Bronwyn about the scrap of paper burning like a guilty coal in my purse. *Get it over with, Allie.*

"Last night." My words tumbled out as I handed the envelope to Bronwyn. "When I was looking at the body I found this. It was windy and I was afraid it would blow away so picked it up and put it in my boot and I didn't remember it until now."

Bronwyn opened the envelope. To my surprise she didn't say anything about me messing up police evidence. She tilted the envelope so she could read the paper inside without touching it. "'M—meet me at the grave. I'll bring the money,'" she read. "So money was changing hands. Did you see any money?"

Verity and I shook our heads.

"No, but it was so dark and people were running around everywhere." How I wish I'd stayed calm so I could have read the paper and looked for the money.

Bronwyn got her coffee black. Verity had mocha cappuccino covered with whipped cream. I decided to save my tea for later and got up to order another one of Verity's drinks.

When I returned with my drink, Bronwyn said, "Take it to the police station. They'll take a statement. Tell them everything." I think at one time Bronwyn had been horrified by the number of times I'd had run-ins with the police, but now she seemed to accept it. Actually, I think she enjoyed having someone to talk to about police stuff.

We rehashed the previous evening over and over, and

as Bronwyn asked questions, I began to see things through her eyes, appreciate her methodical approach.

"That's why I'm back in town from my training in Meriden," Bronwyn said. "I'm going to help with a grid search of the crime scene this morning. They secured the crime scene last night, but couldn't search the area in the dark. All hands on deck today."

"It was gross," Verity said. She made a stabbing motion at her neck. "Bloody."

"I wish I'd been there to see the body." Bronwyn sighed.

"Poor Madame Monachova. There was blood all over her cape," I said.

"There was so much blood," Verity said. "It got all over Kathleen's dress, too."

"That's hard to explain away." Bronwyn drained her coffee.

"Of course Madame didn't kill Max," I said, but then I hesitated.

Verity was right—there had been so much blood. "So how did that blood get on her cape?"

Bronwyn said. "We'll know more after her cape undergoes testing."

I became aware of a growing silence. The usual bustle of the coffee shop had disappeared. People sitting at tables around us were listening, hanging on every word. A man in the corner, a writer who occasionally got a lobster roll at the Mermaid, raised his eyebrows over his metal eyeglass frames, hands poised over his keyboard.

"Let's go." We took our drinks and said good-bye to our server.

On the sidewalk outside, we waved good-bye to Bronwyn as she unlocked her mountain bike from the rack.

"My training session is over Thursday," she said. "I'll check in when I get back."

"Let's take the van to Madame's house," I said to Verity. "Lorel's home so she's driving Aunt Gully in her car."

We rolled out of town and onto the highway, crossing the river into New London. I steered toward the southern part of the city, where beaches and lighthouses were a common part of the scenery. I turned into a cul-de-sac called Captain's Way, a neighborhood of midcentury ranch-style homes.

Madame's house was a gray one-story ranch with a broad front window. Her two cats, Raisa and Rudi, green eyed with thick blue-gray fur, sat on the sill, evaluating us as we approached. They leaped from the sill as I keyed in Madame's code on the security keypad.

"I can't remember. Have you been here before, Verity?"

"I think when you were ten and there was a party after your recital."

Music played as we stepped through the door. I wondered if she had it programmed to start as soon as the door opened. "Her own soundtrack," Verity said. "Nice."

Piano music. "Rachmaninoff, I think—one of her favorites."

Raisa and Rudi circled our heels as we went into the kitchen. The entire house was carpeted in white and there were gold and brass accents everywhere. A baby grand piano a touch too large for the living room stood next to a stone fireplace.

"It's a sixties time warp," Verity said. Madame had had this house for decades, enjoying its proximity to the beach and the college. New London was halfway between Boston and New York, a perfect spot for a woman who loved theater, travel, the beach, and worked in both places.

Her walls were covered with a gallery of art, much of it from her early days in Russia and London. Verity walked the walls, oohing and aahing. "Some of these are really good. I wonder if they're worth anything?"

Raisa and Rudi yowled and stalked off, tails switching back and forth. "I get it, I get it, you're hungry," I said.

"Where's their food?"

"Let's check the kitchen."

I changed the water in the cats' bowls, then opened cabinets until I found some cat food and matching bowls in a small pantry off the kitchen. I took the empty cat food bowls and put them in the sink to soak, then opened the food and set the fresh bowls on a pretty plastic mat printed with a matryoshka doll pattern. Rudi and Raisa pounced on the food as soon as I set it down.

I sat at the kitchen table watching them. Verity went to the sink and started washing the dishes.

"I'll wash that teacup, too," she said. An elegant teacup weighted a stack of papers on the kitchen table. I handed the delicate cup and saucer to Verity.

"This is gorgeous," Verity said.

"Mmmm." The papers drew my attention. The top one had *Mortgage* across the top and was dated a month ago. Madame had lived here so long—surely the house was paid for. Why would she need a mortgage? *None of your business, Allie,* but my mind churned with questions.

Unbidden, a thought slid into my mind. *M—Madame Monachova?* Her first name was Svetlana, but everyone called her Madame. *Don't be ridiculous, Allie. M—Max.* The note was right next to his body. Wouldn't the note writer call her by her first name?

"Madame has beautiful antique china," Verity said, opening a cabinet. I sighed. Everyone did call her Madame.

The note mentioned money.

Madame had been so disappointed by the news that she didn't get Royal's grant. Could she be in financial trouble? Artists of any kind—dancers, musicians, authors—hardly made a good living. She was artist-in-residence at the college—surely that gave her some kind of financial security.

But Madame Monachova's cape had been covered in Max's blood. I had no explanation for that.

Verity poured dry food into Raisa's and Rudi's bowls. I jolted upright and pushed the papers away.

Sometimes I thought Lorel had it all figured out. MBA, high-powered job in Boston, fantastic condo overlooking Boston Harbor. It was hard not to compare with my total lack of a car—always borrowing Aunt Gully's van, the vehicle I'd learned to drive on ten years earlier— my job at the ballet company, which barely covered my rent—of a tiny bedroom in a shared house.

I walked into Madame Monachova's hallway and looked at her photos of herself in starring roles—Odette, Princess Aurora, Juliet.

Nah. I wouldn't trade with Lorel for the world.

"Allie, these are the most beautiful cats I've ever seen."

Verity sat on the floor, Rudi in her lap, stroking his blue-gray fur. "They're such a gorgeous color."

"They're Russian Blues. Madame said they're sometimes called Archangel Cats." I picked up Raisa and tucked her soft head under my chin. She yowled, but I knew she liked me. She let me cuddle her. "They were from the Russian court. Purebred. Probably the most expensive thing in here. Except for her art. And piano."

"Did Madame give you a list of things to bring to her in the hospital?" Verity said quietly.

"Yes." Raisa leaped softly from my arms. "I just hate the thought of her in the hospital."

I looked at the list on my phone. Slippers, sweater, some clothes. Her prayer book. Her Kindle and her reading glasses.

I went into her bedroom, found a small overnight bag in the closet and set it on the bed, which was covered with a lush dove-gray silk coverlet. A dozen velvet and silk pillows topped the bed. Raisa and Rudi leaped onto the bed, watching us with their wonderful emerald eyes. As I packed the bag, Verity picked up a small book from the bedside table. "I think these are jewels on the cover," she whispered.

Madame Monachova had always been an exotic creature to me, as exotic to me as her wonderful cats. No one else in Mystic Bay looked like her—like a star, with designer dresses, Parisian silk scarves, fur coats. But seeing her clothes in the bottom of the suitcase brought home to me the fragile real woman underneath the glamour. I clicked the locks on the suitcase. "Let's go."

"Hospital or police station?"

I sighed. "I better get the police over with."

"Drop me back at my car," Verity said. "I have a feeling that may take a while."

An hour later, I left the police station. As Bronwyn had said, all hands were on deck at the Parish Cemetery. I gave my statement to a guy who told me that the police would be in touch. My stomach churned. I hoped no one thought I had anything to do with the death of Max Hempstead.

* * *

At Mystic Bay Hospital, a policewoman stopped me at the door to Madame's room. "She's sleeping," she said shortly.

"She asked me to bring her things." The woman took the overnight bag.

"Can I wait? So I can speak to her?"

The officer glanced back into the room. Over her shoulder I saw Madame, her hair braided into one plait over her shoulder. She lay on her side, huddled under a sheet, wires attached to beeping machines. Alone.

My shock must have shown on my face.

The policewoman exhaled and her tone warmed. "Listen, I think she's sedated. Come back tomorrow."

Chapter 16

Back at the Mermaid, I had to park on Pearl Street because our lot was so jammed with cars. When I went in the front door, Lorel was at the counter with Hilda, taking orders. Lorel looked cheerful.

Something was up.

As I crossed the dining room to join them, I passed the ceiling-mounted television that was almost always tuned to news, cooking, or game shows. Today it was a travel show, a repeat of *Foodies on the Fly* that had showcased Aunt Gully and the Lazy Mermaid. The show had put us, literally, on the map. The Mermaid was a stop on at least a dozen food tours, their buses inching through Mystic Bay's narrow streets to drop off dozens of hungry tourists at a time.

It wasn't just the food that brought them. The shack was only yards from the sparkling Micasset River. Sailboats, pleasure boats, and even historic ships from the Maritime Museum upriver were a constant, photoworthy backdrop for our diners' selfies. Picnic tables and candy-color Adirondack chairs made it easy for diners to relax and enjoy the scene.

Plus, the inside of the shack was unforgettable. Most shacks and seaside restaurants are decorated with a nautical theme: mounted fish, oars, netting, model ships, carvings of old mariners in yellow slickers and sou'westers smoking a pipe. The Mermaid's walls had that and more, covered with what Aunt Gully called her mermaidabilia, her collection of some of the most unusual and frankly kooky mermaid collectibles imaginable. People sent her mermaids from all over the world—just last week a fan in Singapore had sent her a mermaid carved from jade.

Something struck me. I went back outside. Our mermaid figurehead had no leis.

I went into the kitchen. "Hey, no leis on our mermaid this morning? No prank on Halloween?"

"Not a one and no beer bottles, either," Hector said. "I guess the police patrols have helped."

Hector and Hilda pelted me with questions about the party and Max Hempstead's murder. I filled them in.

"People are saying Otis Parish is walking again," Hector said.

Aunt Gully bustled in. "Nonsense! Allie, you'll be glad to know that Fred called. Lobzilla is safe in a tank at his lab. It was touch and go for a while, but Fred thinks that Lobzilla wasn't out of salt water for very long. God only knows where he'd been."

If only the big fella could talk. He was a witness to murder. "Thank goodness he's okay." I washed my hands and looped my pink Lazy Mermaid apron over my head.

Hector wiped sweat from his brow with the back of his muscular forearm. "Allie, I heard you went to see Madame Monachova." The speed that news traveled in Mystic Bay always astonished me. "How's she doing?"

"She was sleeping. I'll go back later to check in on her."

Aunt Gully stirred her chowder. "Poor woman. How on earth did she get blood on her cape if she wasn't anywhere near the body?"

The same thought had been troubling my every waking moment. How could that happen?

"Hey, everyone." Lorel and a man in his forties wearing a black T-shirt, khaki shorts, and very expensive running shoes edged into the kitchen. "I want you to meet someone."

Lorel's guest had a slim build and his legs were muscular. Runner. His sandy, thin hair was combed over, and his teeth so blazingly white I thought they must be fake. He carried a huge basket of fruit piled into a pyramid and topped with an orange bow.

He inhaled, "Ah! THAT AROMA. That's what I'm talkin' about!" He held out the basket—full of oranges, grapefruit, mangoes, apples, and more I couldn't see. "For you, dear Gully."

"Oh, my! That's too much. Thank you." Aunt Gully took the basket and looked around for a space large enough to set it down. Finally she put it on the desk in the office off the kitchen.

"Greetings." Hector put a lobster in the steamer.

Aunt Gully smiled. "Well, beware of Greeks bearing gifts! May I help you?"

"Aunt Gully, this is Don O'Neill. He's a principal with Chowdaheads. Remember I told you we met at a conference?"

I folded my arms and threw a glance at Hector. *You "met" him after he'd been bombarding Aunt Gully with letters for a month.*

"How do you do?" Aunt Gully said. "Would you like a cup of chowder?" Instead of seeming surprised or annoyed that Lorel had blindsided her, she was being her usual charming self. She ladled the chowder into a mug with a spoon and handed it to him. "Crackers?"

He took the mug. "I could eat this all day, Gully! You're a talented woman. And so's your daughter."

Lorel didn't correct him.

"Niece," I said.

"Well, it's just the resemblance is so strong. I see where she gets her beauty." He shoveled in a spoonful of chowder.

I couldn't help but roll my eyes. *Amateur.*

"Why don't we go outside and chat." As Lorel, Aunt Gully, and Don went out the screen door, Aunt Gully winked at me. I laughed.

If it had been me, I'd have thrown him out, but Aunt Gully took the high road, as always. Well, soon she'd have him laughing, and telling her his life story, and out of here in a few minutes, convinced that he'd convinced her. He'd be wrong.

"Your sister." Hector shook his head. "She's unstoppable. Nice fruit basket, though."

"It's as big as Aunt Gully!"

I watched Don, Lorel, and Aunt Gully sit at our meeting room, the wobbly picnic table just outside the kitchen door. "Watch Aunt Gully work. I give it five minutes. He'll leave smiling, thinking that he's won her over."

Bit banged through the back door and hefted a bucket of live lobsters next to Hector. "Allie! You're okay!"

He ran to me and threw his skinny arms around me. I hugged him back, letting my cheek rest on his silky black hair. Bit looked up, tears brimming in his beautiful green eyes. My heart squeezed.

"I was worried about you! That guy got killed and I heard you were there."

At the steamer, Hector had gone still.

"I'm fine, Bit. I'm fine really." I gave him another hug. "And where's Lobzilla?"

"Good news. I just heard that he's okay. He's in a nice comfortable tank in Fred Nickerson's lab at the college."

Bit brightened. "I'm going to ask if I can go see him." To my surprise, his lips turned down. "Lots of people were making jokes about Lobzilla, but I didn't think it was funny. He's old. He deserved better." Bit ran back outside.

"I hope he doesn't know too much about that business," I said. "It was just awful, Hector, grotesque."

Hector dumped a basket of cooked lobsters on the stainless-steel table for me to pick. "You know how people talk. Saying all kinds of weird stuff. But it is weird."

"True. Why was that lobster by the body?" I went to the stove to stir Aunt Gully's chowder. As my fingers wrapped around the wooden handle of the spoon, a memory surfaced. "Hector, that wasn't the only weird thing about last night." I told him about the Witch's Rock, the wooden spoon, and what Delilah had told me. "By the light of the half-moon, the spell is cast to change a person's mind."

To my surprise, Hector threw his head back and laughed. "Oh, that's rich. Don't tell Hilda—"

Hilda came into the kitchen. "Don't tell Hilda what?"

Hector pressed his lips together. Hilda gave him a look. He sighed. "Tell her, Allie."

I told Hilda what I'd found on the Witch's Rock altar by the Parish cemetery.

Hilda's dark eyes widened. "Not good. Not good."

"Don't worry," Hector said. "Gully's got too much good juju to be bothered by some silly spell."

"Mark my words—bad thoughts become bad actions. I hope I'm wrong, but this is not something to take lightly."

"You know, maybe it wasn't even Aunt Gully's spoon." As I said the words, I didn't believe them. Beltane wanted Aunt Gully to change her mind. The ceremonial candles were arranged just as Delilah had described. The little bundle of licorice for the spell was missing, but it could have blown away, or been burned. I'd ask Aunt Gully if she was missing a spoon, just to be sure.

Minutes later we watched Aunt Gully wave as Lorel and Don O'Neill left.

Aunt Gully came through the kitchen's screen door, thoughtful, quiet.

Hector and I shared a glance.

"Where's Lorel?" I asked.

"Heading back to Boston." Aunt Gully washed her hands and put on her apron.

"Well?" I handed a plate of lobster rolls through the pass-through to Hilda.

"Maybe." She tasted her chowder and added some white pepper. "Maybe I should listen to your sister. Give Don's company a listen."

"Really? Was it the fruit basket that changed your mind?"

"Just kidding." She winked at me, but then turned serious. "You know me, Allie. I'm happy here. This is my dream come true. But—" She stirred and tasted again. "Am I being too hasty? Maybe your sister's right. Maybe I could grow. I should be practical, consider things like retirement. I told Lorel I'd think about it. With all that happened to you last night, I just got to thinking about how life can turn on a dime. That's all I'm going to do.

Think about it tonight in my bathtub with a nice glass of book club brandy." She lifted her hand holding the spoon skyward and started to sing.

"Wait a sec." I pointed at the spoon. "Have you lost a spoon lately, Aunt Gully?"

She shrugged. "Can't say I keep track of my work spoons but I may have left one behind at the historical society. Why do you ask?"

I turned so she couldn't see my face. Hector threw me a glance. "Just wondering."

Chapter 17

I left an hour later for the college. I'd promised to cover Madame Monachova's Sunday-afternoon beginner ballet class. Her students were subdued. Several told me they planned to visit her at the hospital. After class, I packed up, determined to do the same.

Once outside, I saw students hurry across the green toward the chapel and the back entrance to the campus.

"What's going on?"

A girl read from her phone. "Cops are at the frat house."

I remembered the news. Max Hempstead had been a member of a fraternity.

Maybe someone at the fraternity house could tell me if there was any link between Max and Madame Monachova.

I joined the crowd gathered at the back gate of the college. The road here was quiet, flowing past campus into the shady tree-lined lanes and rolling hills behind the college arboretum. Several stately homes lined the road. One sprawling white building had Greek letters nailed over the door. The house itself was in good repair, but several sagging, worn couches lined the front porch. A dozen recycling bins and trash cans stood waiting for pickup outside, several overspilling with liquor boxes and empty bottles. At least the frat recycled.

A gray sedan pulled from the curb—a state police car. I jogged forward but it pulled away before I could see who was in it. Some guys came down the steps and were mobbed by friends.

I crossed the street. As I climbed the stairs onto the porch I noticed a weather-beaten sign: ABANDON HOPE ALL WHO ENTER HERE. Under the Greek letters was a small shiny brass plate: Parish House. The door was ajar and I went in.

Well, that was easy. I paused in a darkened, wood-paneled foyer. A long living room opened to the left, stuffed with couches and several wall-sized flat-screen TVs. The smell of stale beer hit me. I wrinkled my nose. As I turned to admire the ornate chandelier overhead, my shoes stuck—the floor was sticky, with beer and probably other stuff I didn't want to think about.

"Hey!" A guy with sandy hair and tortoiseshell glasses popped up from a leather couch in the living room.

"Hi." From his hopeful expression, I think he thought I was looking for a boyfriend. There was an indistinct quality to his speech and I looked closer at his chapped lips. He had braces on his teeth and there were two tiny pieces of tissue where he'd cut himself shaving his round pink cheeks. I forced a smile.

"I'm trying to find someone who knew Max Hempstead."

The guy puffed out his chest. "I was just talking with the cops about Max."

He's trying to impress me. I suppressed a smile. "I'm sorry. Were you and Max close?"

He stuck out his hand. His fingertips were orange. I hesitated, then shook. The cheesy dust from his snack transferred onto my hand. I wiped it surreptitiously.

"Cooper Forsythe the Third. They call me Coop. I didn't know Max real well, I just moved in here. But he was a fun guy. Pulled the best pranks. We had rush—"

"Rush?"

"Rush Week. It's where you go to the different fraternity houses and interview. Then if you're lucky the frat you want picks you. But this is a small school and there's only one frat, so you either get in or you don't. My dad was a legacy. Same with Max, he's, well, was a legacy, too." He frowned. "I didn't know him well. He was a junior. He was always busy. Double major. History and business."

"Not marine biology?"

Coop held out the snack bowl to me. I shook my head. He swept up the last of the chips and licked his fingers. "Everyone takes marine bio because you get to go out on boats with Professor Nickerson. Max liked being on the water."

"Anyone here who knew him well?"

"His big brother."

His brother? "His brother's here?"

"Not his brother, brother. I think he was an only child. We all get matched with an older fraternity brother. Nate Ellis was Max's big brother, he's president of the frat. He was just talking with the cops. They were close, so he took it hard."

"Can I talk to him?"

"He said he was going to the freshman bullpen." Coop nodded toward the stairs. "After you." I took a breath and headed up. He followed so close behind I could smell the salty snacks on his breath.

"Why do you want to talk to him? Are you a cop?"

"Do I look like a cop?" I turned, not sure I hoped I looked like a cop or not.

He raised his eyebrows. "I get it. You're a private eye hired by the family to solve his murder."

This story was better than anything I had prepared. "Something like that."

"Oh, I know." He tapped his nose, smeared it with orange dust. "You're not at liberty to say."

I gave him what I hoped was a mysterious smile and resumed climbing the stairs.

"One more floor." We went along a gallery lined with beer posters and deer heads, their antlers strung with Christmas lights and—I squinted—multicolored bras and panties of every type, through a doorway, and up a narrow stairway. *Ugh. Everything I'd heard about frats is true.*

We passed a bathroom. Towels and shower slides were piled on the floor. The reek of sweaty clothes and sneakers was overpowering. I held my breath.

"There he is, in the freshman bullpen." Coop hurried in front of me and through an open door. I stepped into a long narrow room that appeared to run the length of the house. Eight beds lined the walls, each with a small desk and chair next to it. Computer screens and equipment crowded every surface. There was a footlocker at the end of each bed. The funk of sweaty workout wear and sneakers asserted itself despite the cool air flowing in open, unscreened windows.

It was incredible that these guys had this elegant old building yet the students slept in a shabby ward furnished with a mix of yard-sale castoffs. At least their bedding matched, probably bought by their doting moms. I tried to ignore the posters of naked women on the walls and stepped around a heap of dirty laundry. The smell and misogyny and the general air of something kept under wraps had me on edge.

A stocky guy bent over a bed, packing a gym bag.

My guide leaned one hip against the door frame. "Nate, you got a visitor."

Without turning, Nate said, "As long as it's not the cops."

"Nope. And no worries with the cops, I kept it on script."

On script? Had they lied to the cops?

Nate looked up. Surprise registered on his face. I, too, felt a shock of recognition. I'd seen him before. Where?

The party. I'd seen him running off with Isobel Parish.

Nate had the same bland good looks that my guide would have when his braces came off and he got more skilled at shaving. Nate's longer, sun-streaked brown hair and impressive beard were at odds with the pressed, button-down shirt he wore. He jutted his chin at my guide. "Thanks, Coop."

Dismissed, Coop slid back around the corner. I watched him go, making sure he headed down the stairs.

"Are you a . . . cop?" Nate nodded toward a chair with socks drying on the back.

"No, and no, thanks, I'll stand."

His brow furrowed; he was trying to place me.

I launched in before I lost my nerve.

"Rough day?"

He nodded. "Max was my little brother—not related," he said. "Not a bad kid. Some of them are real dorks. He was pretty together."

"He was a junior?"

Nate nodded. "But he was older. He did a gap year, built schools in Guatemala or someplace for a month or so, then just traveled around Asia. Wish I'd done that. So who are you, if you're not a cop?"

"My name's Allie. I was at the party last night. Where he died."

Nate nodded and dug in his bag, avoiding my eyes. He'd been so talkative and now he clammed up.

"Were you at the party?" I knew he was.

"Yeah. But only for a while. There were several parties that night. You know, Halloween, right? I jumped around." His evasiveness set me on edge even more.

I had to get to the point. "Listen, did Max do any dance classes?"

"Dance?" he scoffed. "Oh, I thought you looked familiar. I saw you at the Arts Center. You're with the dance department." He relaxed. I guess he didn't remember me from the party. His eyes traveled to my legs. These guys were so predictable. "Max, dance? No. He played lacrosse and sailed. TA'd for Professor Smith."

"Teaching assistant?"

"Yeah, his usual TA left to have a baby. Usually it's grad students who TA, but Professor Smith is the frat adviser and he—" Nate stopped himself and cleared his throat. What had he meant to say?

"Max helped in the office. Research, running papers." At my quizzical look, he said, "Running papers through plagiarism software, catching cheaters."

"Did Max study marine biology?"

"Max is—was a super student. Brilliant. He had to take marine bio for a science requirement but ever since he just liked visiting with Professor Nickerson. He was even visiting him when they found the superlobster." For a moment Nate looked stricken.

I wondered if Nate had seen his friend's body. I

couldn't remember seeing him, but there'd been so many of us in the dark cemetery.

His jaw worked and he turned his back as he swiped at his eyes. I was reminded how young these guys were. I knew I had to wrap this up.

I pictured Max arguing with Isobel, helping Fred Nickerson in the shack at the Mermaid. Both times he'd carried a backpack. "Did the police take his backpack?"

Nate cleared his throat. "Backpack?" He was quiet for a moment, a moment that told me I'd struck a nerve. "The cops took pictures, took lots of stuff." He turned back to me and jutted his chin at the narrow bed next to him. The covers were rumpled. "The cops searched everything. They took Max's footlocker and all his stuff from his drawers."

He edged around the bed. "They told me to come down after I talk to the chaplain about Max's service. I really should go now." He looked me up and down. "We could meet up later to talk."

Ugh, these guys. "Maybe. Do you think the cops found it? The backpack?"

We went down the stairs.

"Probably it was in his footlocker. Max always kept it locked. Guys steal stuff. Morons."

Nate held the door for me as we left the frat and crossed the street. His expression softened as we approached the chapel. "Max was a legacy but he wasn't a typical frat guy. You can't study in the frat—too much going on—unless you've got superhuman study power with all the noise. Max would go to the basement of the chapel. There's a library there and some study carrels. Normally nobody goes there unless they're desperate."

"Thanks for talking with me."

Now Nate smiled and I felt the force of his all-American charm. I imagined him having to beat off his fellow students with a lacrosse stick. "You should come back later. We're having a party in Max's honor."

I gave him the slightest of smiles. "Thanks. Bye."

He jogged across the lawn. I turned toward the parking lot behind the Arts Center.

"That was useless." I fished my keys from my pocket. I wondered how much a kid paid to live in the frat. Eight kids in a room? And no privacy at all. They did have lockers, but the cops had searched the room. If the backpack was there, they would've found it.

I got in the van and drove past the fraternity house. A lot bothered me: how evasive Nate Ellis was. How Coop admitted to lying to the cops. I sighed. I knew they lied. Coop told me he was taking me to the freshman bullpen and Nate Ellis told me that Max Hempstead was a junior. Did these lies have anything to do with Madame? I was sure Nate and Coop were hiding something, but what?

A party in that beer-drenched frat house definitely did not appeal, but I knew I'd go back.

Chapter 18

At Mystic Bay Hospital, there was no longer a police officer at Madame Monachova's door.

"Did the police leave?" I asked a passing nurse.

She shook her head. "Shift change. Though how they think a lovely woman like that could have anything to do with a murder . . ." she whispered, and continued down the hallway.

A man and a woman sat by Madame Monachova's bed. Madame sat up against the raised head of the bed, a few gray hairs escaping from her braid.

As I entered the room, she reached out her hand to me. "Allie!" Her voice was heavy, indistinct.

I took her hand and kissed her cheeks. Her other hand rested on her stomach, curled, clawlike.

Madame took a deep breath. "My sister, Yulia, and her husband—" She hesitated, confusion and then fear playing across her face. She drew another deep breath. "Russ."

I nodded to them. Madame's voice was so strange, her words slurred. Fear quickened my breathing.

A nurse pushed a cart into the room. "Time to take

your vitals and get you ready for bed. Would you all please give us some privacy for a few minutes?"

Russ, Yulia, and I stepped into the hallway.

"Coffee?" Russ asked.

I shook my head.

"Yes, please, darling," Yulia said.

Russ walked down the hallway to the elevators. Yulia and I took seats on a couch in a lounge at the end of the hallway.

"Svetlana has spoken of you so often, Allie." Yulia had Madame's high cheekbones and petite build, but she was younger, her thick chestnut hair highlighted with just a few strands of silver at the temples. "So proud of you." She took a breath. "We came from the city as fast as we could." Her eyes welled with tears.

I handed her a box of tissues. She took one and dabbed her eyes.

"Thank you. The doctor spoke to us. The shock of finding herself wrapped in a bloody cape, being questioned by the police, it was too much." Yulia shook her head "They think she had a stroke. They have to do more tests." She took a deep, shuddering breath.

A stroke? "Can she . . ."

"She can walk but she has"—Yulia closed her eyes and tears spilled to her cheeks—"weakness in her right arm and leg."

Tears pricked my eyes. Yulia squeezed my hand. "You understand. How difficult this is. How difficult it will be."

I nodded, stricken. A woman who lived for dance, who moved through the world with such grace. I couldn't imagine the road she'd have to travel now. I remembered how I felt when I was first injured. Not just the pain and rehab . . . The loss of identity. Madame was a dancer. She had to dance.

"What can I do to help?"

"The college has someone to cover her beginner class. Is there a way you can keep her advanced class going? I will stay at her house and watch her cats so I can be nearby. I think that would be something she'd want."

The classes were evenings on Tuesdays and Thursdays. I could work that into my dance schedule and I knew that Aunt Gully would want me to help. We'd make it work at the shack.

"Yes, yes. Of course."

"Thank you. I still cannot believe something so horrifying happened to her."

I gave voice to the question that had been on my mind since Saturday night. "Did she say how blood got on her cape?"

Yulia shook her head. "She can barely speak and she has trouble remembering things. The police were here earlier, but the doctor told them that she must rest and can't possibly be interrogated further until she's come through this crisis."

The nurse left the room. "She's sleeping now."

We nodded to her. I gave Yulia's hand another squeeze. "I'll come back tomorrow. Tell her not to worry about her class. I'll take it from here."

Chapter 19

The next morning I hurried downstairs, stuffing tights into my dance bag.

Aunt Gully flipped through my rehearsal calendar hanging near her ancient wall-mounted telephone. "Good thing Boston is only two hours away. Your schedule is crazy."

"I just have to be there while Serge builds the dance for me, then for act 1 rehearsals. Things will really kick into high gear in a couple of weeks when we rehearse with the schoolkids."

The Nutcracker was a huge production with a cast of over a hundred performers, many of them children from local dance schools and the conservatory. Traditionally, the ballet's first act is set in the drawing room of an 1800s Austrian family. Serge wanted to update it with a 1930s Hollywood glamour look to the costumes, which meant even more to prepare with new sets and costumes.

"I'm happy that you're back onstage. In your element. Where you belong." Aunt Gully set a plate of scrambled eggs sprinkled with marjoram and thyme on the table, then a plate of still-sizzling bacon.

She nodded toward a bowl of fruit salad. "And we have plenty of fruit."

The ridiculously large fruit basket sat in the center of the dining room table—it was too big to fit on the kitchen counters. "And that's with me giving most of it to Hector and Hilda, and Bit's family."

"Thanks." I grabbed a few pieces of bacon. "Today Serge is choreographing my solo in the party scene." I knew my dance was a consolation prize for losing my role as Dewdrop in act 2, but Serge was so famous that I was buzzing with excitement.

"A dance by Serge Falco—what a feather in your cap!" Aunt Gully took her seat across from me.

"I'm sorry about not being able to help as much at the shack in the coming weeks, Aunt Gully."

She made a dismissive gesture. "I've got the Gals. Business has slowed since it's November already. And I'm so glad you can help Madame Monachova with her class."

The *Mystic Bay Mariner* lay between us on the table. I could see the headline: FRATERNITY BROTHER KILLED IN GRUESOME HALLOWEEN MURDER. A photo of Royal Parish's palatial home ran with the headline above the fold. I flipped it over to a smaller photo of Max, in suit and tie, grinning. Golden boy, I thought sadly. A patch on the jacket pocket, too small to make out, was probably from an exclusive private school. Next to the article was a photo of Lobzilla with Bertha on one side, Fred Nickerson on the other, each holding the beast by one of his massive claws. The caption read: *"Giant crustacean, seen here at the dock of the Lazy Mermaid Lobster Shack, mysteriously appears at scene of death."*

Beneath that another headline read: "Giant Crustacean Returned to Graystone College Marine Biology

Department." The articles had nothing new to tell me about the death of Max Hempstead.

"Thank goodness Lobzilla made it. Losing him would've been another blow for Fred."

Aunt Gully munched a piece of bacon. "He really wanted that grant from the Foundation to make repairs to his boat."

I nodded. "He wasn't alone. Madame Monachova had also applied for a grant."

Aunt Gully's mouth turned down. "Poor woman. Are you going to see her today?"

"Yes, after rehearsal, if that's okay."

"Of course, give her my best." Aunt Gully sipped her tea. "I'm still giving thought to Chowdaheads."

"Really?"

She held up a hand, still holding a piece of bacon. "I know. I don't want to be too hasty. Your sister's right. I should be practical." She sighed. "Sometimes I feel like I automatically dismiss what your sister wants me to do."

"Because it's always the opposite of what you want to do."

Her eyes sparkled. "In a word, yes."

We laughed.

"And now Don O'Neill's wooing me with a fruit basket," she said.

"It is an impressive fruit basket."

The doorbell rang.

"Who could it be this early on a Monday?" Aunt Gully said.

"I'll get it." I opened the front door and took delivery of a beautiful white box tied with black and silver ribbon. I recognized the ribbon—it was the trademark of the most expensive florist in Mystic Bay.

I set the box on the kitchen counter.

"Well, what on earth?" Aunt Gully untied the ribbon and lifted the lid.

An intoxicatingly sweet scent filled the room as pink roses, with cupped petals and ruffled edges, were revealed. Aunt Gully buried her nose in them.

I read the card and handed it to her.

A pleasure to meet you. Don O'Neill.

"Well, I must say these are some nice blooms." She sighed.

"This is some serious wooing, Aunt Gully."

She inhaled the roses' scent again and smiled. "Maybe I'll think about Chowdaheads a little longer."

Chapter 20

Faces and thoughts jumbled together as I drove north on 95, hardly seeing the traffic. I pressed PLAY on the van's ancient CD player.

Madame Monachova, so small in her hospital bed, hovered in my mind. How on earth had she ended up with blood on her cape? Had she brushed against the murderer? My hands tightened on the wheel. There'd been too much blood for the contact to be accidental.

Had there been any connection between her and Max? I thought of the note promising money that I'd found by Max's body. Madame also needed money for her dance project, but I simply couldn't believe she was connected to Max's murder.

So much of what had happened at the party was unbelievable. What was wrong with Kathleen Parish? Her response to the news of Max Hempstead's murder had been so extreme. Of course she would have been shocked, but she'd been panicked, afraid. No, terrified. Then it dawned on me. I'd seen Isobel fight with Max. Isobel, who from what I'd observed was governed by extreme emotions. Was Kathleen afraid Isobel had killed Max?

Kathleen had also mentioned Royal. Did Royal know about Isobel and Max, know that they had a relationship?

Max kept running through my mind. Max at the shack. Max with Isobel. Fighting with Isobel. Both times he'd worn a black backpack. It had been odd, at the shack, that he didn't leave the backpack in the car even though it had gotten in the way.

Why?

Nate Ellis had also been upset, naturally. He and Max were friends, fraternity brothers. I remembered him dancing with Isobel at the party, so he knew her as well. He'd also reacted strangely when I asked about the backpack.

What was in the backpack?

Well, the cops would find it. *Or would they?* Coop's words came back to me over the pounding eighties soundtrack of Aunt Gully's CD.

On script. The fraternity brothers lied. Lied about Max, a junior, sleeping in the freshman bullpen. That meant they didn't want the police to see his room.

My fingers tightened on the wheel. I had to find and search Max Hempstead's room.

And more than anything, find out how Max's blood had gotten on Madame's cape.

At company class, everyone gathered around but I was relieved they weren't asking about the murder. Everyone wanted to know about Madame Monachova. A hushed feeling spread throughout the company. She was beloved, an icon, and a stroke was a devastating blow that any dancer could relate to.

I was glad when Serge took me to a studio to work out my solo. I loved him because he pushed me hard, as hard as he had before my injury. The only difference was that I wouldn't be dancing this role on pointe or do any difficult jumps. My ankle strength just wasn't reliable yet. But Serge took that as a challenge and the dance he created for me was just as beautiful and satisfying as any I'd danced before.

After rehearsal, Serge gave me a quick kiss. "When you see her, give my love to Svetlana. Oh, and go see Virginia in the costume shop. She has surprise for you."

As I left the studio, music seeped out of a practice room next door—the music for the Dewdrop's dance— the role that was supposed to be mine.

I couldn't help it. I peeked in the glass door.

Margot Kim spun past, her trademark ponytail whipping the air. Margot lived in the same group house where I'd lived with some dancer friends. Well, I wouldn't call her a friend. Margot was phenomenally talented and phenomenally mean. The only time she'd really been nice to me was the day I'd fallen down the steps and broken my ankle. She'd called an ambulance and stayed with me as I lay, dazed, on the cement floor at the foot of the cellar stairs.

I watched the assistant artistic director coach her in the Dewdrop's dance, which calls for incredibly quick and precise footwork.

"No, no, Margot. Quick, quick, quick." She clapped her hands. "You're behind the music."

Margot, face red and sweaty, nodded, her chest heaving as she panted.

I stepped away from the door before she could see me. Margot was struggling.

Good.

* * *

Downstairs in the costume shop, a woman with gold curls and impish sea-green eyes looked up from a worktable, pins in her teeth. Virginia Aldous was our costume maven.

"There you are!" In her broad Boston accent, *are* came out as *ah*.

We hugged.

"Got something special for ya!" She led me to a mannequin wearing a floor-length gown. "Serge wants 1930s Hollywood glamour, so that's what Serge will get. Based this on a Rita Hayworth number, copied the lines, don't tell anyone. Top's fitted, but the skirt's pretty full so you can move. This gold silk's gonna look great with your hair. Serge himself wanted gold. He never comes down here, but for you—"

She squeezed my arm. She knew how hard this was. I could see the Dewdrop costume hanging on a rack behind her, a pink and silver dream, with a tiny abbreviated tutu that wouldn't get in the way of all the crazy difficult footwork.

I turned back and ran my fingers along the satiny fabric of my new costume.

"I love it." It was the truth.

"Hope so, it was a royal bee yotch—excuse my French—took me three hours to get that beading right." We laughed and I slipped it on. The costume fit perfectly but still my eyes strayed back to the Dewdrop costume.

Virginia tilted her head. "Here, look."

She took down the bodice of the Dewdrop costume and flipped open the back. Ballet costumes are shared— several dancers will rotate through a role and the costume is cleaned after performances. The bodice is separate from the tutu. A row of hooks and eyes go down the back, so each ballerina can adjust the fit.

Name tags are sewn inside for each dancer taking the role.

Margot Kim. Kellye Garrett. Dawn Atkins. Allegra Larkin.

"I left your name in. I figure you'll be back. Like a bad rash."

I could barely get out the words. "Thanks, Virginia."

Chapter 21

I drove to Mystic Bay Hospital. Inside, I waved to a group of dance students from the college as we passed each other in the hallway outside Madame's room.

Yulia sat beside the bed as her sister slept. "So nice her students came. She could only speak for a few moments, then fell asleep," Yulia whispered.

Under a thin white blanket, Madame lay so still.

"Should she be sleeping this much?" I whispered.

"The doctor says it's how the brain heals."

I nodded. "When she wakes up tell her that everyone at the ballet sends their love. Especially Serge."

Yulia's lips curved in a small smile. "He's still a devil?"

"Yes."

"Your aunt came. She left that." She nodded at a vase of pink roses and a bowl of fruit. "Such a generous lady."

"Did the police say anything?"

Yulia shook her head. "A woman detective came. Very professional and businesslike, dark hair pulled back very tight, tailored suit. Very"—she searched for a word—"controlled."

I'd met her before. Detective Rosato. *Good grief.*

I managed to smile and wish Yulia good night before slipping out, my mind whirling.

Detective Rosato was with the state police. Like many towns in Connecticut, Mystic Bay was too small to have its own expensive homicide squad or crime labs. I'd endured her probing, unblinking gaze, her emotionless, precise, almost robotic voice.

How on earth could anyone think Madame Monachova could kill a strong young man like Max Hempstead? He was a junior in college. A lacrosse player and a sailor.

But . . . she was a dancer. In her seventies, true, but in great shape. Maybe she'd surprised him. It was not probable, but possible . . . I hated to think this way about Madame, but I'd learned in the past summer that people could be capable of things you'd never expect.

Still, I'd never believe she was guilty.

Who'd want to kill Max Hempstead? Isobel Parish. I'd seen her fight with Max. *I hate you,* she'd screamed.

I swallowed—Isobel had been wearing a sword at the Halloween party.

Was that why Isobel's mother Kathleen freaked out so badly when she heard Max was dead? Did she know that her daughter and Max had fought? That would explain her extreme reaction when she'd heard Max was killed. She'd totally lost it.

Kathleen had also asked about Royal. Old-fashioned Royal Parish. I couldn't believe the way he'd pulled his daughter aside at a party to talk about the family honor.

A thought jolted me. Maybe Kathleen didn't think Isobel killed Max. Maybe she thought her husband had. Part of me hoped this was true. I'd liked Isobel and I didn't like the way Royal had grabbed her.

Still, Detective Rosato had come to the hospital to see Madame. The police focus was on her.

My mind settled as I got into the van. Detective Rosato was a dogged investigator. I'd be just as dogged to prove that Madame was innocent. With Detective Rosato on the case, Madame would need me in her corner to find the truth.

I'd talk to Isobel. I knew where to find her. The fencing class met right down the hall from Madame Monachova's dance class at the Arts Center.

Chapter 22

The next day, I received a text from college administration asking me to fill out some paperwork in their office. While Madame Monachova was in the hospital, I'd be the instructor of her class. I wouldn't be paid more, of course, but paperwork must be done.

I'd go after my shift at the Mermaid.

Officer Petrie came in for chowder to go. "I was just up at Parish cemetery. State police released the scene but we had to set up a security perimeter. Had lots of trespassers disregarding the crime scene tape. Lots of crazies going up to the graveyard to visit old Otis. Some say Otis is walking again."

Aunt Gully snorted. "Pish!"

I headed to campus at four, giving me an hour before my class started and time, I hoped, to see Isobel Parish at her fencing class after I handled the paperwork for Madame's class.

The administration building was one of the oldest on campus, three stories of gray granite with a broad outdoor stairway leading to tall glass doors. I ran up the steps and went in.

As I hefted my bag and ran upstairs to the second floor, I passed giggling girls and a guy who almost bumped into me since he was looking at the screen of his phone instead of where he was walking.

Sometimes I envied students here—the luxury of studying topics that intrigued them, no responsibilities outside those of class or sports.

I'd been a nontraditional student all my life. I'd left my junior year at Mystic Bay High School to attend the New England Conservatory, a school of the arts in a quiet town in northern Connecticut. There had been academic requirements, but mostly it was dance class, music, history of dance, and performance. Instead of going to college, I moved from the conservatory into the preprofessional level at New England Ballet Theater, sort of a farm team. I danced in the corps de ballet, but in a couple of years moved into more important roles. As Dewdrop, I'd finally have the coveted title soloist.

I pulled up short. I'd been so lost in my reverie that I'd walked down the wrong hallway. Now I stood in a reception area with wood-paneled walls, a cushy leather couch, huge leaded windows, and a large fireplace. A discreet sign read HISTORY DEPARTMENT.

Four doors led off the reception lobby. A familiar painting hung over the fireplace: A man in colonial garb, pilgrim hat, flowing black cape, his pointed chin held high. His very arrogance was a magnet. I stepped closer. Deep-set dark eyes looked to the distance, which included a harbor, as he pointed to a map on the table. The artist must have imagined him standing on this very hill, since the college looked out over the same harbor.

I'd seen this painting before in the library at Royal Parish's house. Isobel had shown it to me. The Parish sword had hung next to it over the mantel.

A student sprawled on the couch, headphones on, head bobbing, his arms and legs spread wide, hogging the couch. I sat in a hard, straight-backed chair and angled my camera at the portrait to snap a picture. I wanted to look at it later.

There were four magazines on the coffee table, all issues of *New England Scholarly History*. The subhead on the top one read: "The Diary of Rosamund Parish: Colonial Women, Emerging Voices." Rosamund Parish? I did a double take, then flipped the magazine open to "The Diary of Rosamund Parish" by Lyman Smith, an alphabet soup of initials and degrees following his name.

A door behind me opened and I heard a familiar voice.

"Glad we had a chance to make sure we're on the same page." I remembered his satisfied tone from the grant presentation. Royal Parish, Isobel's father. I lifted the magazine to cover my face.

"Thanks again for stopping by, Royal. It's rough, but I'll manage. You know Max was really important to the department and the frat. We'll continue, certainly. I'll have another TA very soon." The deep voice that answered belonged to Lyman Smith.

I set the magazine in my lap, turned away from them, and hunched over my phone. I hoped they wouldn't recognize me. They'd think I was stalking them.

Just then Fern Doucette wheeled Prudie in a stroller around the corner. Fern's hair was glossy, held back with a headband. She wore a sweet floral dress, marred by an orange splotch on one shoulder. Prudie saw me, reached out, and bounced in her seat.

Fern blinked, then smiled. "Seems you've made a friend. Prudie remembers you."

"Hi." I tried to keep my face angled away from Royal and Lyman. "I remember her, too."

Royal passed by, his shoes ringing on the polished floors. Fern nodded to him and he gave her a brief nod back.

Fern raised her chin, her fingers tightening on the stroller handles. "Lyman, may I"—she cleared her throat—"speak to you for a few minutes? About my job?"

I threw a glance over my shoulder.

Professor Smith made a show of looking at his watch. "I have another appointment very soon."

She looked at the magazine in my lap. Her voice shook. "It's important. It won't take long."

"Very well. I have only ten minutes, Fern."

I remembered—Max had taken Fern's job when she went on maternity leave. Maybe she'd know if there was a connection between Madame Monachova and Max Hempstead.

"Can I talk to you about something? When you're done? Just for a couple of minutes?" I whispered.

Fern nodded. "Sure." She frowned. "It looks like I'll be out of this meeting soon."

"I'll meet you here."

I gathered my things as she passed by me. I threw another look back.

Lyman Smith looked every inch the history professor. Stylish dark glasses, bow tie, vest over a button-down shirt. His corduroy jacket even had suede patches on the elbows. With his high cheekbones and firm jaw, he looked like a model playing a professor.

"Thanks for squeezing me in, Lyman." Fern's voice

had an edge at odds with her sweet round face and floral dress.

They went into his office.

I rushed down the hall to the administrative office. Thank goodness there was no line and I was able to sign my paperwork and rush back to the history department. Moments later, Professor Smith's door opened and Prudie's wailing filled the hallway.

Fern's broad face was crumpled. She was trying to keep her composure but her lips trembled and her eyes brimmed behind her thick glasses.

"What happened?" I said.

She shook her head. Prudie reached for me.

"Do you have time for a quick cup of coffee?" I asked.

She took a deep breath. "There's a café in the basement."

We took the elevator and minutes later we sat with hot drinks on a patio behind the building.

"Sorry. I'm a mess. I just went through hell to get child care set up for Prudie so I could get my TA job back, but then Professor Smith tells me that he doesn't have an opening. Max died three days ago! He'd promised to rehire me when I was ready to come back. He said my work was exemplary. Now he said he'd give me a recommendation for a job elsewhere—oh, the way he said *elsewhere*—but how does that look? He didn't rehire me himself? Like he couldn't wait to get rid of me."

"That's awful." I'd heard Lyman Smith tell Royal Parish, *We'll have another TA soon.* Lyman lied. Clearly, he didn't want Fern back.

Prudie chewed on the ear of a terry-cloth puppy dog.

"So what did you want to ask me?" Fern said.

"Do you know, did Max Hempstead ever take any dance classes? Or know Madame Monachova?"

Fern blinked. "Max? Dancing? I'm sorry I don't know a Madame Monachova. Oh, wait, Svetlana Monachova. She was one of the grant applicants. I don't remember Max ever mentioning dance classes. He might have met her at the grant presentation?"

Somehow, I didn't think so. It was worth a shot. "I know Madame Monachova. She was questioned by the police about Max's murder."

"How terrible," Fern said, but I could tell her mind was elsewhere.

"Damn Professor Smith." She rooted in her pocket for a tissue and blew her nose. "Max replaced me when I left for maternity leave, though generally TAs are grad students, not undergrads. While I was on leave, I started doing my own research, showed some of my projects to Lyman Smith. Max handled the paperwork. Which he could barely do."

I remembered what Nate Ellis had said. "Running papers?"

She grimaced. "There are some web sites out there that sell papers to kids who don't want to bother to research and write their own." Bitterness made her words sharp. "Or they don't quite get the meaning of plagiarism. You know, that's hard for a college student. Don't take other people's words and pretend you wrote them."

She nodded toward the fraternity house. "There's a rumor that the frat keeps a drawer of A papers that the brothers can use if they get in a bind."

"Would the software catch that?" *Had Max discovered some student's cheating? Would it be worth murdering him, to keep it silent?*

"Not if the original work wasn't in the database. Besides, some kids just hire someone to do their papers. Easier, the work is original, nobody gets hurt. Except for the integrity of the entire educational process." Blotches bloomed on her pale cheeks.

"Are you okay?"

She took a deep breath. "Professor Smith is such a jerk. I did a lot of research on women in colonial times. Lyman and I authored a paper together. Well, I thought together. There was no mention of me as his second on the paper that just got published in *New England Scholarly History*." The magazine I'd seen in Lyman Smith's office.

"Second?"

"Coauthor. Big deal to publish an academic paper. Lyman told me that Max sent in the article but made a clerical error that left me off. A clerical error! He says he'll get it fixed, but in the meantime, he's getting all these accolades for his groundbreaking work. And I get no job and no credit because Max Hempstead made a fricking clerical error."

"You don't believe that, do you?" *Had her professor stolen her work?*

Fern laid her head in her hand. "No. Not for a minute. Lyman took all the credit. But that's the story I'll stick to if I want a job. Lyman is the only professor I've ever worked with. I need a recommendation from him to get into any decent PhD programs. There's no proof that he stole my work."

"I'm so sorry."

Fern didn't seem to hear. "My word against his."

The clock chimed the quarter hour. "I'd like to hear more but I have to teach a class."

She gathered her things. "And we have to get to Mommy and Me Yoga."

"At Blissful?" I took Pilates there.

"Yes."

"Where are you parked?"

"By the Arts Center."

"I'll walk with you."

As I stood and tossed our cups in a trash bin, I looked up. Two stories up, Lyman Smith stood at the window, watching Fern go. I shouldered my bag. Fern followed my gaze. Smith turned from the window.

"God, I don't owe him anything anymore." She shot me a look. I was surprised to see a small smile playing around her lips. "Did you ever go to the grave of Otis Parish? Hear the stories?"

We hurried down the sidewalk to the Arts Center, Fern pushing Prudie's stroller.

"Yes," I said slowly.

She laughed bitterly. "Oh, how Royal Parish hates those stories. That's why . . ." She hesitated then continued, "We did studies in the graveyard. To disprove all that business about Otis Parish and Uriah Parish."

"What kind of studies?"

She seemed to come to a decision. "Lyman and Royal can screw themselves. Royal wanted to prove once and for all that the stories about Otis Parish were just stories. We did research. Of all kinds."

Her face took on a sly look. "Absolutely fascinating. They dug up lots of new discoveries."

"Dug up." I remembered the stakes and string in the graveyard. It dawned on me what they reminded me of— an archaeological dig. "You mean . . ." *Oh my God, did she mean . . .*

The clock in the tower tolled five, breaking the spell of her words. Fern laughed.

"Royal Parish is so arrogant! He thought he knew

better than three hundred years of folk wisdom. Come on, Prudie. Let's go get mommy some Zen." Prudie waved to me as they turned into the parking lot. "Sorry about your friend, Madame Monachova."

"Thanks. Um, did you mean—"

"I'll see you at Blissful!"

She pushed the stroller across the parking lot to a battered gray sedan with several stickers on the rusted bumper. I ran toward the Arts Center.

Dug up. Did she mean they had dug up the grave of Otis Parish? I'd felt the soft earth beneath my feet.

I shook myself. *Overactive imagination, Allie.* One thing was certain, there was no love lost between Professor Smith and Fern Doucette. Had that animosity spilled over toward Max? Had Fern been jealous?

Had she been at the Halloween party? I didn't remember seeing her. I'd assumed she'd taken Prudie home after the grant presentation. I could imagine how Fern would feel, not getting any credit for her work. Would she be angry enough to kill Max for his part in derailing her career?

It was too late to go to the fencing class to speak to Isobel, so I ran to the dance studio. There was an envelope taped to the door, "Allie" scrawled on it in bold, black marker.

I tore it open.

"Allie, could you please come see me? I want to talk to you about something I found." The note was signed Isobel Parish, with her cell number.

My mind whirled. *What could she have found? Something to do with Max's murder?*

Thank goodness dance class went smoothly. Even though my thoughts were distracted by Isobel's note, I enjoyed the class. The joy I felt, watching the students as they mastered complicated steps, surprised me. The hour-and-a-half class flew by.

I wished the students good night, turned off the lights, and closed the door. I watched the last students leave the building then dialed Isobel's number.

She didn't pick up. I left a message and drove home, mulling what news she had for me.

Chapter 23

Isobel didn't return my call so I texted her the next morning that I had to be in Boston for rehearsal. She texted back. *Come to Parish cemetery 7 P.M. Meet me at gate at Old Farms Road.*

The cemetery? I hesitated but texted back, *See you then.*

In Boston, I did a rehearsal with two dancers who would understudy my role, Dawn Atkins and Kellye Garrett, terrific dancers and good friends. Then we dressed in our costumes and joined the rest of the company for some publicity shots.

No surprise, Margot pushed to the front of the group, smiling coquettishly. I straightened my shoulders, determined to stay positive. Margot in her Dewdrop costume was the epitome of ballet pretty. Her pink lipstick matched the costume perfectly, her dark hair pulled back into a high bun, not a hair out of place.

"Oh, I'm in love." The photographer started shooting her, having her pose in different positions. "Perfect."

"Am I your cover girl?" Margot said.

The photographer laughed. "The editor will let us know."

Kellye squeezed my hand.

"I'm okay." And I was. The gorgeous dress Virginia had designed for me made me feel powerful. My dancing was going well. I was having fun and I wasn't going to let Margot spoil it.

"Oh my gawd." The photographer's eyes lit up. He took my hand and spun me around. "Baby, you sure do Hollywood glamour right."

"It's easy in this outfit."

The photographer took several shots and gave me a thumbs-up.

As I drove back home from Boston, I basked in a glow. The shoot had made me feel great. Plus, somehow, I finally felt confident that my ankle was completely healed. It was only a matter of time until I could dance full-out again.

But as the familiar exit for Mystic Bay approached, I grew restless as I remembered what I planned to do at 7 P.M. Should I be wary of meeting Isobel Parish alone in the graveyard? And wasn't it a crime scene? Was this legal?

A few minutes later I pulled into the driveway of Gull's Nest and called Bronwyn.

"Can you come with me?"

"Rats, I'm still up in Meriden at training. So, Isobel Parish invited you to the cemetery? Then it's not trespassing. It's her property. Just don't go into anything taped off by the cops, okay?" Bronwyn sighed. "I'll be back tomorrow morning. You'll have to tell me every detail. And don't do anything stupid, okay?"

"Okay." It wasn't stupid to go alone, was it? I liked Isobel, but . . . I needed backup.

I called Verity.

"Hmmm," Verity said. "Tell you what. I can go with you and wait safely in the car. Then we can go get dinner at that new Ethiopian place."

My mouth watered. I'd barely had more than some cheese and crackers and an apple in the van as I drove back from Boston. "I love Ethiopian. It's a plan. I'll just have a quick shower."

"I live to serve. I'll drive. If we need a quick getaway, I'd rather have the Tank than Aunt Gully's rust bucket, no offense. I'll be there soon."

I went inside, took a quick shower, then went to the kitchen, stopping to inhale the scent of Aunt Gully's glorious pink roses. A giant box of chocolates sat on the table next to the vase. The box was tied with an elegant red velvet bow. I reached to untie it.

Aunt Gully came into the kitchen, carrying a stack of folded aprons. "Caught in the act!"

"Busted." I picked up the card. "Let me guess."

"Mr. Persistence. Don O'Neill."

I flipped the card over. *Dear Gully, Hope you're doing well. Thinking of you and that great chowder. Don O'Neill.*

She lifted the lid and offered me the box. At the rich aroma of chocolate, we sighed in unison. I took the lid and turned it over—it had a diagram showing the different types of chocolates. I love chocolates that have a map of the different types under the lid. I want to avoid getting one with coconut—my least favorite. I selected a chocolate and bit in. Salted caramel and bittersweet chocolate. *Yum.* "Died and gone to heaven."

Aunt Gully picked up her book—*Trouble Is My Busi-*

ness by Raymond Chandler—and tucked it in her tote bag. "I'm bringing the chocolates to share at book club. It's next door at Aggie's tonight."

"You're not really still considering Don's offer, are you?"

"No." She patted the box. "But Don O'Neill doesn't have to know that."

Verity honked from the street. I got in the Tank and we headed toward Rabb's Point.

"I can't remember—did I tell you about the Peeping Tom at the Shack?"

The Tank swerved. "No. What! Are you sure it wasn't Beltane? Trying to cast another spell on Aunt Gully?"

"I'm pretty sure the Peeping Tom was a guy. But . . . Beltane's pretty tall and has strong shoulders," I mused. "No, it was a guy. And this guy could run."

"Beltane gets strong muscles sacrificing goats at the Witch's Table."

I snorted. "It's strange. When we had the break-in at Gull's Nest, the only thing that was disturbed was the kitchen—and now this guy from Chowdaheads is trying to buy Aunt Gully's chowder recipe."

"Maybe you just scared off the thief before he got past the kitchen," Verity said.

"Don't be so reasonable. I don't trust Don O'Neill."

"At least now he's buying Aunt Gully flowers and fruit baskets—"

"And he just sent her a box of fancy chocolates. He changed tactics, is all."

Verity's brow wrinkled. "Aunt Gully's not interested though, right?"

I shook my head. "She's not interested in selling her recipe, but Lorel has her thinking she has to be more practical. I do think she's enjoying the attention."

"Clever woman. I wonder what he'll give her next."

Lorel must think Don O'Neill was a respectable businessman but I would be keeping an eye on Aunt Gully.

Just past a rusted DEAD END sign, Verity steered into Old Farms Road. There were no streetlights and the dark closed in on us. We passed a small cottage at the end of a driveway, yellow light glowing through small mullioned windows.

"That's Beltane's house, isn't it?" Verity said.

"Leave it to her to live here, right down the street from her buddy, Otis Parish. This is the creepiest street in town."

Tree branches overhung the narrow road that threaded between stone walls. It felt like we were driving into a tunnel. The silence grew thick as we followed the yellow headlight beams down the rutted road.

Verity cleared her throat and spoke softly. "Why did Isobel want you to meet here?"

"I don't know." Now it really seemed odd—why didn't she just tell me what she'd found? Or invite me to her house? Hadn't Bronwyn and Officer Petrie said this was a crime scene? "I wonder if there are any cops posted here."

But there were no cars parked in the lane. "Shouldn't there be? Don't murderers always go back to the scene of their crime? Or maybe that's funerals?"

Verity gave me a look. "You sound like Bronwyn."

The Tank drew up to the stone wall by a large willow tree. The dangling branches clawed the roof of the car as Verity pulled as far as she could onto the gravel shoulder of the narrow lane. The cemetery was just on the other side of the wall. Verity cut the engine.

A loud knock rattled my window. Verity and I

screamed. Isobel Parish waved through the glass, up-lighting her face with a flashlight, turning it into a ter-rifying mask looming out of the darkness

I rolled down the window. "You scared the living day-lights out of me!"

"Yeah, sorry. I don't want my parents to see what I'm doing. That's why I wanted you to come in this way." Iso-bel leaned into the car. "Oh, hi, Verity. Thank God the cops have finished up."

I took a deep breath to steady my nerves as I got out of the car.

"How's Madame?" Isobel asked.

For a second her question surprised me, but then I remembered how close her mother and Madame were. "As far as I know she's still in the hospital."

We followed her away from the car, our footsteps loud on the gravel, then swishing through a dense carpet of leaves. Birds called and bats flicked overhead. I pulled my jacket tighter.

Isobel shook her head. "It's awful. I heard the police wanted to question her about . . ." Her voice trailed. "My mom said you were her TA."

I was a TA. Just like Fern and Max had been. "Yes."

There was a bit more moonlight than the night of the party, but still we followed the powerful beam of Isobel's flashlight. I wasn't taking any chances on stumbling over a tree root. I wasn't sure what I'd done with the flash-light Aunt Gully had given me. Verity huddled close and kept an arm on my elbow. I didn't know who was cling-ing to whom, but it helped.

Isobel turned abruptly as the path passed the entrance of the graveyard—a yellow ribbon of police tape sagged across it. The graveyard was encircled by a rough wall of stones. In some places the rocks had collapsed or given way, and those spots were jagged. Isobel kept to a path that curved into the woods.

"Years ago, there was an old dirt road that led to our barn. It's kind of overgrown now," Isobel said.

Something stirred in the woods. Verity and I froze.

"Just squirrels." Isobel waved us on.

I was sure we were passing somewhere near the Witch's Table.

"Don't you worry about witches?" Verity said, giving voice to my thought.

"Bunch of dried-up old sticks who think they're witches," Isobel huffed. "We just hope they don't burn the woods down. Tramp right past all the NO TRESPASS-ING signs like they own the place."

Verity and I shared a guilty glance. Years ago, in high school, we'd been trespassers, too.

"My dad tried putting up a fence years ago, but kids just climbed over," Isobel said over her shoulder as she strode ahead. "One got hurt and sued. Can you imagine? My dad's a lawyer. He knew he'd spend a fortune just set-tling with people looking for a payout. So he took the fence down."

"Don't you have security?" I asked.

"Cameras. But not where the—where Max died," Iso-bel said. "Plus, they were off the night of the party. I don't spy on my party guests." Her tone was defiant, but I knew we were all thinking the same thing: the cameras might have caught Max's killer.

We continued walking in silence.

The path widened to a clearing where two stripes of dirt crested a hill and led to a barn. Spotlights blazed around the building.

I heard the sound of water lapping as we passed a

small in-ground pool. "My dad's lap pool. Salt water's pumped in."

"Ah." I hadn't thought about the role Lobzilla had played in Halloween's events, but now I realized that to keep the giant lobster alive, the thief would have put Lobzilla in salt water. A thought took shape.

"Max—"

Isobel didn't seem to hear me as she strode to the barn. She yanked open the door. Verity and I shared a glance, then followed her into the dark building.

"The cops have been over every square inch of this place, the woods, the graveyard, the house even." Isobel flipped on the lights and slammed the door behind us.

Now that I could see Isobel clearly, her appearance shocked me. Her hair, pulled back into a ponytail, was matted and greasy. She had dark circles under her eyes and her eyeliner was smeared. I wondered if she'd showered since the night of the party.

She kicked a pile of dried newspapers. I stepped closer. Dark strands of seaweed were mixed with the papers.

I crouched and picked up a piece of the newspaper. I sniffed.

There's no getting around it. Lots of things from the sea—drying seaweed, fish, and definitely lobsters—do not smell good. The paper smelled like lobster.

Isobel folded her arms.

"Did you tell the police?" I said.

Verity looked from Isobel to me. "What?"

"The thief must've used a box to transport Lobzilla. And to keep him alive, Lobzilla had to be kept moist. The seaweed and paper would've been soaked in salt water and put around him," I said.

Had the cops missed this? Maybe it didn't start to smell until today? Lobster smelled all the time, but the night of the murder, perhaps Lobzilla hadn't been the cops' first priority.

"What about the box?" Verity asked.

Isobel pushed back her hair. "The cops found one behind the—" She looked away. "Headstone near Max."

I let the newspaper fall from my hand as I stood. "So you kidnap a lobster and bring it here. Why?"

Isobel paced. "Dad's lap pool is filled with salt water, pumped in from the beach. The pool by the house is salt water, too."

I remembered the leis. Max was in the frat. Stealing Lobzilla was a fraternity prank. But he needed a safe place to put Lobzilla. The saltwater pool had been perfect. Most people wouldn't know the Parishes had a second saltwater pool, but Max did.

Isobel wrapped her arms around her waist as if she felt ill. She curled over and walked slowly down the middle of the stalls to a row of hay bales. She sagged onto one of the bales.

"Are you okay?" I joined her, careful not to sit too close. Isobel put her head in her hands.

Verity walked past the stalls, looking into each empty one. "Where are all your horses?"

"Sold. My dad lost interest. He didn't care that I loved them. He needed money for something at the fraternity."

"So you think the frat guys brought Lobzilla here for a prank?" Verity said.

"My dad had a very close relationship with the frat. His blessed frat!" Isobel balled her fists.

"Parish House." I remembered the sign by the frat's front door.

"My grandfather was the founding member. My dad loved it. He's legal counsel for the frat. That means when they get in trouble they come running to my dad. And that's all the fricking time."

She wiped her nose on her sleeve. "They were his surrogate sons. When my mom had me and then couldn't have any more kids, he lost interest in me. According to him I can't carry on the family name. But the guys at the frat—he takes them sailing, let them ride here when we had the horses, throws them parties, gets them internships.

"I started dating Max in September. We met at a big fancy dinner for the frat." She rubbed her arms. She was wearing a denim jacket over a sweatshirt, but still she looked cold. She spoke quietly. "We spent time here. Went swimming in the pool. Max knew this was salt water."

"But Max seemed to like Fred Nickerson. Why would he steal Fred's prize find?"

"Max, when I first met him, wouldn't have. The Max I thought I knew. But the real Max, the frat Max, he loved stupid jokes. He'd stab you in the back to make his stupid fraternity brothers laugh."

"What happened?"

She shook her head. "He was such a liar. A thief and a liar."

"A thief?"

She took a deep breath.

"Our house was broken into last week."

"I remember." Johnny Sabino had gotten the call as we stood in the lobster shed at the Mermaid. "The burglary took place the night before Lobzilla was found."

She nodded. "Our house wasn't really broken into." She swallowed. "Max said it would be fun if he pretended to be a burglar and climbed up the balcony to my room."

Oh, Isobel.

Verity said, "That's romantic."

Isobel gave Verity a withering look. "I was an idiot. So I turned off the security system. And he came over just like he said he would. And the next morning he's gone and my dad's going crazy because stuff was missing from his office."

"Stuff from his office?" I remembered what I'd heard. "I thought on the news your mom said nothing of value was stolen?"

Isobel pushed back her hair. "Dad was missing papers. Important papers. But he can't say that because then his clients would freak out. My dad was beyond livid. I've never seen him like that. And"—she sniffled—"I couldn't tell him it was Max. But I knew it was Max and Max was gone. Ergo . . ."

"Max took the papers," I said.

She buried her head in her hands.

"Did you tell your dad now that Max is . . . ?"

"Are you insane?" Isobel shouted. "Nobody knows, but the way he looks at me! He knows somebody had to have turned off the security system. He knows it was me, for a guy. He just doesn't know which guy."

"You should tell the police," Verity said, echoing my thoughts.

"I don't even know why I'm telling you! I just had to tell somebody!" She jumped to her feet and paced, her voice rising. "I'm such an idiot! Why did I even think he liked me? Max played me. And now he's dead and I'm happy! I'm glad he's dead! I wish I'd done it myself!" Sobbing, she flung herself next to me on the hay bale.

Verity and I exchanged glances, then I moved closer to Isobel. I laid a hand on her shoulder. She jerked away, but remained seated.

"I still hate him." She sobbed but her tears belied her

words. We waited until the storm of her weeping passed. "My mother thinks I killed Max. She knew I was angry with him."

"I thought you were with that other guy at the party?" Verity said.

I'd been thinking the same thing. "Nate Ellis." I thought Isobel would blow up, but she shook her head. "I thought that would help me forget Max." She shrugged.

I thought back to the graveyard and the note I'd found. "Halloween night, I found a note, near Max. It said that he was to meet someone in the cemetery, someone who was going to give him money."

She swore. She let her head fall back and wiped her eyes. "Max needed money. His parents cut him off because he got caught selling drugs. My dad made it all go away for him, but still his father was pissed. He was big on tough love, but without the love. He told Max he had to pay his own fees for the frat."

The barn door jerked open.

Isobel jumped to her feet.

Kathleen Parish ran into the barn, her cheeks flushed, her chest heaving. "There you are!" She flung her arms around Isobel.

Royal Parish followed, his broad frame filling the doorway, his face stern. With a shock, I wondered if they'd seen us on one of their security cameras.

Isobel threw off her mother's arms and pushed past her father into the darkness.

"Isobel!" Royal turned and ran after her. "Young lady, you stop right now!"

Kathleen started after them, but stopped at the door. "You girls—"

Verity and I looked at each other. "We were just going."

Kathleen's eyes darted from me to Verity. She did a double take. "Allegra." Her expression softened.

"Mrs. Parish. Are you okay?"

She ran a hand through her hair. "This has all been awful. It's a nightmare and I cannot awaken." Her expression hardened. "What did Isobel tell you?"

Verity and I glanced at each other.

I thought of the safest thing to say. "She's upset."

Kathleen took a deep breath, trying to compose her face. "Yes, she's upset, she doesn't know what she's saying. Please don't pay any attention."

Kathleen slipped out. Verity and I followed slowly and peered around the door frame. Kathleen and Royal stood just outside, in an embrace. No, he was holding her back as she struggled to escape his arms. We jerked back.

"Kathleen, let her go. Now this is between her and the police." Royal spoke as if trying to calm a small child.

"Royal, how could you? She needs us!" Kathleen shouted.

"She's made her bed." Royal's voice rose. "She has to lie in it! All she's done is brought disgrace to this family."

I peered around the door frame again. Royal's and Kathleen's bodies were illuminated by the light over the door. He held her by her elbows as she fought him.

"This family!" Kathleen wrenched away. "Your perfect family is a disgrace! They were just as barbaric and superstitious as anyone else! And still all you care about is your family name! Not Isobel, not me!"

She pushed him away and stumbled toward the house. Royal swore and stalked after her.

Verity and I looked at each other then hurried in the other direction, toward the dirt road to the cemetery.

"Wow, what was that about?" Verity's whisper was urgent. "She's unhinged."

"They're all unhinged." Isobel's outburst had shaken me, but hearing her parents saddened me, too. "Talk about a dysfunctional family. I feel sorry for Isobel."

We walked as fast as we dared on the uneven ground, our cell phone flashlight beams pulling us along. "There are tire tracks here. Too bad I know nothing about tire tracks."

"So Max took the lobster here because he wanted to leave it on Otis Parish's grave as a prank. Why? Why take it in the first place?"

"Let's face it, Verity. It's a bunch of frat guys. They don't need an excuse to do anything stupid. Max liked pranks. The frat was invited to the Halloween party, right? Max probably figured everyone would go to Otis's grave and wouldn't it be funny to find a giant lobster there. It seems like he didn't mean for Lobzilla to get hurt. He did put him in the right type of water," I mused. "You know, it's funny, did you see Max at the party at all?"

"I wasn't really sure which one he was," Verity said. "He looked like all the other guys in those costumes, with the capes and the pilgrim hats."

"I don't remember seeing him at the party." A memory struggled to surface. When Isobel showed us Royal's office, I'd seen someone with a cape in the hallway. Could that have been Max? He'd been very busy. The party had been in swing for no more than an hour and a half or two hours before his body had been found. He'd probably gone straight from the grant presentation, along the path through the trees behind Parish House, to the saltwater lap pool where he'd stashed Lobzilla. Then he put the lobster back in the box and dragged him to the cemetery. And met—I shivered—his killer?

Verity had been following her own train of thought.

"And didn't you say Max worked with Professor Nickerson? Why would he hurt nice old Fred Nickerson by taking Lobzilla?"

I remembered them in the shack together. There had been affection there. But what had Isobel said? There was Max and there was frat Max.

When we got close to the Witch's Table, Verity turned off her light.

"What are you doing?

"I don't want the witches to see us."

The wind stirred tree branches; something rustled in the underbrush.

"I can't take it. Run!"

We ran back to the Tank.

Chapter 24

Bronwyn texted me the next day. *Meet you at lunchtime. I'm dying for a lobster roll.*

At the Mermaid, Aunt Gully greeted Bronwyn with a big hug. "We haven't seen you in ages."

"My criminal justice classes have been pretty intense," Bronwyn said. "Finally I'm getting into more of the hands-on stuff, less of the theoretical stuff. I'm thinking that I'll apply for the police academy next year."

"How exciting!" Aunt Gully beamed.

We heard a commotion outside the front door of the shack and—violin music?

The door to the shack burst open.

A broad-shouldered African-American man in a tuxedo, top hat, and cape made an entrance, holding a single red rose before him. He wore a half mask like the Phantom of the Opera.

"I'm looking for Gina Fontana," he sang as he set an iPod and speaker on the counter.

Aunt Gully's eyes widened. She spread her arms and stepped around the counter. "Here she is," she sang back.

Hector, Hilda, and Gully's Gals gathered at the kitchen door. Customers rummaged in pockets and purses, then raised cell phones.

Bronwyn and I exchanged glances. *What on earth?*

Holding his cape to one side, the "Phantom" swooped up to Aunt Gully and presented the rose. Her cheeks pinked and she made a little curtsy as she took it. He pressed a button and the violin music segued into the introduction to a love song from one of Aunt Gully's favorite weepy old movies, *Love Story.*

Her eyes lit up. Unfortunately, Aunt Gully knew the song by heart. She and the "Phantom" sang along to the swooning, sappy accompaniment.

I tried not to laugh, but his over-the-top rumbling bass and Aunt Gully's squawking set off a torrent of giggles. Bronwyn's face reddened. She bit her lip as she tried to hold back her laughter but it burst like a dam. Thank goodness Aunt Gully was in on the joke. She loved singing but also knew her nickname was "Gully" for a reason. She was a ham and was enjoying every moment of this spotlight serenade.

"Sounds like a seasick gull caught in a thunderstorm," a customer next to me muttered between torrents of laughter.

I swear the singer's deep bass voice made Aunt Gully's collection of mermaid bric-a-brac rattle on the shelves. Customers raised their cell cameras and filmed. The Lazy Mermaid and its quirky owner would once again go viral.

As the last notes mercifully faded, the crowd in the shack burst into applause. The singer presented Aunt Gully with a small box tied with a black bow and swooped out again.

"Open it!" Bronwyn cried.

Aunt Gully chuckled and high-fived customers. She wiped her eyes. "Oh, I haven't laughed so much in ages. What fun!" She untied the bow and opened the box. Her eyes widened. "Oh, my! Four basketball tickets!"

Hector leaned over her shoulder. "Not just any basketball tickets—those are courtside for the Celtics."

"Lady, your boyfriend must be crazy about you!" a customer said.

Aunt Gully's mouth made a little red O. She looked up and caught my eye.

"Don O'Neill?" I said.

She nodded. I saw a flash of doubt in her eyes before she was swept up by the Gals into a group hug.

Hilda handed Bronwyn a tray with lobster rolls and two cups of hot chocolate. I slipped on a jacket as Bronwyn and I went outside to the splintery picnic table by the shed.

"Aunt Gully has a boyfriend?" Bronwyn set our tray on the table.

I explained what was happening with Chowdaheads and Don O'Neill.

She shook her head. "As long as she's having fun."

"I think." I hesitated. I had no proof that Don O'Neill had broken into Aunt Gully's house.

"What?" Bronwyn prompted.

"Remember we had the Peeping Tom and someone broke into Gull's Nest? I think Don O'Neill is trying to steal Aunt Gully's chowder recipe."

"I'll look into him." Bronwyn took a bite of her lobster roll. "Oh, that's good."

My relationship with Bronwyn, one of my oldest friends, had become complicated by her decision to study criminal justice. Now it looked like she was going to the police academy. I knew that I shouldn't ask her for inside information about Max's murder and I knew I should probably tell her everything I knew about Max's murder. Why did this have to be so difficult?

I sensed Bronwyn was thinking the same thing.

"Allie, this investigation is turning into a political minefield. Royal Parish has been leaning on the police to clear up Max's murder—fast. He's telling them to"—she took a breath—"keep the focus on Madame Monachova."

I gasped. "She wouldn't hurt a soul. Never!"

Bronwyn nodded. "I agree. But he's so well connected. People listen to him. He knows everyone—I mean *everyone*. Of course he's a lawyer, but he's powerful, too. People are afraid of him."

I thought back to the man in Pilgrim garb at the grant presentation. "Have you met him?"

She shook her head.

"He looks so much like his ancestors." I pulled out my phone and showed her the portrait I'd photographed at the history department office.

"What about the daughter? Isobel. Does she look like him and all the ancestors, too?"

"She's got the same nose and chin. I wouldn't say she's pretty, but she's striking. She's intense. Aggressive. Volatile. Like a bomb waiting to go off." I filled her in on the fight I'd witnessed between Max and Isobel. I hesitated, then said, "She's torn up by his theft of papers from her dad."

Bronwyn set down her lobster roll. "Holy crap. You're telling me that Max Hempstead stole papers from Royal Parish?"

My stomach twisted. "That's what Isobel told me. I feel like a rat telling you this." I was a rat. But if Isobel was guilty of Max's murder that had to be brought to light. Madame Monachova was still in the hospital—any further stress brought on by being part of the police investigation would only harm her more.

"Think of what might be in those papers. Maybe that's why people are afraid of him. He knows their secrets." That must be what was in the backpack. No wonder Max didn't let it out of his sight.

Bronwyn looked away, toward the river. There were a fair number of diners at the picnic tables overlooking the water, but now everyone wore jackets and scarves. The sunlight was beautifully golden, but didn't have much warmth. I pulled my own jacket tighter.

"Allie." She took a sip of hot chocolate. "You know what? You have a fan. Detective Rosato."

Her words kindled a satisfied glow in me. I certainly didn't like Detective Rosato—to be honest, she scared me—but I respected her.

"She told me that you have good instincts. So what do your instincts tell you?"

I chewed the last bit of my lobster roll, savoring the combination of the rich lobster meat and buttery toasted bun.

"First of all. Isobel." Could she have been lying to me and Verity? No, it was easy to unburden herself to us because she didn't know us well. "I think she was so upset that she actually would've told us that she killed Max. Her words were, 'I wish I had killed him.'"

Bronwyn, chewed, watching me.

"Second, Max's frat. They're lying."

Her eyebrows flew up. "But I heard they cooperated fully. We got a ton of stuff from them." I noticed she said *we*.

"The police took a bunch of stuff from a room they call the 'bullpen'—it's just for freshmen. Max was a junior. When I went upstairs, Nate Ellis, the frat president, was there, putting stuff into a sports bag. I wonder what he was taking. And one of the guys told Nate that he stayed 'on script' with the cops."

"Whoa," Bronwyn said.

"Did the police find a black backpack?" I told her about the way Max hadn't let it out of his sight. She shook her head. Bronwyn held her body very still. She blocked out everything when she was listening intently.

"Back to Isobel. She and Max had a huge fight when I saw them leaving her fencing class the night before the murder." I swallowed. From what I'd seen she could've killed Max. Maybe she had lied to me and Verity. I explained how Max had pretended to care about Isobel, but was just using her to get into Royal's home office to steal legal papers.

"And then there's a Halloween party two nights later and he's dead." Brownyn tilted her head. "What was her costume?"

"She was a pirate."

"With a sword?" Bronwyn's gray eyes were steady.

"With a sword." I tried to remember what Isobel had called it. "An épée."

"A what?"

"She had a long narrow sword. It was part of her costume."

A cool breeze stirred my hair around my face. I smoothed it back into a bun. "Was Max stabbed with a sword?" I held my breath, wondering if Bronwyn would share that information with me.

Bronwyn said quietly, "Max was hit over the head with a heavy object, probably a rock. Then he was stabbed with a long narrow"—she hesitated—"implement. They're not sure exactly what. In the heart and in the throat." She sipped her cocoa.

I winced. "A lot of kids said Otis Parish killed Max."

Bronwyn rolled her eyes. "And then there's the giant lobster, just to add to the crazy." Bronwyn rubbed a hand through her short brown hair, tousling it.

"Speaking of crazy"—I lowered my voice—"at Witch's Rock I found a bundle of licorice, candles, and a wooden spoon that's part of a magic spell Beltane Kowalski cast to make Aunt Gully join her coven."

Bronwyn burst out laughing, rocking back and forth. "Look what happens when I'm not here." She sipped her hot chocolate and looked toward the parking lot. "Speaking of crazy," she muttered.

Delilah limped toward us and stood by the table, the breeze stirring her coppery red hair, the onyx pendant of the Egyptian cat god nestled on her ruffled purple top. She wore a swirling patchwork skirt that brushed the top of well-worn shearling-lined moccasins. "My bunions are killing me." She leaned on the table. "I came to see how your aunt's doing."

"She's fine, thanks."

Delilah looked at me over white plastic Jackie O sunglasses, her heavy-lidded eyes lined with a peacock's palette of colors. "You owe me a cup of chowder, remember?"

"Oh, that's right." I'd completely forgotten.

Bronwyn looked from Delilah to me. She was trying not to laugh. "I've got to get back to the Plex. Thanks for the lobster roll." She gave me a mischievous grin as she waved and took off.

"Delilah, do you want your chowder for here or to go?" I asked.

She spread her skirt and arranged herself on the seat across from me. "Right here's fine. Fresh air is good. And come back and chat for a minute."

"Oh—kay." I wondered what she wanted to talk about.

I returned with the chowder. Hilda watched, eyes narrowed, from the back door as I sat down with the psychic.

Delilah rubbed her hands, her nail polish bright purple, when I set a tray with the chowder, crackers, and a spoon in front of her. She inhaled. "Ah, the aroma. It's wonderful."

"Thanks."

"Sit down, sit down. You've got a sec, right?" She parked her sunglasses on her head. "Everything's slowed down so much in the fall. Well, for you. Halloween was gangbusters for me."

"I suppose it would be."

"You know, a long time ago redheads were automatically assumed to be witches."

I laughed. "We're dangerous, right?"

She smiled. "Give me your palm."

I hesitated, then held out my hand. I hoped I wouldn't owe her anything else. I felt like everything with Delilah was an exchange.

She took my hand in hers. Multicolored stones sparkled in the rings she wore on almost every finger as she spooned up soup with her other hand, like people scroll their phones or read while they eat. "Hmm . . . good life line. Creativity." Her eyes flicked up. "Very strong curiosity. Love line—a bit of rockiness." She smiled, genuinely. "But then smooth for a long, long time. Just like your aunt."

Despite my mistrust, I said, "You mean with Uncle Rocco?"

She nodded. "Those two were two peas in a pod."

I pulled back my hand. I didn't want to get personal with her. "So what did you want to talk about?" This odd woman was a cross between a gypsy and a witch and an ordinary housewife you'd see at the Big Y squeezing tomatoes.

"Ah, that chowder's so good." She patted her lips with a napkin. "But like I said, I wanted to see how your aunt's doing. If she'd made any changes, you know, decisions."

"You mean about Beltane's group?"

She nodded. "Or anything else."

For a second Don O'Neill and Chowdaheads flashed in my mind. Delilah couldn't know about that. Could she have been the one to put a spell on Aunt Gully instead of Beltane? "Why are you so interested?"

Delilah's lips twisted. "Beltane and I do not have the best relationship. Who am I kidding? I hate her guts. She gives all the rest of us a bad name."

Hilda stepped out the kitchen door carrying a trash bag. She dropped it into the Dumpster and let the lid fall back with a bang. She walked back, waving to me as she passed.

Hilda, my watchdog.

Delilah scraped the last of the chowder from her bowl. "Drama, drama, drama, that's Beltane. She has an orgy in the woods and who does the *Mystic Bay Mariner* call for a quote? Me, that's who. I'm trying to run a respectable business. I can't put up with that crap. It makes me look bad."

"Orgy in the woods?" *In Mystic Bay?*

"She takes her name seriously. Beltane is a holiday halfway between the spring equinox and the summer solstice. It's a celebration of fertility. Long ago there would be, oh, what were they called?" She squinted, trying to remember. "Ah, greenwood marriages, where couples would try each other out, see if they'd have children together. Simpler times." She tugged on her gold hoop earring and burped quietly. "Anyway, Beltane takes herself too seriously and the rest of us pay." She looked out at the river. "And I'm not being entirely honest. " She set down her spoon. "She wanted to oust me, can you believe it? A power grab! When we are a sisterhood!

"So she left. None of us were as extreme as she. None of us. She hooked up with some folks"—she shifted uncomfortably—"I don't know."

"Where do they meet?" I asked, although I was sure I knew.

Delilah lowered her eyes. "A vortex of evil. Of sacrilege and broken taboo so strong, I don't dare go. The echoes are too strong, too dangerous."

"The Parish graveyard," I whispered. She was giving me the creeps. I rubbed my arms.

Delilah nodded.

I stood. "All's good with Aunt Gully. She's not interested in joining the group."

Delilah sighed. "We could use someone a bit younger. We have some members who can't drive at night and the carpooling can get hard to arrange. We're always taking new members, if she's interested in joining a coven, I mean."

I thought of all of the Gully's Gals. "She already has one."

Hilda called from the door. "Code Red. We've got a tour bus rolling in!"

"Sorry, I have to go."

Chapter 25

"Did she try anything weird?" Hilda said.

"No," I said. "Though that was one of the stranger conversations I've had in a while."

When the tour bus rush subsided, I scrolled on my phone to search for information on Delilah. All I found was a Facebook page with a twenty percent off coupon for readings.

I mulled what Delilah had told me about Beltane. A distant memory struggled to surface. Aunt Gully had said something about Beltane having an affair that went wrong with the president of the historical society two years ago. That affair had sent her over the edge, into a new persona.

I also searched online for Mystic Bay Historical Society. Mystic Bay Historical Society and Old Otis Parish House was the name of the site. What a mouthful.

There were dozens of photos from the Parish Family Trust Grant announcement. I scrolled through, surprised by a photo of me talking to Fern. The photo credit read "Photo by Beltane." I shivered. I hadn't noticed Beltane taking the photo. There was a photo of Aunt Gully waving a wooden spoon, her hair frizzing out from under her white bonnet.

I stopped at the photo of a group around the lucky grant winner, Professor Lyman Smith. This must have been shot after Verity and I—and I recalled, Madame and Kathleen—had left the room.

I enlarged the photo.

Royal Parish stood with the Parish sword, well, its reproduction, behind him on the wall. I enlarged the photo to see the details of Royal's costume. He had a long black cape over a white linen shirt with a stiff collar that stood out from his neck and black pants that ended beneath his knees. His calves were covered in lace-up leather, and his shoes were adorned with pewter buckles. He was a tall man, so his broad-brimmed pilgrim hat almost brushed the low ceiling of the room.

To his right, Lyman Smith held the winner's plaque, his chin high, chest puffed out, looking extremely pleased with himself. It was quite a coup to win that much money. I imagined most history departments weren't exactly rolling in cash. His outfit was a carbon copy of Royal's except that his shirt was more beige in color and his hat was tucked under his arm.

The college kids stood behind them, also in long capes, trying to look like they were at attention. Of the college students, only Max had the same Pilgrim-style hat as Royal and Lyman. A couple of guys held pikes, long wooden poles topped with long leaf-shaped blades. I zoomed in. They were dangerously sharp.

To my surprise, the photographer had captured Fred Nickerson and his watchdog Gladys Burley, standing in a corner of the room. Fred looked lost, Gladys looked daggers at . . . It was hard to tell from the angle, but it appeared she was looking at Max Hempstead.

Strange.

Photos by Beltane. I tried to remember. Had she been at the Halloween party? I didn't remember seeing her, though her typical garb was practically a Halloween costume. She would have blended right in. Even if she hadn't been invited to the Halloween party, it was a short walk from her house on Old Farms Road to the Parish House. She'd just have to cut through the woods behind the house—the path ran right by the cemetery.

Beltane's love affair gone wrong had been two years ago. Who was president then?

I went to the counter, where Aunt Gully was serving lobster rolls to a group wearing LOBSTAH LOVAHS T-shirts. She posed for a photo, then I tugged her back into the kitchen.

I lowered my voice. "Aunt Gully, do you remember telling me that Beltane Kowalski had an ill-fated love affair with someone at the historical society?"

"Yes, I'd heard it from Aggie. She said it was civil—eventually." She stirred her chowder and shook in some white pepper.

Hector laughed. "Probably civil because she had a voodoo doll of the guy hanging over an open flame at her house."

Hilda shook her head. "Now, Hector."

"Who was the president then?"

"Oh, let me think," Aunt Gully said. "This year it's Royal Parish. Last year, it was a history professor from the college."

"Lyman Smith."

"Yes, Lyman Smith."

Chapter 26

That evening, I stopped by the college fencing studio. Several student fencers practiced, their faces covered with mesh masks, their steel blades flashing and ringing when they made contact. I could tell Isobel wasn't one of them—her confident movement was so distinctive.

Dance class went well. The students were eager, quickly catching on to the combinations of steps I gave them. It was good that they were so focused because I kept thinking of all I'd learned from Bronwyn and Delilah. My gaze turned repeatedly out the windows to the glowing lights that illuminated the chapel and the fraternity house just past the exit gates. Coop's words kept echoing: *on script.* What were Nate and Coop hiding?

After class, I drove to the hospital. As I walked down the hallway I heard a low murmur of voices from Madame's room. I wondered who was visiting as I hurried in.

"Allie!" Madame was sitting up, a dinner tray on the table in front of her.

"How are you?" I took her hand.

Her voice was stronger, but her speech was still indistinct, slurred. "I had a stroke. I have started my rehab.

My good brother-in-law has done research." She paused for breath. "The sooner I start, the sooner I can recover. I refuse to believe I won't get better. The body can heal. I believe that."

"I'm glad to hear that!"

The nurse came in. "She exhausted her therapists today. When they wanted four repetitions she gave them eight. When they wanted eight she gave them twenty!"

"I will work hard," Madame said simply. "Now you must tell me about the ballet and the class."

While I spoke, the nurse took away the tray. I noticed that Madame had barely touched the food. Russ and Yulia stepped out to get some air.

"They get tired of my dance talk," Madame said.

"You know I never get tired of it."

I filled her in, watching her face brighten and color return to her face.

"My schedule is crazy, but I'm making it work."

"Dancer's life, Allie. Not easy. Most wonderful and most difficult of the arts. You must live your art in a way that other artists don't, in your body."

"So true," said a woman's voice behind me.

I turned. Kathleen Parish stood at the door, carrying a bouquet of roses. Huge dark crimson blooms, at least two dozen, spilled from her arms. A black belted trench coat emphasized her dark brows and eyes, filled with worry. Her eye makeup was smudged.

"Kathleen!" Madame held out her hand.

Kathleen rushed to Madame. I stepped back as they murmured to each other. The pang of jealousy I felt surprised me. I knew that Madame must care about Kathleen from the way she acted at the party.

"How is Isobel? And Royal?" Madame whispered.

"Royal." Kathleen shook her head. "Madame, the

police took Isobel to the station to question her. It was the worst moment of my life."

"Maybe I should . . ." I took the flowers. "I'll get these in some water."

As I left the room the nurse appeared. "Oh, let me put those in water for you."

"Thank you!"

I'm not proud of what I did next. I sat in the chair outside the open door and pulled out my phone. But I listened. And I exulted. If the police were questioning Isobel Parish, did that mean that they no longer suspected Madame of Max's murder? I let myself hope. Still, listening to Kathleen weep and Madame try to comfort her, I felt like a rat.

"Isobel knew the boy who died, Max Hempstead," Kathleen said. "She dated him. He, he broke her heart. No, that's too nice. He used her. And you know how she is."

What did that mean?

"I'm afraid, Madame." Kathleen's voice shook. "I'm afraid that she did kill that boy. He was stabbed. It could've been her sword. She wore it with her pirate costume. The police kept asking her if she fought with him. She lied—I knew she did! I heard them."

I had, too. I prayed that the nurse would take her time.

Kathleen continued, "But she won't talk to us. She left the house for a while during the party. We can't account for her movements and she refused to tell us what happened!"

"My dear, my dear . . ." Madame murmured.

I'd seen her slip away with Nate Ellis. Was that what Kathleen meant? They'd seemed more interested in hooking up than murder. I held my breath.

"Royal is furious. He said terrible things to her. Called

her terrible names. But he's been so hard on her. Saying she didn't keep up the standards of the Parish family because she has no morals dating all those boys. I think she tries to hurt Royal with all of her boyfriends. He's hurt her so badly I don't know if they can ever repair their relationship."

She hiccupped. "Royal's trying everything he can to keep her from being thrown into jail, but even he might not be able to—"

Madame Monachova whispered something I couldn't make out.

"I'll tell you one thing. My marriage is over." Kathleen laughed bitterly. "Maybe I never really had one. He never loved me. He loves my money. He loves his family, those dead ancestors, more than he ever loved me."

The nurse reappeared with the flowers. I jumped to my feet.

Russ and Yulia returned, carrying paper cups. "I brought you some tea, Allie," Yulia said.

"Thanks." *Drat.* Now I couldn't eavesdrop any more.

Kathleen jumped to her feet as we entered the room. She forced a smile, but there was no hiding her blotchy cheeks and smeared eye makeup. "Yulia, Russ. How are you? Sorry, I have to go. I'll come back tomorrow." She slung her bag over her shoulder. "Good night." She hurried from the room, swiping her eyes with a tissue.

"What's going on with Kathleen?" Yulia stood next to the bed and put a cup of tea on Madame's table. Russ took a chair. I perched on the bed and sipped my tea. Madame used one hand to lift the other, trembling, to her cup. She wrapped both around it. "Success."

Her eyes were red and she'd lost the spark I'd seen just minutes before. Now her face looked gray against her white pillowcase.

"Haven't seen Kathleen for years," Russ said. "Do they still live in Rabb's Point?"

Madame nodded.

Yulia smiled broadly, straining to keep things light, to change the emotional weather of the room. "Allie, you of course wouldn't have known Kathleen, but she was one of Madame's first students here. Years ago."

"Very athletic girl." Madame's voice had dropped to a whisper. "Tennis. Horses. Skiing. Not the best technique, but she fell in love with the ballet and helped the studio get off the ground."

I watched with concern as Madame lifted the cup to her lips. Yulia hovered, holding her hands around Madame's to steady them. Madame took a sip but then her hands shook so badly Yulia took the cup and set it back on the table.

I blinked back tears, my throat closed up. I coughed and said, "It's great that Kathleen supported the studio."

"Remember those American women who were married off to British aristocracy?" Yulia said. "The buccaneers? The men had the title, the property, the name, but needed the money. That was Kathleen. Her father made a fortune with an auto parts chain. She didn't have the pedigree of Royal's family,"

"Her pedigree is better. She has Micasset blood—her family was here before Royal's even thought to come," Russ said. "But that big house needed taking care of, repairs, never mind the historical society house. It takes a lot of money to keep houses like that running. Don't get me wrong, Royal's family had plenty of money, but Kathleen had real money."

Madame's eyelids fluttered and she sank back against her pillow. Yulia moved the table away and I helped her settle Madame's blanket.

I wished everyone good night and left, my mind whirling with worry for Madame. As I got in the van I took a deep breath. She was getting good care. She believed she'd get better. I had to believe it, too.

As I drove home my thoughts turned to Isobel Parish. So devastating with her sword.

From what I knew, it was no surprise that volatile Isobel Parish had fallen under the eye of the police. Had her pirate sword been the "sharp, thin" weapon Bronwyn had mentioned? Had Isobel met Max at the grave and killed him? I'd seen her several times over the course of the evening. The graveyard wasn't far from the house. It was possible but incredibly improbable. She'd been with me and Verity, then dancing with some guy, then arguing with her dad, then I'd seen her with Nate Ellis. It looked like they were running off to hook up. Was that the secret Isobel was keeping? Why would she keep quiet about an alibi?

A memory stirred. When Isobel, Verity, and I had left her father's library, I'd seen someone in a black cape running down the hallway. Was it Nate Ellis looking for Isobel? Could it have been Max? Hiding, waiting for us to leave Royal's library? He needed money. Isobel had said how valuable the Parish sword was.

I shoved in Aunt Gully's Pat Benatar CD. I loved her 1980s power ballads. Benatar's voice filled the van with ferocious passion. I imagined the force of a passion like that, turned against someone who'd betrayed me. Hurt me. Like Isobel's love for Max.

Isobel was the perfect suspect. She had means, motive, opportunity. But still—why didn't it feel right?

Chapter 27

This was the first day that my commuting to Boston for rehearsal had gotten to me. I'd slept badly and traffic had been a nightmare. Even as I rehearsed my dance, I couldn't keep my thoughts from returning to Madame and Isobel Parish and what she'd been doing the night of Max's murder.

Then, as we finished company class, Margot passed me, smiling and humming the Dewdrop music.

Maybe Beltane could whip up one of her little potions for Margot.

"Hey, Allie!" Cody Walton rushed over. Tall with sandy blond hair and broad shoulders, Cody and I have been friends since our conservatory years.

"I really like the dance Serge made for you in act 1. You look like a movie star, you know, not like a lobster roll slinger."

I laughed. "Well, you make a pretty good Nutcracker Prince."

"Don't let Margot get you down," he whispered. "Check this out." He showed me one of those action cameras that shoot video. "This one is motion activated. I left it on the floor by my dance bag." He replayed the video. He'd captured the class dancing—from the knees down. We laughed. He gave me a kiss on the cheek then he ran off to his own rehearsal.

Smiling, I headed to the van for my drive back to Mystic Bay. Before I got in the car my phone dinged with a text from Lorel. *Call me.*

I sighed, but called.

"Aunt Gully told me you had rehearsal today," Lorel said. "Can you stop by my office? I had the certificates made—"

"Certificates? For what?"

"Remember the Lobzilla Wanted poster? I want to award certificates to the winners."

I'd forgotten about Lorel's Wanted poster scheme. "I'll be right there."

Lorel's office was in a massive new building right on the Boston waterfront. It cost more to park there than a dinner for four at the Mermaid. Thank goodness I could get my parking validated by Lorel's office.

I took the elevator up to the top floor.

Lorel greeted me wearing a navy blue linen sheath with a designer silk scarf. Suddenly I was aware that my leotard was sweaty and that my yoga pants had a rip in the thigh. I moved my bag to cover the tear.

Lorel's secretary, a Swedish guy who was a ballet fan, rushed over to greet me. "How is my walking work of art? Lorel said you have a special dance choreographed just for you!"

He made me forget my ripped pants.

"Come see me." I smiled. "I'll take you on a backstage tour after the performance."

He beamed. "I've died and gone to heaven!"

Lorel and I went into her office. Her sleek desk overlooked the harbor through floor-to-ceiling windows.

"Look at this. I had the art department whip it up." She held up an oversized check made out for dinner for two. In the upper corner was Lobzilla's photo and FOUND underneath.

I folded my arms. "This just doesn't seem right, Lorel. After he was stolen, Lobzilla was found at the scene of a murder." I shuddered at the memory.

"I still think Lobzilla's a gold mine," Lorel said. "So go present the check to the winners and be sure to take pictures. At their houses. I need the photos for the campaign."

I sighed.

"Allie." She gave me the I-know-better-than-you look she'd been perfecting for years. "There is no such thing as bad publicity."

It was easier to give in. "Who's getting the check? The cops who found Lobzilla? The first ones to find him were probably the frat brothers who led the party guests out to the cemetery. Or the killer?"

As soon as I said the words something clicked. The frat brothers had led us out there after they heard the story of Otis Parish.

Most of the partygoers weren't from Mystic Bay. They were out-of-towners from the fraternity at the college. I remembered the two freshmen who had asked me and Verity about Otis Parish. But before that Lyman Smith had been telling a big bunch of guys about Otis Parish. Funny that he'd do that, wasn't it? The Parish family hated the rumors and old stories. Surely Lyman Smith would know that, as a friend of the Parishes. He'd know to keep it quiet. By telling the story he'd had to have known that he was luring a bunch of drunk frat boys to the grave.

Or was Lobzilla on the grave supposed to be the lure? Was that why Max was there? A Halloween prank to end all Halloween pranks?

Both?

"Earth to Allie," Lorel said. I told her what I'd been thinking.

Lorel sat on the edge of her desk. "I see your point but it was a Halloween party. Of course people would be talking about Otis Parish." She was right.

"Back to the campaign," Lorel said, "I decided to switch it to focus on the people who *originally* found Lobzilla. That's a feel-good story."

I rolled my eyes. "Maybe not for Lobzilla. Who are the winners?"

"Fred and Bertha. And whoever they want their dates to be. Don't forget." Lorel pushed the check into my arms. "Photos."

Gladys would be Fred's date, of course. Bertha and her date? I wondered who she'd bring.

"Did you tell Aunt Gully?" I asked.

She pushed me toward the door. "She'll love it." That meant the answer was no.

On the drive back I barely saw the traffic. A memory was struggling to surface, some detail, something important.

I kept coming back to Halloween night.

My footsteps swishing through the leaves. The flashlight beams playing in the dark, illuminating the headstones.

I could practically feel the soft, recently turned earth beneath my feet, see the wooden stakes connected with string. I recalled a television show about an archaeology dig. The archaeologists had used the stakes and string to mark off areas to dig.

Had Fern told me the truth? Had they actually dug up the body of Otis Parish? Fern said that Royal wanted to prove that the rumors and old stories about Otis and Uriah weren't true. But to dig up bodies! Didn't you need permission from, well, who? The police? Health department? What was the word for that?

Exhumation. Would you need some kind of legal permission if the graves were on your own property? If you were digging up your own family? My stomach twisted. I wanted to talk to Fern again.

Max had clearly kept his appointment to meet his killer at the grave. What a macabre touch—meeting at the grave of Otis Parish on Halloween night. Why there and why then?

Chapter 28

The sun was gleaming low along the horizon as I turned off the highway into Mystic Bay. Trees blazed with autumn color, their leaves drifting across the road as I drove to the Mermaid.

"Allie!" Bertha greeted me as I entered the shack. Bertha hitched her hip onto a stool, grimacing.

"Hi, Bertha. How's your sciatica?"

"Been worse."

I joined Hilda and Aunt Gully behind the counter. "Have you heard the news about Lobzilla?"

Hilda set a lobster roll in front of Bertha.

Bertha nodded her thanks. "I did indeed. I feel sorry for the old guy. After many a peaceful year under the waves, look at what his senior years have brought him." She tsked and took a bite of her lobster roll. "I have a good mind to liberate him from the marine biology department and set him loose."

"I do feel for the guy. I'm just glad he lived through it all," I said.

"Barely." Bertha patted her lips with a napkin. "Fred Nickerson called to tell me. Old guy was a bit worse for wear. Tough on that poor lobster to be out of water for however long he was. He was barely alive when the police found him. Thank goodness they got him back into water right away." She turned her bright eyes to me. "Is it true? He was on top of the kid who died?"

I hesitated. I hadn't wanted to look too closely. "Not exactly. More next to him."

Hilda shuddered.

"Who does that to a lobster? Why would you kill someone and then put a lobster on him?" Bertha shook her head. "Poor lobster's been traumatized."

Nobody said anything about the irony of talking about a lobster this way while eating one for dinner.

I stopped short. "Max was in the fraternity. It was a prank, you know how our mermaid was getting stacks of leis around her neck?"

"Leis?" Bertha choked. "Lei-ing the mermaid! That sounds just like a guy."

Hilda blushed. "Oh, my. Is that what that was?"

Bertha slapped her knee, roaring. "You gotta admit, that's funny."

I shook my head, then remembered Lorel's giant check. I hurried to the van and brought it in through the kitchen.

"What's your sister up to now?" Aunt Gully adjusted her glasses and held the two checks at arm's length.

After explaining Lorel's idea to Hector and Aunt Gully, we went back into the dining area.

"Bertha, may I present this check entitling you to two free Lazy Mermaid dinners, for you or for you and a guest of your choice."

"For what?" Bertha said.

"For finding Lobzilla, of course!" Aunt Gully beamed.

Bertha's ruddy face turned an even darker shade of

red. Her wide mouth turned up. "Me? All I did was pull the old guy out of the water!" But Bertha was pleased, I could tell. She laughed and slapped some money on the counter. "I'll use the certificate next time I'm in. You know I'll be back."

I took photos and sent them to Lorel. She sent back a thumbs-up and minutes later the photo was on Facebook with ten likes.

After closing the Mermaid, Aunt Gully and I drove home. It had been a long day and my mind was spent from churning out scenarios for the murder of Max Hempstead. I was happy to join Aunt Gully in the living room, putting my feet up and watching a rerun of *Columbo* while eating pumpkin pie with whipped cream.

"I wonder who Bertha will invite to be her guest at the Mermaid," I said.

Aunt Gully shook her head. "Bertha's private. I don't know if there's ever been someone special in her life. Far as I'm concerned she could just use it for two dinners." She set aside her plate and let her head fall back against the soft leather of the recliner. "I let your sister win this one. But now I must call Don O'Neill and let him know that my answer truly is no."

I licked my spoon. "Right after the Celtics game."

"Right after." Aunt Gully smiled serenely.

Chapter 29

This morning we moved to the Opera House for a rehearsal. It would be the first time stepping onto the magnificent stage for many of the children joining the *Nutcracker* cast as mice, snow maidens, toy soldiers, flowers, and angels. How well I remembered my first time dancing on this famous stage.

Aside from a couple of kids who still had a hard time telling stage right from stage left, all went well until I saw Margot. She was arguing with Kellye, who burst into tears and ran from the room.

I sidled up to Cody. "What's going on with them?"

Cody whispered, "It's been tense at the house lately." He still lived in the group house with Margot and several other dancers. "Margot's been making no secret of the fact that she thinks Kellye isn't good enough to share Dewdrop with her. She's been cutting Kellye down to anyone who will listen."

A group formed around Serge. Several heads swiveled toward Cody and me as he called us over.

"*Bay Fashion* just sent over the images from our shoot." Serge beamed and turned his tablet toward me.

The first photo was a solo shot of me in my gorgeous gold gown. I blushed. "Virginia did such a great job on that dress," I said as friends patted me on the back.

"And this is the cover shot," Serge said. It was a photo of Kellye.

Margot pulled the tablet from Serge's hands and swiped through. Then she shoved the tablet into Cody's hands and stalked away. There was an uncomfortable silence as we shared glances. Serge followed Margot's exit then shrugged. Cody swiped through the photos and gave the tablet back to Serge.

Chatter resumed.

Cody and I crossed the studio to get our bags.

"What was that about?" I said.

Cody shook his head. "There'll be hell to pay. Aside from the group shot, there were no photos of Margot in the article."

As I drove into Mystic Bay and headed to the Mermaid, I passed the playground at the end of Pearl Street. Fern Doucette was by the swings with Prudie.

I slammed on my brakes and pulled over.

Fern pushed Prudie in a rubber swing shaped like a bucket. Prudie chewed on the strap and kicked her chubby little legs as I approached.

"She likes you," Fern said. As she pushed up her sunglasses, I noticed dark circles under her eyes.

"How are you?" I said.

"Prudie's teething and we had a rough night. But she's okay now."

I caught Prudie and tickled her little legs, then let the bucket carry her backward. She chortled.

Fern took a deep breath. "I keep thinking about Max Hempstead's murder. I feel bad. I mean, I didn't wish

Max ill, exactly. It's just that I wasn't happy that I was pushed aside, is all. Nobody deserves what happened to Max."

I shuddered. Dying in a graveyard. It was something out of a nightmare.

Her lips curled. "Some kids were here talking about it. They were saying that the ghost of Max Hempstead now walked along with Otis Parish. Funny, people never talk about Uriah, or Mercy, or Rosamund Parish."

I was confused. "Mercy? Rosamund Parish?"

"Mercy was Otis's daughter. Rosamund was a great-niece. She's buried in the Parish cemetery, too. I got interested in her when I found her diary in the historical society library."

I didn't want to interrupt, but I wanted to keep her from going off on a history lesson. "Fern, something had struck me as odd Halloween night. The wooden stakes in the ground, connected with twine. You weren't kidding when you talked about digging up secrets? You meant it literally?"

She laughed, which made Prudie chortle again. Fern gave Prudie a big push. "I'm not lying anymore. Royal Parish made us sign a confidentiality agreement about a project he wanted to do in the Parish cemetery. Me and Max. Forget confidentiality! I'm done with Lyman Smith and Royal bloody Parish.

"When I went into labor and had Prudie prematurely. I had to leave work. Didn't hear any more about the project. Lyman would occasionally send me an e-mail when he needed a question answered, then the e-mails stopped and then I got one saying my services were no longer required.

"This summer I went back to volunteering at the historical society. Lyman and I had worked together on an article, and we'd worked well together. I wanted to know what was happening with it. But still he wasn't returning my calls.

"A few weeks ago"—she hesitated—"a friend told me there was activity at the graveyard. I went with her. You see, Royal decided that he was tired of the old stories about ghosts and vampires in his family. He wanted the legends about Uriah and Otis being vampires disproven."

"How could you disprove it?" I whispered. I knew.

She raised her chin defiantly. "Only one way. Dig them up. My friend and I—" She hesitated.

She'd just mentioned volunteering at the historical society. Whose name would she hesitate to mention? "Beltane."

She nodded. "She'd heard them talking. So we went through the woods—Beltane knows them very well, she lives right down Old Farms Road from the cemetery—and watched."

"And," I breathed.

"Royal and Lyman Smith did the dig with Max."

"They removed all those stones?"

"Well, not all the stones. That's how Beltane knew something was up. She was walking through the woods one night as a bunch of frat boys cleared the stones. It was some kind of initiation."

I remembered all the stones, the freshly turned earth. "And?"

"We weren't the only ones watching."

I met her eyes. "Isobel Parish."

She nodded. Prudie fussed and kicked. Fern reached in the swing and lifted her out gently. "I've got to get her home so she can nap."

"What did they find?" I picked up her bag and followed her to her car.

"Thanks." She put Prudie in her car seat. "What did they find? Exactly what that arrogant bastard did and didn't want to find. Otis wasn't a vampire. But Uriah Parish was."

"What? How could they tell?"

She shook her head and laughed. "Nobody's a vampire, Allie, though there are reasons why people might imagine they are." She closed the door and leaned against the car. "It was the way he was buried. I've been doing my own research on Rosamund Parish's diary and it's way worse than Royal feared."

"How could it be worse?"

"Listen." She got in the car. "I'll be at the Historical Society Harvest Fair tomorrow. Come see me and we can talk then? I'm volunteering between four and six."

"Okay, thanks." I ran to the van. How could she leave me hanging like this? I got in the van and caught my eye in the mirror. *She's pulling your leg, Allie. No such thing as vampires.*

Still. What was worse than a vampire?

As I pulled out, I saw the check in the backseat. I sighed. I had to do the other check presentation. It would be more fun if I took Verity. I called her.

"Could you take off an hour? I have to deliver a giant check to Fred Nickerson and I'll have to get past his guard dog. And I have to tell you something that Fern just told me about Otis Parish. Well, Uriah Parish."

"I've got help today. Pick me up."

Chapter 30

Verity gasped when I told her about Fern's revelation. "They dug Otis and Uriah up! I wonder what they found exactly?"

"As soon as she tells me I'll tell you every word," I said. "Listen to us. There's no such thing as vampires, right?"

Verity shrugged. "Maybe there are people who think they're vampires? Right? Is that the same thing? I was in line at the grocery store behind a guy who said that Otis Parish killed Max Hempstead for desecrating his grave with the giant lobster."

"That's completely nuts." But I thought back to all the stories I'd heard about Otis Parish. "Maybe Max's death will be the start of a new Mystic Bay legend."

I parked the van under an oak tree in front of a cedar-shingled Dutch colonial two streets up from the Mermaid. Mystic Bay had a program where historic houses could hang a sign with the name of the original owner and the date the house was built. A sign on the house read EZEKIEL NICKERSON 1840. Gladys, in baggy jeans and a paint-splattered sweatshirt, bent over the bushes by the door.

Next door was a Cape, covered in gray siding with exceptionally tidy, geometrically cut bushes by the door. The mailbox by the road had BURLEY written on its side in block letters.

"Isn't Fred's girlfriend named Gladys Burley? So the gray house is hers, and she's doing yard work at his house?" Verity said quietly.

We watched Gladys prune the bushes by Fred Nickerson's front door. She attacked them with her shears, cutting with ferocity, as if they'd insulted her. Her house and his were tidy to the point of psychosis. A single leaf drifted to her feet. She threw down the shears and grabbed a long pole with a pointy end, like the trash picker-uppers convicts used by the side of the highway. She gutted the leaf and stuffed it in a trash bag.

"Whoa. Glad I'm not on the receiving end of that stick," Verity said. "Maybe we should come back later."

I thought of one of Aunt Gully's old sayings. "Fortune favors the bold."

"Here's one for you. 'Beware of the dog,'" said Verity. "Or how about 'Avoid crazy ladies with pointy objects.'"

I hauled Lorel's giant check out of the backseat, pasted on a smile, and approached Gladys warily. "Hi! I'm looking for Fred."

"What do you want?" Gladys said, clutching the stick. She had deep-set small dark eyes that made me think of a bear. Her chapped lips curved down under a hint of mustache.

"Hi, I'm Allie Larkin. Remember, we met at the Lazy Mermaid Lobster Shack? This is my friend Verity Brooks. I'm here to make a presentation to Fred. May I speak to him?"

Fred opened his front door and stuck his head out. He wore glasses, had a pair of sunglasses perched in his thick, unruly hair, and another pair hung from a lanyard around his neck. He held a sheaf of papers in his hand.

"Well, hello, Allie. And that's Veronica Brooks, isn't it?"

"Verity."

"Yes, yes, of course." He joined us outside.

I held up the supersized check. "The Lazy Mermaid would like to present you with this gift certificate for two free dinners at the shack for your role in finding Lobzilla."

Fred grinned and bounced on his toes. "Well, my, my. Look here, Gladdy, isn't this wonderful?"

Gladdy? I couldn't think of a less appropriate nickname.

"Is it okay if we do a photo?" I asked.

"Sure, sure." Fred grinned.

Gladys scanned the poster as if looking for small print that would scam Fred out of his home.

"Would you help me get a picture, Verity?" I handed her my phone. "Would you like to be in the picture, too, Gladys?"

Gladys, apparently finding nothing amiss with the check, edged close to Fred. I straightened the check in Fred's and Gladys's hands and ran behind Verity to see what the photo would look like. Gladys still held her stick like a spear. Inwardly, I sighed. It would have to do. "Perfect!"

After Verity took the photos, Fred said, "Why don't you girls come in for some cider? Gladys just bought it."

"Oh, so sorry, we don't have time." Verity started toward the van.

"Thank you anyway," I said.

Gladys looked relieved.

"Oh, the penny just dropped," Fred said. "Verity, you're Chief Brooks's niece. He must be very busy with the terrible murder. I'm just so glad that Lobzilla made it through. Traumatized, of course. Who wouldn't be? At least I had a nice comfortable tank ready for him at the lab but it was touch and go for a while."

"I'm so glad to hear that," I said.

"He's a tough old codger." Fred grinned.

"I remember Max working with you the day you found him." I ignored Verity's pleading look. "Did Max often help you?"

Gladys stiffened, tightening her grip on the stick.

Whoa.

"Yes, well, no." Fred scratched his head. "He did last year, when he took my Introduction to Marine Biology class. Handy to have on the research vessel. Good sailor, good kid."

Gladys turned away, her knuckles white on the stick. I wondered at this reaction. She didn't agree with Max being a good kid?

Fred continued, "Max was a very good student. He told me his plan was to start his own law firm. Well, this was before that business with his father."

"His father?" I asked, "What happened?"

"Not sure, Max never explained why, but his father cut him off. Completely. I helped him get some funding to pay his tuition and school fees, that sort of thing." Fred shook his head, dislodging his glasses.

Max and his money again.

Fred pushed his glasses up his nose. "Smart kid. Ah, well."

"Some of my customers said today was the funeral," Verity said.

And the fraternity ceremony, I remembered.

"Yes, we attended the service this morning at the college chapel. Such a sad ending for such a bright boy, right, Gladdy?"

Gladys kept her baleful eyes on us, but said, "Yes."

"His family was there. His father, I was glad to see. Broken up, of course."

"Of course," I said.

"I think the fraternity will do something later; of course I won't go but I'm sure Lyman Smith will."

"Lyman Smith?"

"Yes, he was the fraternity's faculty adviser. He was very close to Max."

Inside Fred's house, a phone shrilled.

"Sorry, I'll have to get that. Good day, ladies." He went into the house.

Gladys dismissed us with a curt nod and put the certificate next to the pile of leaves, just another bit of trash to throw away. She picked up her shears and started hacking at the bushes again.

I wondered what Gladys was thinking. She was upset about Max but didn't want to say anything in front of Fred.

"Gladys, did you know Max well?" I said.

She stopped and straightened slowly. "Only what Fred told me."

My eyes followed the clippers.

"You didn't like him." That was plain.

Gladys threw a look toward Fred's door. "Max was a user. Fred has the kindest heart. When he heard Max needed money he didn't hesitate to give it to him. A lot of money. But did that kid care about Fred? He couldn't be bothered to stick by the man who helped him."

"Stick by?" Verity and I exchanged a glance.

Indignation drew Gladys's lips further downward. "Max was close with the Parish family. Could have put in a word for Fred to get that grant. But did he? That grant went to Lyman Smith, who's all buddy-buddy with Royal Parish. The kid was an ingrate." She turned back and decapitated the bush with one forceful clip.

Verity and I rushed back to the car.

"You know, I'd almost feel bad for poor Gladdy if I weren't so afraid of her. Imagine doing yard work for someone who thinks fish are more interesting than you are," I said.

"That's devotion," Verity said. "If she'd do that I guess she'd do anything for him."

"So Max didn't help Fred get the grant from Royal Parish. So what? How much pull could a college kid have?" I sent the photos to Lorel. Then I scrolled on my phone to the historical society Facebook page and the photos posted by Beltane.

"I know you," Verity said. "What are you thinking?

"Do you have time for ice cream? I can't think. My blood sugar must be low." I pulled from the curb.

"Yes, let's stop at Scoops."

Scoops by the Bay was our favorite ice-cream shop. We didn't go much during the summer since tourists made the lines insanely long. Leaf peepers made up the line now, but it was much less busy than during the summer.

Verity and I ordered two-scoop cones, rocky road for her and chocolate-chocolate chip for me. Scoops had several picnic tables overlooking the water. We took seats and licked our cones in silence for a few minutes.

"So what are you thinking?" Verity said.

"Look at this." I showed her the picture of the group at the grant presentation. "What do you notice?"

"Royal looks great and so does this guy"—she pointed at Lyman Smith—"and this is Max, right? They all look like they stepped out of the history book. Maybe they all got their costumes at the same place."

"Exactly," I said. "They're all dressed the same. Maybe I'm looking at this the wrong way. What if the killer didn't mean to kill Max at all? It was dark. Maybe the killer followed him to the graveyard in the dark because the killer thought he was Royal. Royal had the same build, the same cape and hat."

I crunched my cone.

"But," Verity said, "what about the lobster? Wouldn't the killer see the lobster and think, wait a sec, Royal wouldn't be caught dead carrying a lobster?"

"Good thought. Maybe the killer didn't see the lobster. Just thought, tall guy in a cape and pilgrim hat."

But why kill Royal? I sighed. "I hate to say it, but I think Isobel might have wanted to kill her dad. No love lost there. I heard her mother, Kathleen, talking to Madame." Kathleen had no love lost for her husband, either.

"That's awful. Well, we heard him yelling at her at the party."

"So Isobel may be the killer even if she thought it was her dad and killed Max by mistake. It was dark. Or she knew it was Max and killed him on purpose." I finished my cone and sighed. I should have gotten three scoops.

Verity finished her cone and licked her fingers. "She seemed nice. And she bought a lot of jewelry from me. You're still so preoccupied."

"Didn't Gladys look like she was hiding something?" I said.

"All I could think was that when I was little my mom would tell me if I kept making faces my face would freeze like that and I'd be stuck with it forever. I figured that's what happened to Gladys."

I told Verity about Fern, and how she'd been shouldered out of her job. About Beltane, and how her love affair with Lyman Smith had soured.

A car full of guys pulled into the Scoops parking lot. They wore sweatshirts from Graystone College. I remembered that there was supposed to be a ceremony tonight at the fraternity for Max. I searched on my phone. "Remembrance celebration at 7:30 P.M. in the college arboretum." *Remembrance celebration* sounded so civilized. This was a frat. I could imagine what kind of party there would be after the ceremony.

I wanted to learn more about Max Hempstead and find his black backpack.

"Verity, would you like to go to a frat party tonight?"

Chapter 31

At eight P.M., Verity met me at the Arts Center. "Sorry I'm running late," she said. "I had customers who would not leave."

We walked down the green toward the chapel entrance to the campus, across from the frat house. Music pumped. The street was lined with cars.

"I haven't been to a frat party in years," she said. "I don't know how to dress for one anymore." She wore vintage designer jeans and a silky teal top with an Asian print. "I have my Graystone sweatshirt still." Verity had gotten degrees in art history and business while she grew her vintage shop. She knotted the sweatshirt around her neck.

I'd tossed on a black sweatshirt and yoga pants. I didn't want to call attention to myself. I knew where I wanted to go.

The frat house was already alive with music. Dozens of kids spilled out the door and porch, all holding red plastic cups. I wrinkled my nose. "I can smell the cheap beer from here."

Verity and I turned toward tall cast-iron gates that led

to a broad path, which was lighted by luminaria, the candles set in brown paper bags giving off a soft, wavering light. A sign over the entrance swung in a light breeze, visible in the golden light of an old-fashioned gas lamp. GRAYSTONE COLLEGE ARBORETUM.

"Wait. I thought you said the party was at the frat," Verity said.

"We're checking out the remembrance ceremony first."

"Were we invited?" Verity said.

"It was on the Web site so everyone must be invited. I want to see who shows for the ceremony."

The backyard of the frat house abutted the arboretum, a hundred acres of natural beauty where the botany department of the college gave classes. Plays and dance performances took place at a large amphitheater at the end of a broad lawn. The amphitheater was ringed with four tall stone columns, a fanciful gift from an alum. I'd danced here in two shows.

"I bet the ceremony will be in the amphitheater. But let's stick to the shadows," I whispered.

We edged down the broad lawn, skirting the line of luminaria on the path. The luminaria made me certain we were headed in the right direction.

As we neared the amphitheater, we dodged into the trees.

A group of young men in blazers and matching striped ties stood around a brazier, alight with a flame leaping into the night sky. A large group of people, men and women, ringed them.

Nate Ellis stood before the assembled guests in a somber black suit. I saw Lyman Smith and Royal Parish in the inner circle. Nate and another guy poured large urns of water onto the flame.

They muttered some words, then the inner circle raised glasses. "To Max. Our brother forever. Now the sacred rites are concluded."

"Rats, we missed it," I whispered.

The crowd processed up the path.

Verity and I dived farther into the trees but followed the group as they headed back up toward the street.

Royal Parish and Lyman Smith got into expensive black sedans and left along with the other adults. The students streamed toward the frat house; Verity and I joined them.

Music now pumped more loudly from the frat house. We followed a group of giggling girls who looked barely out of high school up the stairs. Two hulking guys, the bouncers, waved the girls in and did the same with me and Verity.

"I don't think anyone's checking invitations at the door," I said.

We stepped inside into a wall of music and a crush of writhing, dancing bodies.

"What's the plan?" Verity shouted in my ear.

"Let's get the lay of the land. Learn about Max Hempstead," I yelled in her ear. "And keep your eyes peeled for a black backpack."

"A backpack?" she shouted.

"Remember Isobel told us about the papers stolen from her house? When I saw Max with Fred Nickerson at the shack, he wore his backpack while he was working with Lobzilla. I thought that was strange. That was the day after a burglary at the Parish house."

"So you think the papers are in the backpack?"

I remembered what Nate Ellis said. *Guys steal.* "Yes, I think he didn't want to let those papers out of his sight."

We slid through the crush into the kitchen. The table

was covered with dozens of bottles of alcohol and one small bowl of pretzels.

"Hey." The two freshmen we'd met at the Parishes' Halloween party stepped into the kitchen holding the ubiquitous red plastic cups. I peered past them into a bathroom. An old-fashioned claw-footed tub was full of murky brownish liquid that guys were stirring with a paddle as another poured from a bottle of vodka.

"So, you came to the party," one said.

Verity and I shared a glance. Small talk wasn't their strong suit.

"Yes."

"Hope it doesn't end like the other party." One guy swayed. *God, drunk already and the party has just started.*

"That was sad," Verity said. "Did you know Max well?"

"Max? Nah." One guy reached for a handful of pretzels.

The other said, "He owed me money."

"He did?" *Max needed money.*

"He shook me down for fifty bucks. Now I'll never get it back."

"I liked your outfit the other night better." One guy waved his cup at me and slurred. "Pirates are hot."

Verity said, "Let's get out of here."

"I lost my cape—did you find it?" Red Cup said.

Cape? "You lost your cape?"

"After the party they were in a big pile in the coat room. I couldn't find mine. Had to pay the party store twenty dollars because someone took mine."

My pulse kicked up a notch. "Sorry, no."

Verity grabbed my arm. "Are you thinking what I'm thinking? The capes were in a big pile—"

"Maybe that's what happened to Madame Monachova." I pictured her, a pair of glasses on her head always. The lights had been turned down until the police came. She couldn't see well. She must have picked up the wrong cape at the party.

I pushed Verity through the kitchen, waving good-bye to our stalkers.

"Verity!" I hit my head. "I should have known. When we saw her on the patio, her cape was too long for her. I stepped on it!" My words tumbled out. "She must have taken off her cape when she went in to the party because it was warm. She left it in the coat room. When she went back to get it, she picked up somebody else's cape."

"Her cape was awfully long. So the killer was a tall guy in a cape." Verity picked up a bowl of pretzels. "There were a lot of tall guys at the party. But the police can get the killer's DNA off the cape. That's great."

I shook my head. "You just heard that kid. They were all jumbled up together. Lots of different people's DNA rubbing off everywhere. Probably wouldn't stand up in court."

"Now you really sound like Bronwyn. We should have asked her to come." Verity munched a handful of pretzels.

"No, we shouldn't. She'd want to arrest everyone here. Half these kids are underage." Plus I didn't want her to stop me from doing what I wanted to do.

Several guys looked at us appraisingly as we went into the living room. I picked up a cup and handed it to Verity. "I'm so glad I'm old and don't have to do this anymore. Don't drink anything. We'll just look like we're drinking."

"I'm not touching anything," she said.

"Unless it's a black backpack."

"Is there anything that makes the backpack stand out?"

"It had keys and tools and one of those orange foam floating key chains on it. Like the kind sailors use."

Verity sniffed the drink and put it down with a grimace. "Okay, you take me to a party where I could get salmonella or worse if I eat or drink anything, not to mention all that weird ritual stuff. Now what do we do?"

"Now we go upstairs." I nodded toward the staircase.

Verity put her hands on her hips. "Are you kidding? I know you didn't get to go to many college parties because you were at the conservatory, but there is one rule: you do not go upstairs in a frat house. Or the basement. Definitely not the basement."

I grinned at Verity and pulled her hand. "We are tonight. Keep your eyes peeled for that backpack."

We eased through the crush of bodies and went up the stairs. "Remember I told you that the frat showed the police Max's bed? But a kid here told me that only freshman slept in the bull pen. So I think Max's room must be on the top floor."

We passed kids crowded around an air hockey table and continued upstairs.

As we climbed, the music quieted enough that I could hear the floorboards of the stairs creak as we ascended.

"I don't have a good feeling about this," Verity said.

At the first room we came to, the door was open. I glanced quickly behind me and stepped inside. The room was narrow, with two beds, computer equipment, tennis rackets, and duffel bags. My quick search found a green backpack and a black leather briefcase.

The next room held two backpacks, one blue, one with a camouflage pattern.

The next room's door was closed.

"Is the light on?" Verity whispered.

I bent to look.

A door across the hall opened. "Ladies?"

I whirled. Nate Ellis pulled up short, his hand on the doorknob. He'd changed from the suit he'd worn at the ceremony and now was dressed in jeans and a GRAY-STONE LACROSSE T-shirt. He quickly pulled his door shut behind him, his brows knitted, trying to place us. He nodded. "I remember you. The dance professor."

"Hi," I said weakly.

"And who's your friend?" Nate said.

"Sade Wellington." Verity batted her eyelashes.

"Looking for someone?" He wasn't smiling.

"The little girls' room," Verity said in a sultry voice I'd never heard her use before. I almost laughed.

"Oh, downstairs." Nate looked from me to Verity, confused.

"Too kind."

I had a feeling that Nate knew we were up to something but didn't know what. But with Verity by my side and a bunch of kids downstairs, I wasn't worried.

"This way." He led us back downstairs.

Back on the first floor I turned to Nate. "I'm sorry about your friend Max," I yelled as we entered the living room. The music thumped from speakers at a deafening volume. Verity danced at my side.

Nate shouted back. "He was a good guy."

Coop was on the couch, a bowl of corn chips on his lap. His eyebrows jumped when he saw me. He waved. I waved back. He scurried to the kitchen.

"Ooh, a boyfriend already!" Verity said in my ear.

Coop returned with two more cups. "You ladies all set for drinks?"

"Ah, okay," Verity said in her breathy voice. She took

the drink and continued dancing. I nodded thanks to Coop.

"Was Max's family here? For the ceremony?" I shouted over the music.

Coop leaned back, pulling my drink away, and slurred, "I thought his family hired you, didn't they?"

He and Nate exchanged glances. Nate frowned. "I think you'd better leave. You, your friend."

"We're just—"

Shouts came from the kitchen, then the sound of crashing bottles and falling bodies.

Nate swore. "Geez, those morons. See the ladies out, Coop." He rushed toward the kitchen.

Coop made an exaggerated just-this-way gesture toward the front door and staggered drunkenly in our wake. When we got outside on the porch, the sound of the fighting behind us, I took a deep breath of clean air. "Coop, honestly, we're not cops. I just want to know what happened with Max. He was dating a friend of mine." That felt true. I did like Isobel.

Coop touched his nose. "Nope. I kept on script for the cops and I'll keep on script for you, too."

So he did lie to the cops.

Someone shouted from inside. Coop and the bouncers headed in. Coop slammed the door.

"Well, there's one for the books." Verity put her drink down on the railing. "I've been kicked out of a fraternity."

I inhaled deeply as we went down the steps.

"Follow me." I circled the house, stopping to turn back and beckon Verity. She groaned but followed.

A black iron fire escape clung to the back of the building. I reached up and pulled down the ladder. "Back in we go."

Chapter 32

A few minutes later, after a lot of moaning from Verity, we climbed to the top level of the fire escape. "These are the rooms we didn't get to look in," I whispered. "I especially want to know why Nate Ellis pulled his door shut so quickly."

"Well, we better hurry. I don't want to see those kids again. The little drunk one is fine, we could knock him over with a pinkie, but the big ones looked a lot more serious."

I peered through the window into the first room. There was nobody inside and they'd helpfully left the light on. Piles of what appeared to be dirty clothing were heaped next to unmade beds. Sports equipment and more clothes spilled out of a closet. I spotted a green backpack by the door.

The next room had the curtains pulled and the unmistakable shadows and sounds of a romantic encounter. "Oh, no."

"Aren't you going to look?" Verity said.

"You look."

·"No, you look! You're the one who dragged me up here."

I stepped quietly past the window. "We'll come back later."

I hoped that wasn't Max's room.

Soft sounds of sitar and temple bells came from the next room; the window was open but screened. A lava lamp swirled the walls with clouds of red and yellow, and the scent of pot flowed out the window. Several bodies lay on two beds, one of which was an empty mattress next to a desk that held only bongs and candles. Everyone in the room wore Hawaiian leis.

"Leis," I muttered. Just like the ones on our mermaid at the shack.

One kid strummed a guitar. He gave me a friendly chin jut as I passed the window. I waved back. Maybe people on the fire escape weren't unusual. I crept carefully past some pots, some quite large, which were growing luxuriantly healthy marijuana plants.

"They're growing their own," I said. I wondered if they were grown in the basement and had been moved outside when the cops came to search? The frat brothers could have hidden the plants in the arboretum. Talk about blending in.

The next room was dark, the window open a few inches at the bottom. I listened. Despite the thumping music and shouting downstairs, the room was quiet. Empty.

"I think this was the room Nate Ellis came out of." I gripped the window frame and raised it, then hooked a leg over the sill and eased inside.

Verity stayed put.

"Aren't you coming?" I whispered.

Verity shook her head. "I'll be the lookout."

This is breaking and entering. I shouldn't be here. But I couldn't help myself. I had to find that backpack, had to see what was on the papers Max stole.

The room had a sense of order that was at odds with everything else I'd seen at the frat. There was one queen-sized bed and the bedspread was smoothed neatly over the mattress. I pulled open the closet door: all the clothing was neatly hung, shoes arranged, not tossed. No backpack. There was a laptop computer on a desk with a hutch over the top. I brushed a finger across the touchpad and the screen sprang to life.

A spreadsheet.

"What's on the computer," Verity whispered.

"Lots of numbers. Names and phone numbers."

I slid open a panel on the hutch revealing plastic baggies of pot.

"Do you think that was what was in Max's bag?" Verity whispered from the windowsill.

"Maybe. But Isobel told me that Max had stolen her father's papers. Royal was furious. That seemed a lot more serious than weed." I pulled open a drawer with vials of white powder—coke. "Holy crap! I think he had something more dangerous than a few bags of weed in his backpack." I slid open a top drawer. Inside were stacks of dirty and wrinkled bills.

Footsteps approached and the door opened.

I whirled toward the window and was halfway out when Nate came in.

"Hey, you!" He grabbed me from behind, wrapping his arms around my waist, knocking me to the floor. I kicked and squirmed and somehow managed to buck him off. I jumped up as Nate scrambled back to his feet and ran at me again. Bracing myself against the windowsill, I kicked out with both feet, knocking him to his butt.

I twisted around and threw my leg over the windowsill. I was almost out when he scrambled back to his feet, grabbed my hair, and pulled me back into the room. I shrieked and fumbled for his hands as he swung me off balance. I fell to my knees.

"What the hell are you doing here!" he bellowed as he shook me. "We—"

Out of the corner of my eye, I saw a green blur, then I heard a crash. Nate groaned. He went limp and collapsed on top of me. Something soft and damp dropped onto my hair and my arms. Clumps of dirt and shards of clay lay scattered around us.

"Verity?" I rolled to the side and Nate slumped onto the floor.

Verity sat half in, half out the window, still holding the broken pot of pot in her hands. She dropped it and stepped back onto the fire escape. I staggered to my feet, threw my leg over the sill, and hopped out the window. I looked back inside. Nate rolled on the floor, groaning and holding his head.

"Are you okay?" Verity grabbed my arm and brushed dirt off my shoulder.

I took stock. I was winded and shocked, and my scalp hurt where Nate had pulled my hair, but I was okay. "Hurry, let's go before he gets up."

We scrambled down the fire escape and ran across the darkened campus back to our cars. No one followed, but still I jumped at every shadow, even when it was some guy carrying an armful of books or girls in party outfits walking to meet friends. My adrenaline slowly dropped and by the time we got to the Arts Center parking lot, my heart rate was somewhere near normal.

"Well, that was a drag and terrifying and dumb, all at the same time." Verity flung herself onto the hood of the Tank and fanned herself. "We'll just wait for the cops to come and arrest us for trespassing."

"I don't think they will. They have a lot to hide at that frat, Sade." I laughed and rolled on the hood of the car. "Miss Sade Wellington."

"Really, Allie, you have to plan ahead. I had my story all ready to go. Sade Wellington, exchange student from Washington, D.C., studying government. And what was your story?"

I was laughing so hard I had to wipe my eyes. "Didn't have one. Didn't think we'd get caught." Then the reality of what we'd done washed over me and I was struck by a wave of fatigue. What I'd done was so incredibly dumb. Thank God we hadn't gotten caught or arrested. "Well, Verity, thanks for coming out with me tonight."

"No worries," she said. "That was too much excitement for one evening. I have to go home and get the dirt out from under my nails. Besides, with this outfit I might as well stay home."

We got in our cars. I watched the red taillights burn as the Tank rolled out.

I started the van and followed. Were the drugs reason enough for Max to keep his backpack by his side? It explained the frat's subterfuge with the police. The frat couldn't let the cops search that room.

But I knew that Max had stolen papers from Royal. Where were they?

I drove past the college library. Through the floor-to-ceiling windows, I could see kids in study carrels hunched over books and laptops. It was surprising that so many were studying on a Saturday night. What had Nate said? Max had been a good student. He studied sometimes in the chapel library, a place you went if you were desperate for a quiet spot to study.

Desperate.

I made a quick decision and pulled into the empty parking lot behind the chapel.

I ran up the slate steps and pushed through the heavy wooden doors into hushed silence. In the vestibule, three doors faced me, one into the main church, one labeled RESTROOM, and the other labeled STAIRS TO LIBRARY, with an arrow pointing down. The chapel door fell shut softly behind me as I headed to the stairs.

The stairs turned into a narrow, whitewashed hallway. At the end of the hall was a door marked LIBRARY. I turned the knob slowly. A library inside a chapel—it was so quiet my breathing sounded not just harsh but sacrilegious.

I slipped through the door and eased it shut behind me. The library was a single room with rows of bookshelves at one end and two long wooden study tables in the middle. On the wall opposite the shelves were two doors, one marked STUDY ROOM A the second STUDY ROOM B. The only people in the library were a guy sleeping at one of the tables and a tall girl with an Afro nodding to music on her headphones as she shelved books from a cart.

I peeked inside study room A, then study room B. Both were dark. I slipped into study room B and hoped nobody was sleeping in it. Talk about quiet—a study room in a library in the basement of a chapel. This must be the quietest spot on campus. There was a mustiness that made me think the door to this room was rarely opened. My pulse thundered in my ears as I flicked a switch and fluorescent lights buzzed on overhead. There was a single wooden carrel and chair. I checked to be sure— no backpack stashed there. I turned back to the door.

On a coat hook on the wall behind the door hung a navy blue Graystone College windbreaker. I pulled it aside, hardly daring to hope.

Underneath the coat was a black backpack. It had the same key ring with the same pocketknife, marlin- spike, and floating orange key fob attached I'd noticed at the Mermaid.

I took the backpack to the carrel, my hands tingling. This had to be Max's.

I thought for a moment, rushed to the door, and turned the knob. There was no way to lock the door. The staff probably didn't want students to be able to lock the door. I could imagine what kids would get up to here—if they even knew this quiet spot existed.

I went back to the backpack and unzipped it, reveal- ing folders stuffed with papers and a magazine, *New England Scholarly History,* the same one I'd seen in Ly- man Smith's office. Tucked inside was a stack of papers clipped together. Max's homework? There was also a map. I traced the lines with my finger. Old Farms Road. The map showed the Parish property and the cemetery. I set it aside.

Underneath were three file folders. I flipped open the first folder. I'm no lawyer, it was page after page of le- galese, but a name made me stop turning the pages.

Maxwell J. Hempstead III. Possession of a controlled substance. Intent to sell. Injury to a minor. This was why Max's father had cut him off.

I flipped through the papers.

Another name jumped out. Nathan Adams Ellis. The frat president who'd dated Isobel and who'd just tackled me at the party. I scanned the papers. Destruction of property. Hazing. Assault. I wondered if he'd hazed Max.

Other names came into focus. Loida. Wyman. Shaw. These were some of oldest and wealthiest families in not just Mystic Bay, but New England. One of them, Shaw, was running for U.S. Senate. I scanned the paper with his name. It looked like a contract, with several signatures at the end. The words *sexual assault* leaped out at me.

Oh my God. This was dynamite. From what I could glean, these were not papers filed with the police. These were settlement contracts to hide what these well-connected young men had done, to pay off their victims.

So why take the papers? Royal had defended Max—successfully. Why would Max take these contracts, want these secrets?

Max's dad had cut him off. Max needed money.

It came into focus.

Max was a blackmailer—or was planning to be. All these secrets, indiscretions, outright crimes Royal had swept under the rug would be brought into the bright and humiliating light of day by Max—unless he was paid to be quiet. I considered. The theft at the Parish mansion had taken place just three days ago. Max had probably been silenced before he could blackmail anyone. Or had he? He stole the papers on Wednesday and he was dead Saturday night. He'd have to be the world's fastest blackmailer.

I stuffed the papers and files into the bag and slung it over my shoulder. I remembered Bronwyn telling me once about something called chain of evidence. I should call the police immediately. But I couldn't leave these papers lying around. Surely a custodian would come in here to vacuum? They wouldn't close the door. A student would eventually come in to study and shut the door and see the coat and backpack. The papers could end up in the wrong hands. Again.

Your hands are the wrong hands, too, a little voice said.

I ignored it.

Though I tried to be as quiet as possible, the door banged shut behind me and the backpack's canvas fabric rasped against my shirt as I hurried up the stairs and through the front doors of the chapel.

As I swung into the driveway at Gull's Nest, my headlights illuminated Lorel's blue BMW sedan. *Lorel's home again?*

I needed to think.

Lorel and Aunt Gully sat together in the living room. Aunt Gully had her feet up on Uncle Rocco's Barcalounger, her head resting against the well-worn brown leather as she sipped tea and turned the pages of a book. Lorel had her feet curled beneath her, a glass of red wine on the coffee table. She paged through one of Aunt Gully's *People* magazines.

Lorel really wanted this Chowdaheads deal to go through if she was willing to sit at home on a Saturday night and read *People* magazine with Aunt Gully.

"There you are! What were you up to tonight?" Aunt Gully said.

"Verity and I stopped at a party." *And I got tackled by an enraged frat boy when I broke in looking for Max Hempstead's backpack. Verity hit him over the head with a potted marijuana plant. Then I found a backpack full of secrets that probably got Max Hempstead killed.*

"Fun?" Lorel asked.

I shrugged. "I've been to better parties."

I grabbed a cup of tea and slice of coffee cake, called, "Good night," and ran upstairs. I hung the backpack on a hook in the back of my closet and shut the door. Then I settled into the rocking chair by the window and sipped tea as I flipped through the folders again.

Think, Allie.

I had a bag full of secrets, secrets someone might have killed to get. I had no idea what I should do with them. Well, I did. I should turn them in to the police. But I hesitated. Was there anything in that backpack that would hurt Madame Monachova? I had to look through them more carefully first, make sure there was nothing in there that had to do with her.

The only normal things in the pack were the magazine and stack of papers held together with a paper clip. Homework? I read the title. "Rosamund Parish: A New Perspective on the Legend of Otis Parish" by Fern Doucette.

It wasn't Max's paper. It was Fern's. Why did Max have a paper written by Fern Doucette?

Chapter 33

Sunday

For once I woke up feeling refreshed. Thank you for the extra hour of sleep, daylight savings time! My favorite day of the year.

I ate a quick breakfast and drove to Boston for company class and rehearsal. I jogged into the studio and instantly noted the subdued mood of everyone in the room. I ran up to Cody.

"What's going on?"

Cody pushed back his sandy hair. "It's Kellye. She broke her arm."

"No!" I gasped. "What happened?"

Cody threw a glance at Margot, who was warming up at the barre. "Kellye fell down the stairs to the basement."

The same stairs I'd fallen down. "I can't believe that." Impossible, just impossible.

His jaw hard, Cody folded his arms. "Believe it."

We both turned and looked at Margot. "Allie, I don't know what to do. I mean, there's no proof, but Margot was jealous of you and look what happened. She's been putting down Kellye for weeks and look what happened."

Serge came into the room and called, "Places."

I was so shocked by Cody's news that I could barely pay attention to my steps. After class, I headed toward Margot. I had questions I needed her to answer. But Serge called me over, and Margot hurried out the studio door.

My thoughts churned as I drove back to Mystic Bay, but thoughts of Max's murder pushed Margot from my mind. After a quick shower, I grabbed the backpack—I didn't want to let it out of my sight. Lorel and Aunt Gully had taken her BMW, so I drove the van to the Mermaid. The parking lot was full, so full that patrons were even sitting at our rickety meeting room table. They were soaking up the beautiful day—the sky was that deep autumn blue, such a perfect backdrop to the scarlet and orange leaves of the trees.

I carried Max's backpack into Aunt Gully's office and hung it on a peg next to some extra aprons. I shut the door firmly, my hand lingering on the knob. Guilt thrummed through me. I had to take it to the police.

Before leaving for rehearsal, I'd gone through every file and had been thankful that Madame's name didn't show up once. But the presence of Fern's paper baffled me. Why did Max Hempstead have her homework? I wanted to talk to her.

What did I really know about Fern Doucette? Besides the fact that she had a cute baby and was friends with Beltane. I did know there was no love lost between her and Max. Was her anger about being replaced as Lyman's TA enough to drive her to kill Max?

Through the pass-through, I noticed Aunt Gully, Lorel, and Don O'Neill seated together at a table by the door. Don slid his sunglasses into a pocket on his safari vest, which he wore over a BOSTON MARATHON T-shirt.

I washed my hands. "What's up with Don O'Neill? What did he bring Aunt Gully today? I didn't see a pony in the parking lot."

Hilda looked up from the worktable, her gloved hands flecked with bits of red lobster shell. "Get this. Don O'Neill offered Aunt Gully her photo on the label of Chowdahead's takeout cups. It's not credit exactly, but they will pay a hefty sum and it's a nice gesture."

"We got a hefty sum for catering that party on the Fourth of July and she hasn't spent a dime, even though that van is being held together by rust," I said. "Money just doesn't motivate Aunt Gully."

"True. Well, we have things under control here. Go see what's up. I'm dying to know."

As I joined the group in the dining room, Don leaned back in his chair. ". . . Chowdaheads franchise. The chowder will be made in a big state-of-the-art facility—"

I slid into the fourth seat at the table, nodding to everyone.

"Facility?" Aunt Gully wrinkled her nose.

Don smiled. "Don't you worry. It has the most modern safeguards and purity rules. Top-notch scientific standards."

"Science?" Aunt Gully frowned.

Don leaned forward. "Then the chowder will be frozen and—"

"Frozen?" Aunt Gully's eyebrows shot up

"Trucked and reheated in—"

"Facility? Frozen? Trucks?" Aunt Gully shook her head. Then to my surprise she laughed.

"You've given me a lot to think about. Thank you."

She patted Don's hand and gave him her twinkliest smile, her dark eyes warm, her head tilted slightly. The guy smiled back, a genuine, wide smile. Lorel and I exchanged glances, mine pleased, hers panicked.

Don actually thinks he's won her over.

When Aunt Gully used her hypnotizing smile, I knew exactly what it meant. Lorel's mouth dropped open. She knew what it meant, too.

"Don, my answer is no." Aunt Gully stood and spread her arms. Uh-oh. Here comes a song. She launched into the song from *Dreamgirls* but changed the lyrics.

"And I am telling you I'm not giving you my recipe!" Aunt Gully warbled. "No no no no no!"

Then she chuckled as she took him by the arm and helped him to his feet. Don looked dazed. His mouth moved but he didn't make any sound.

"You're a nice man and all the gifts have been very nice. But no means no."

Don O'Neill finally found his voice. "But—"

"It's been fun. My answer is no." Aunt Gully pushed him out the screened door and it closed with a bang.

Lorel rushed after Don, throwing a frosty look at me. *What did I do?*

"Did she just show him the door?" one customer said to another. "Maybe he didn't tip enough."

Aunt Gully went back into the kitchen to a smattering of applause. I followed her.

"The poor man. He'll look silly when he realizes that the answer was really, truly no. He just didn't want to hear it." Aunt Gully washed her hands and grabbed a spoon, stirring her chowder vigorously.

Lorel came in, her shoulders slumped. "Aunt Gully, that was a lot of money walking out the door."

Aunt Gully scoffed. "Don doesn't realize that my

chowder is different every time I make it. There is no recipe."

Lorel frowned. "But it always tastes the same."

"You know I don't use recipes. Sometimes the clams taste a bit different. Sometimes, I need to add more stock. Sometimes I'm feeling spicier than other days." Hector, Hilda, and the Gals nodded in agreement with this arcane cooking wisdom.

True. Every time someone asked Aunt Gully for the recipe, she cheerfully gave it to them. "All they have to do is ask." The one thing they'd never get is *the* recipe. She measured nothing, tossing in ingredients and tasting. A little of this, a little of that. When I asked for measurements, she'd say, well, a handful . . . unless it needs more. It was the same with her secret Lobster Love sauce for her lobster rolls.

Lorel held up a hand, "Wait a minute. So you don't really care what they put in the Aunt Gully's Chowdahead brand chowder."

Aunt Gully's cheeks pinked. "Of course I do. So don't you get any ideas about selling them any old recipe and calling it mine just for the payday, young lady."

Lorel sighed and looked away. Just what she'd been thinking. I laughed.

"If people want Aunt Gully's chowder, they can have my chowder. All they have to do is come to the Lazy Mermaid." Aunt Gully waved her spoon. "And that's all I have to say about that."

Chapter 34

We were slammed for a few hours with leaf peepers and tourists who'd been to the Historical Society Harvest Festival. Even Lorel threw an apron over her designer dress and pitched in. She looked lovely behind the counter while I picked lobster and hefted bags of trash into the Dumpster out behind the shack.

I was dying to talk to Fern about the paper in Max's backpack. Why did he have her paper? He needed money. I couldn't imagine why he'd blackmail a grad student who had no money. Unless . . . there was something in the paper that was valuable.

I glanced at the clock. Fern had said she'd be at the Harvest Festival until six and it was already five thirty. "Aunt Gully, could I—"

"Go!" chorused Aunt Gully and the Gals at the work-table.

I washed my hands, tossed my dirty apron in the basket by the door, and grabbed the backpack. "Thanks!"

I drove down the twisting road to Rabb's Point, my mind returning to Halloween night. Cars lined the road this afternoon too, jammed into any available spot, for the Harvest Festival. Since it was getting late, some folks had left and I found a space in the lot directly in front of the house. I turned off the engine.

A group gathered to the north of the house around a tall rack where fish were arrayed. Gladys Burley and Fred Nickerson stood on either side. A long-ago memory from a school field trip surfaced: the fish-drying demonstration.

Royal Parish, in his tall pilgrim hat and flowing cape, stood by the front door shaking hands with a visitor. I scanned the crowd but didn't see Isobel or Kathleen. I remembered what Kathleen had said that night by the barn: *All he thought of was his family history. Not his family.*

From the parking lot I could see Fern in the kitchen garden leading a tour group, her face alight with happiness. I'd have to wait until she was done. I stuck my head out the van window and waved. Fern waved back and held up both hands palms out, fingers spread. Ten minutes. I nodded.

The backpack lay on the passenger seat. A thought struck me. Maybe Fern wouldn't want me to read her paper.

Maybe I should read it now.

I opened the backpack and pulled out the magazine and paper. I hadn't paid much attention to the magazine when I'd been in the chapel library. I turned it over. *New England Scholarly History.* The magazine with Fern's article. I was sure Lyman Smith had lied to Fern about the "clerical mistake" that left her name off the article. I was certain she also realized that. It was too bad that she felt that she couldn't publicly accuse Lyman since she needed his recommendation for work or a PhD program. He must have realized that the position she was in would make it impossible for her to accuse him of his theft of her research. Besides, how could she prove it?

A slow suspicion kindled in me. *Prove it.*

Maybe Max had blackmailed Lyman Smith. What had Fern said? Max "ran papers" for plagiarism. Maybe he'd discovered that the history professor had stolen Fern's work, or maybe even had plagiarized from other students. Maybe Max had discovered a pattern of intellectual theft. Talk about a lot to lose, especially for a man just named head of the history department, who'd just received a plum grant.

Fern's paper was titled "Rosamund Parish: New Perspectives on the Legend of Otis Parish." I riffled through the pages. The last page had different-color ink and different font.

It wasn't part of Fern's paper. It was a report headed "PASS: Paper Assure for Scholars: Academia's Number One Plagiarism Software." I scanned graphs and columns of ID numbers. The report had been requested by M. Hempstead and compared two papers, one by Author S and one by Author D.

My heart rate kicked up a notch.

Paper by Author S and Paper by Author D had a match rate of ninety-five percent. Max hadn't gone too far out of his way to hide the identities of the authors. Smith and Doucette. Still, there were no names listed. Not quite the smoking gun. Maybe, having run this software for Lyman herself, Fern would have some insight into this report.

I set it aside and settled in to read Fern's new paper.

There was an introductory paragraph with a lot of academic terms like *folklorist* and *fixed text,* but then I skimmed to this sentence: "This story of blood, disease, fear, community pressure, and yes, love, has passed through the years, hidden away in the pages of a teenage girl's diary."

This sounded good.

Now we have a chance to verify the tale. Was it true?

I knew the outline of the Otis Parish story but this account went in a completely different direction than the legend I'd heard growing up. Fern was a talented storyteller. The sounds of the volley of colonial muskets, fiddle music, and bleating sheep in the shearing exhibition faded as I read, as I went back in time to Mystic Bay more than three hundred years earlier.

The house was illuminated only by meager candlelight . . . a figure ran toward the door, black cape flying like the wings of a bat. A woman wringing her hands, her white apron and cap glowing in the dark, stood waiting for him.

Otis Parish had indeed come from British gentry, having been given a royal grant to lands in the area of what local Indians called Micasset. The name survives as the name of the river that flows alongside the hundreds of acres once owned by the Parish family. The Parishes cleared land, sold the timber, grazed livestock, then farmed and traded with the native people. The small settlement grew into a prosperous village under the leadership of Otis Parish.

But diseases ran rampant, unchecked by modern medicine or scientific knowledge. Alone in a world lit by tallow tapers and offered only the chilly comfort of a hard Puritan religion, people in isolated areas struggled when diseases swept through.

One such outbreak, which historians believe was tuberculosis, took place in the area renamed Mystic Bay. The Parish family's affluence could not shield them from the epidemic.

Otis and Ann Parish had three children: Pardon, Mercy, and Uriah. Ann died giving birth to Uriah.

Pardon was in Boston when the epidemic began and was spared. He is the father of the line that ends with the family of Royal Parish, the current inhabitant of Parish House.

The scourge visited Mystic Bay and the community was decimated. When the outbreak began, Mercy had been engaged to marry a young man named Thomas Fletcher, who was one of the first to die.

The family thought they were safe on their isolated farm on what is now called Rabb's Point, but just as winter turned to spring Mercy started showing symptoms. The violent coughing of the disease brings blood to the lips. The pale skin of the sufferer, along with the drawn face, pulling back the skin from the mouth and exposing the teeth, all combined to turn the victim from an object of sympathy to one of fear.

Rumors started to spread that Thomas Fletcher had walked from his grave and returned to feast on the blood of his love, drawing her life's energy to sustain his. Mercy died and the family was wild with grief and fear, since shortly after they buried her, Uriah started to show the same symptoms. Had his sister, Mercy, come to drain him of his life's blood?

The diary of a distant cousin, Rosamund Parish, recently discovered in the archives of the Parish House Library, relates the terrible turn of events that followed.

I turned the page. I'd never heard this part of the story of Otis Parish.

Otis, so robust and steady, had unraveled. He'd already buried Mercy in a remote part of his property away from hallowed ground. Uriah, his younger son, was his favorite. As the most powerful man in Mystic

Bay, Otis had met with other community leaders—the parson, Reverend John Taylor, the schoolmaster, Parish's cousin Isaiah Goodnight, other prosperous farmers—bemoaning the evil that plagued their village. That's how the epidemic was seen, like one of the plagues that struck Egypt. What evil walked among them, taking the lives of so many in such a gruesome way?

How to stop it?

After weeks of prayer, death, and despair, the people of Mystic Bay turned to superstition. Surely it was vampires, those fell monsters of stories heard long ago. People heard that there was a way to strip the vampire of its power. They turned to a crone by the name of Wealtha Runnell. Shunned by the community, she lived in the marshes near the river and was known to make spells and charms. She was tolerated for her skill as a midwife, as other midwives with difficult deliveries would sometimes turn to her for guidance.

Otis was desperate. When Wealtha told him what he had to do, he begged to be spared from the task. But as a leader in the community he couldn't shirk his duty. He had to break a taboo to save his beloved son and all the people of Mystic Bay. Desperate villagers turned to him. He was their leader. He had to take action.

That night, with lantern light to guide them, in the company of his minister and several trusted friends, and the crone, he went to the graveyard where they'd buried the wasted body of young Mercy Parish. They disinterred the young girl, opened the simple wooden coffin. They set their lanterns on a large flat rock nearby.

To their dismay, her body retained its ghoulish appearance and blood still spattered the lips. Shaken, they almost turned from their brutal task, but duty drove them forward. At the direction of the crone, they opened the chest of the young girl and removed her heart, then burned it on the flat rock. When they were done, they took the ashes and mixed them in a cup of wine and brought it to Uriah to drink.

I squeezed my eyes shut and took a deep breath.

The men reburied the girl, taking care to turn the body in the coffin facedown as the crone directed them, so she could not rise again.

Uriah drank the mixture prepared for him, but it did not restore him to health. He died a few days later.

When they interred his body, the same grim men took measures to ensure that he would not walk among them after death. His head was removed from his trunk, the arms crossed, and again, buried facedown.

I shivered and skipped to the end. *Rosamund's diary entry is poignant: "I swear this to be true. It was related to me by the son of the Reverend John Taylor who did penance for the rest of his life for his crimes against the bodies of Mercy and Uriah Parish and his sin in following the commands of the witch, Wealtha Runnell."*

"'I have never seen a man weep so,' Taylor said of Otis Parish."

Finally my eyes focused and I was no longer seeing the grim faces of those men, lit only by lantern light, as they gathered around the large stone to burn the heart of Mercy Parish.

I'd never given thought to the other people buried in the graveyard near Otis Parish, so many buried in what I'd always heard was unhallowed ground.

I took a deep breath. Perhaps it had been an attempt at quarantine. They didn't really understand disease back then. They probably would've thought it was some kind of divine punishment, or a curse, like the one on Otis Parish for his crimes against the native people.

With a shock I realized that Otis Parish was buried there near Uriah and Mercy. Had he also been a victim of the epidemic? That wasn't in the history I'd ever heard. Or was his burial there an act of penance? Of punishment?

A face appeared at my window, jolting me back to the present day. Fern. I started, dropping the top page. "God you scared me!" I scrabbled on the floor to pick it up.

"Hi! How you're doing?"

"I was just reading . . ." Too late to hide it.

Fern's eyes flicked from my face to the stack of papers in my hand. "Is that my paper?"

"Can you talk for a sec?"

She ran around the van and got in the passenger side. She gathered the map and magazine then slammed the door. She jerked the paper from my hand.

"How did you get my paper? And that map? That should be in the files at Lyman Smith's office!" Fern shouted.

I took a deep breath. I owed her the truth.

"That was in Max Hempstead's backpack. He left it in a study carrel at the college chapel library."

Fern stared openmouthed at the stack of papers, then started putting them in order, her movements agitated.

"Your paper's amazing," I said.

She shuffled the papers into order and took a deep breath. "Thanks." She sat back against the passenger seat, her forehead creased. To my surprise, she laughed.

"The chapel library? Yeah, nobody goes there. Why was he hiding my paper?" she said more to herself than me. "That little rat must have gone into Lyman Smith's files and downloaded it. Lyman's the only other person who's seen this."

The backpack was on the floor at her feet. Though I liked her, I didn't think anyone but the police should know what else was in there. She noticed my glance.

"Is that Max's backpack? Why do you have Max Hempstead's backpack?" Her words were slow. I wondered if she was thinking that I had something to do with his death.

I told her everything, starting from when I saw Max guarding his backpack at the lobster shed.

"So you'll have to bring it to the police. I agree. But still, why did he have my paper?"

"Blackmail. I think, maybe, he was blackmailing people. Or at least was planning to. Let me show you this." I took the papers from her hands and found the report from PASS. "Is ninety-five percent—"

"Yes, that's egregious. Lyman was stealing my work and Max ran the comparison between my paper and his article. I'm furious about Lyman Smith, of course." She pressed her fingertips to her temples. "He said it was a mistake. He promised to fix it. I can't get him mad. I'll need his recommendation to get into a Ph.D. program anywhere."

"Fern, can I take this home to finish reading? This is fantastic."

My praise calmed her. "Yeah, you might as well read it. No one else will. I can't imagine Lyman would publish that one."

"Why not? It's a gripping story."

Fern's lips twisted. "This isn't the kind of family history Royal Parish wants to see published."

I put the manuscript inside the magazine and tucked

both next to the driver's seat. "I was transported back in time. The large stone—"

"The Witch's Rock. There are many of those structures throughout the woods. Colonists didn't think much of them—they weren't interested in the native people's culture. It's a coincidence that the Parishes used it for that terrible stuff they did to Mercy's body."

"Where did you learn all this? It's from Rosamund Parish's diary?"

Fern's eyes gleamed. "Yes. Would you like to see it?"

"Yes!"

I reached for the backpack. I still didn't want it out of my sight.

The festive crowd was beginning to thin. We threaded through the tourists who were streaming toward their cars. The bitter scent of wood smoke from the cooking fires blended with the rich aroma of earth and fallen leaves as we stepped inside the historical society building.

"The library's in the annex. Only board members have keys. I'll get the key from Beltane and I'll be right back." *Beltane.* I stiffened. Fern said it like you'd say the name of any normal coworker. I guess to Fern, Beltane was.

I stepped into the large front room where the grant presentation had been held just last week. How many things had changed since then. A life lost. Isobel—she'd lost Max, who I suspected she'd cared for quite a bit before the betrayal. Madame was in the hospital, facing the challenge of recovering from a stroke. Dreams— Madame's for a grant to create a ballet; Fred's for a grant to repair his boat—deferred or lost forever. Lyman Smith had been happy, though. That rat.

I stood in front of the same case of artifacts I'd seen

at the grant presentation, the case with the little white cards noting that some of the artifacts had been loaned out. I read the cards again.

Many items were familiar. Fishhooks. Marlinspikes.

Marlinspikes. Most sailors had one—a metal tool, sometimes curved, used to untie knots in ropes or to splice line. The one loaned out by the historical society was huge—a foot long. I'd never seen one so big.

"May I help you?" Heavy, spicy perfume surrounded me like a cloud of incense. Beltane.

Today the tall woman had her dark hair braided and coiled around her head. She wore a gray version of the colonial dress that she'd worn at the grant presentation, but on her it looked right. Actually, she looked like she belonged in the 1700s, except for the eyes ringed with Cleopatra-level kohl and general air of bat crazy.

Her eyes flicked to the case. "Oh, yes. Last-minute loans to the history department at the college." She pursed her lips. "Patriarchy."

"Patriarchy?" I blinked. "Excuse me?"

"Certain male professors think they own the place," Beltane said.

"Oh, Beltane, there you are." Fern ran up. "I thought you were upstairs. Can I have the key to the library, please?"

"Researching still? I thought your paper was complete."

"I want to show the diary to Allie."

Beltane took the key off a chain she had tucked in her pocket. "Fern is so dedicated to the history of Mystic Bay. She's made some great discoveries, brought into the light those who were so unjustly forgotten, so erased. Those whose stories have been suppressed."

Does she mean Rosamund and Mercy Parish? I nodded tentatively.

She gave me an appraising glance.

"It's okay, Beltane," Fern said. "I told her what's in the paper."

Beltane nodded. "The woman's voice, so often silenced. I'm so glad that Fern is giving Rosamund a voice beyond the grave."

"Yes, me too."

Fern tugged my arm. "Let's go."

Chapter 35

We cut through the kitchen garden and took the path to the small red barn. "The original barn burned down years ago. This was custom-built as an archives and library, so it looks old and charming on the outside but inside it's state-of-the-art." She pointed to the sign over the door. THE PARISH FAMILY TRUST ANNEX.

We stepped inside. A foyer was decorated with more dour-faced Parish portraits and a dozen shield-shaped plaques with brass name plates. I looked at the one closest to the door, with the shiniest name plates. "Board of Mystic Bay Historical Society. Guardians of Mystic Bay History."

Current President: Royal Parish
Past President: Professor Lyman Smith
Manager: Beltane Kowalski
Secretary: Gladys Burley

"Royal Parish loves his family history, but he wasn't interested in my research into the diary of Rosamund

Parish, because it led to the truth behind the legend of Otis Parish," Fern said. "I only showed my research to Lyman Smith, but he put me off. I'm sure he wanted to keep his friend Royal happy. Royal didn't want our discoveries made public. The truth made public. It's his version of Parish history or the highway."

A memory surfaced, confused me. Hadn't I heard Lyman, Royal's friend, telling the frat boys about the legend of Otis Parish?

"You could make sure people know that he stole your research."

She laughed. "How would I ever get another job? Lyman Smith is my reference. He's the only boss I've had for years. The academic world is small, Allie. I need the jerk."

"You'd think he'd want the truth. I mean, isn't history supposed to be true?"

"Oh, you poor misguided girl." She unlocked a door at the end of the hallway. "History is written by the winners. Why do you think the first thing conquering armies do is destroy the libraries and art of the conquered? That's how you erase people. Then your story is the only one left."

As she reached inside and flipped a light switch, Fern said, "This is the archives and library." We stepped into a long room lined with windows on one side, shelves on the other. The room was quiet, hushed except for the buzz of fluorescent lights. Long wooden tables set with wire baskets that held scholarly magazines stretched the length of the room

The door clicked shut behind us. "The room is climate controlled and has a state-of-the-art security system."

She took a key from the key chain and opened a glass-fronted cabinet. "Here's the diary of Rosamund Parish."

Fern pulled a book from the shelf, its cover brown and mottled, and set it in a V-shaped holder, its spine falling open easily.

"It's so small!" The diary was barely as wide as my cell phone.

"Look at the writing." She opened the pages lovingly, carefully. "Paper was precious back then. Look at how tiny the writing is." We bent over it, our heads close together.

"I like to imagine Rosamund bent over a table, lit only by candlelight, scratching out her thoughts on that rough paper with a quill pen," Fern said.

The writing was crabbed and faded. "It's hard to read."

"Look through this." Fern slid a magnifying glass on a wooden stand close to me.

I aimed it over the book. Fern turned the book to the inscription on the first page.

This booke is mine. Rosamund Parish, aged 14 years.

Seeing Rosamund's handwriting made her come alive. "This is amazing!"

Fern nodded. "A first-person document from that time period, by a woman, and not just a woman, but a young woman. We hardly have any surviving accounts from that viewpoint. This was stuck behind some old books. That's what I've been focusing my research on and"—she lowered her eyes—"I've started a book."

"How wonderful!"

Fern straightened her shoulders. "Lyman was always underestimating me. When I left on maternity leave, it was as if I disappeared. I kept researching. That was the nail in my coffin—he never took me seriously. Now maybe he'll finally give me the credit I'm due, with all I've discovered about Rosamund."

"Fern." Lyman Smith strode into the room. Had he been listening?

"Oh." Fern blushed. "Hello, Lyman."

His eyes flicked to me. I froze, praying he wouldn't notice Max's backpack on the table

Fern cleared her throat. "This is my friend Allie Larkin."

"This space is only for researchers approved by the historical society. We both know you're not on the list anymore." Lyman Smith spoke as if chastising a small child.

Could he be any more condescending?

Fern's cheeks blazed, but she gathered herself. Her look begged me to remain silent. "Excuse me." As she carefully placed the book back onto the shelf I slid the pack off the table, hoping he wouldn't notice. "Come on, Allie."

I shouldered the backpack, angling my body to conceal it. Lyman Smith's eyes lingered as he watched us leave. I hunched my shoulders under the disapproving looks of the Parish portraits in the hallway. Fern practically broke into a run as we burst from the door into the cool night air.

I rushed to keep up with her. "What did he mean? You're a researcher, right?"

"I am." Her voice was thick; she was trying not to cry. "Lyman took my name off the list of approved researchers when I stopped TAing for him."

"But Beltane let you—"

"He and Beltane have a contentious relationship. That's putting it mildly. She's the manager, he's a past president and friend of Royal Parish. He's always making demands, as if he were the only historian who mattered around here. Though I guess"—her shoulders drooped—"he is."

"Was Max a researcher?"

"Max? A historian?" She laughed. "He was more of an errand guy, Lyman Smith's right-hand man. And clearly I wasn't qualified for that role." She swiped her nose with the back of her hand. "Listen, I've got to go."

I watched her rush back into the house through the kitchen garden, her head bowed.

Chapter 36

I got back in the van, troubled by what had happened in the annex.

Under strings of lights, volunteers packed equipment and took down displays. Visitors drove back down the road toward Mystic Bay. A pang of guilt struck. They were probably all heading to Aunt Gully's for a lobster roll.

I drove back home. Danger emanated from the backpack on the seat next to me. Max had dug up all kinds of secrets that should have remained buried.

As had Fern. Her research had shown proof that the vampire story was even more grotesque than the stories that had been common lore in Mystic Bay for hundreds of years. When would the historical society start selling OTIS PARISH VAMPIRE KILLER T-shirts? Offer tours to the Witch's Rock? What an embarrassment for a man like Royal Parish, whose family history meant more to him than his actual family. His version of history, anyway.

Where was Isobel? How was she handling being questioned by the police? I thought guiltily that I hadn't visited

Madame Monachova in three days. I drove to the hospital.

I checked in with the hospital receptionist. She tapped her computer screen. "Good news. Ms. Monachova's been released."

"Released! She's gone home?"

The receptionist shrugged. I ran back to the van. Finally some good news. I turned the wheel toward New London, thinking guiltily that I should take Max's backpack to the police station. But it would be too late to bring it to the police by the time I finished visiting Madame, I mused. I'd bring it tomorrow.

I pulled up to the curb in front of her house. The lights were on and a Mercedes sedan gleamed in the driveway. The curtains were drawn on the broad front window, but twitched aside as I threw the backpack over my shoulder and ran up to the door—Raisa and Rudi were watching. I rang the bell.

Isobel Parish opened the door. I was so shocked I stood speechless for a moment. My hand flew to my shoulder. What if Isobel recognized the pack? I turned so it was angled behind me. Regaining my composure, I said, "Isobel! You're—"

"Not in jail." Her lips twisted. "Good old Dad was good for something."

"Can Madame have visitors?" Raisa and Rudi threaded around our ankles.

Madame's voice called from inside. Her words were so soft and indistinct I couldn't tell what she said. But Isobel held the door wide and went back into the living room. As I stepped inside, I slipped the bag from my shoulder and hid it as best I could behind an umbrella stand.

Madame Monachova sat in the corner of the couch

against oversized silk pillows. She wore a pale yellow quilted bathrobe with a gold and blue pashmina stole around her shoulders. A plate of cookies and delicate teacups covered the coffee table in front of her. I rushed to her and flung my arms around her. "You're home! I'm so glad!"

She laughed and took a deep breath. "Me, too." She still slurred her words, but she looked stronger.

Isobel sat cross-legged on the floor, scrolling on her phone. She took a cookie from the tray.

"Hello, Allie." Kathleen Parish sat on the piano bench, wearing jeans, a sweater, and shearling slippers. This was the most casual outfit I'd ever seen her wear. She looked at home, comfortable.

"Hello." I settled on the couch next to Madame Monachova. My eyes fell on a walker in the corner by the fireplace. Madame followed my glance.

"My new best friend." She laid her hand on mine, her words slow and deliberate as she worked to form each word. "Don't look so shocked, Allie. It's only a matter of time before I'm better. With the walker they will let me be at home, instead of a rehab center. I will have an aide to get me around. She starts tomorrow." Madame patted my hand. "The doctor says my prognosis is very good. Evidently, I have the body of a thirty-year-old. Who knew?"

We laughed. Raisa leaped into my lap and I nuzzled her.

"The therapist asked me if I have a goal. I said my goal is to choreograph my ballet."

Kathleen filled Madame's teacup. "And I'm going to make it happen."

"I have a particular dancer in mind for the lead role." Madame squeezed my hand. "You."

* * *

My heart was lighter than it had been in weeks as I grabbed the backpack and left Madame Monachova's house. I tossed the pack on the passenger seat as my phone rang.

"Hi, Verity."

"Hey, what are you up to? Do you have developments in the case?"

"Yes. Get this. I found the backpack."

"Are you kidding me?" she shouted.

"How about getting some ice cream? Scoops is still open."

"Meet you there."

I pulled away from the curb and did a U-turn to head back to the highway to Mystic Bay, humming the music from my solo.

Movement drew my eye. Madame's street was broad, lined with several one-story ranch-style houses on fairly large lots. Most people parked in their driveways, but I noticed a car pull from the curb down the road. Its headlights weren't on.

Who forgets to put on their lights? A drunk? The car followed but didn't get too close. My unease grew as I left the busier streets of New London, but as I crossed the brightly lit Gold Star Bridge, the car fell back in traffic. I exhaled.

Get a grip, Allie.

I put on the Pat Benatar CD and sang along.

I exited the highway onto a narrow, curving country road that led into Mystic Bay from the north, a quiet stretch by the reservoir lined with ditches and stone walls. Scoops was a mile down on the banks of the Micasset River. I glanced at the clock. Eight thirty. They closed at nine. There wasn't any traffic. We'd be in time. I couldn't wait to tell Verity what I'd learned.

The growl of an engine made me look to my left. A dark car swerved alongside me, its engine roaring. The next second, it rammed into the side of the van. The impact forced me toward the ditches. Shock surged through my body as the steering wheel jerked in my hands. I fought to regain control, swerving back onto the road. Again, the dark car thudded against the van. A vision of Max's murdered body flashed in my mind. *Could this be the murderer?*

I gripped the wheel, trying to avoid the gaping ditches bordering the road. The car rammed me again. This time the impact wrenched the steering wheel from my hands. I screamed as the van hurtled toward the trunk of an oak tree.

Chapter 37

A car door slammed. "Allie!" Verity's voice edged into my consciousness. An EMT shone a light at my eyes. I winced.

"You're going to be okay. Good thing you had your seat belt on."

"Does she have a concussion?" Verity asked the EMT. He shook his head. "Thank goodness! When you didn't come to Scoops I thought maybe the van broke down!" Verity flung her arms around me.

I sat on a tree stump, surrounded by first responders. Every bone in my body felt like it had been jarred loose. "A car." My words wouldn't come. I cleared my throat. "A dark car. Forced me off the road." It all came back to me slowly. "Then somebody came to the van. Opened the passenger side door. Oh, no." I stood up quickly, then swayed.

"Sit still." The EMT lowered me back onto the tree stump then looked at Verity. "We're going to take her to the ER—"

"No," I moaned.

"Just a precaution," the EMT added.

I grabbed Verity's arm. "Check the van. I think the guy who ran me off the road took the backpack."

Verity ran to the van, where a tow truck was hooking onto its rear bumper. The impact against the tree had smashed in the front end of Aunt Gully's van. *Oh, no.*

Verity gestured wildly as she spoke to the tow truck crew. They shrugged but let her look in the front seat. She ran back, empty-handed.

"Not there."

The EMT gestured to the ambulance. "Do you think you can walk?"

"Wait a sec, Verity." My mind cleared and I remembered Fern's paper tucked in the magazine. "Check the van one more time. I left a magazine next to the driver's seat." Verity exchanged dubious glances with the EMT. "It's important."

She ran back a few minutes later, waving the magazine. "I got it."

Chapter 38

Thank goodness the next day I had a day off from rehearsals, one of my last before the *Nutcracker* madness began. The doctor at the emergency room had given me an all clear and a prescription for muscle relaxants. Aunt Gully told me to sleep in, that I could come down to the shack when and if I felt up to it. Without the van, she'd get a ride with one of her Gals. Normally if I didn't have the van I'd ride my bike to the Mermaid—it was only ten minutes away—but Hilda offered to get me if I decided to go in to work.

My body still ached. I stood slowly and did a mental check—gingerly moving my arms and legs. I tested my ankle and sighed when I stepped onto it—no pain. My neck and shoulders hurt but the doctor said that would be better in a few days.

I took a deliciously long soak in the tub, borrowing some of Aunt Gully's lavender bath salts. Afterward, I felt better, sore but better. I did some stretching, then some of my usual routine. Relief flooded me. I'd still be able to dance.

I took a canvas tote bag from my closet, one printed

with an image of Audrey Hepburn in her big *Breakfast at Tiffany's* sunglasses. Before falling into bed after a cup of Aunt Gully's tea, I'd hidden the magazine and Fern's paper inside.

Bronwyn called. "I just heard about last night. Are you okay?"

"Yes. Do the police know anything about the guy that hit me?"

I heard her exhale. "Dark car on a dark road." Relief battled with exasperation in her voice. "No buildings with security cameras anywhere near. The guy picked a good stretch to hit you."

"Remember I told you about the papers Max took?" I took a deep breath. I had to tell her the truth. "I found them, in his backpack. The driver who hit me took it."

I could practically feel Bronwyn's dismay. "Allie, you should've—"

"I know, I know. Bronwyn, I'll come talk to the police. I promise." I hesitated. "Anything new about Max's murder?"

She was quiet for a moment. I crossed my fingers that she'd have new information and that she'd tell me.

Bronwyn sighed. "No, nothing new here. They're having a heck of a time with the murder weapon. It wasn't a sword, no matter that the crazies think the ghost of Otis Parish used the family heirloom to slay the lacrosse star."

"So they know that it wasn't the Parish sword? So what was it?"

"The medical examiner said it was a weapon that was tapered and slightly curved."

"Tapered? Curved?" What could that be? A memory struggled to surface.

"Listen, I have to go. Talk to you later?"

"Okay."

* * *

At the Mermaid, everyone fluttered around me making sympathetic noises. I was thankful they settled down quickly after it became apparent that I wasn't badly hurt.

"I feel so bad about your van, Aunt Gully."

She hugged me. "The cargo is the only thing I care about. Besides . . ." She looked out the window toward the river flowing by our dock. "You and your sister were right. It's been time for new wheels for quite a while." She shook herself and spread a red checked tablecloth over a table in the corner, then set a miniature pot of yellow chrysanthemums on it along with one of those candles stuck in a Chianti bottle.

"Have you heard the news?" Hilda said. "There was a break-in at the historical society."

"I was just there last night!" I said.

She nodded to the television in the corner of the shack. Leo Rodriguez and Beltane stood in front of the Parish Annex, the small library building I'd visited with Fern the night before.

"I'm with . . ." He looked at his notes. "Beltane."

She regarded him with serene disdain. "Just Beltane." Her look said, *Silly mortal.*

He paused a beat. "Beltane is the manager of the Mystic Bay Historical Society. Tell us what happened," he said.

"Early this morning I came in to work." Beltane gestured toward the annex. "I noticed that several shelves in our research library had been disturbed, with books scattered to the floor. I called in our librarian and some of our researchers. They are going through our collection to see what, if anything, has been taken." She looked Leo right in the eye, her voice smoky and deep. "Our historical objects are precious, and irreplaceable, as you must realize."

"Yes, ma'am," Leo said, then shook himself. "Was anything damaged?"

"So far, it doesn't look like anything was badly damaged." Beltane's words were measured, but tension simmered underneath her unruffled exterior. Her fists were balled. Of course she was angry.

"How did the vandals, or thieves, get into the building?" Leo continued.

"The police have yet to determine that."

He turned toward the camera. "Well, yes, we'll keep you up to date on this breaking news. From the Mystic Bay Historical Society, I'm Leo Rodriguez."

"Oh, the way she looked at him. Like she was going to pull his soul out through his eyes," a woman at the counter said, shivering.

"Maybe the thief was the ghost of Otis Parish," a customer said. "Looking for something to read."

"Allie, weren't you there yesterday?" Hilda asked as she handed a customer a cup of coffee.

"With half of Mystic Bay at the Harvest Festival." Who would knock a bunch of old books off the shelves? Perhaps some were valuable and the vandalism was supposed to hide the theft? Fern's words stirred in my memory: What's the first thing conquering armies do? Destroy museums and libraries. I remembered Beltane's word, *silenced*.

Silenced. Erased.

I pressed the tote bag with Fern's paper and the magazine to my side. I wasn't letting this get away from me. I felt like a fool. I'd lost the backpack and I wasn't losing this.

Gladys and Fred came in through the screen door, Fred carrying the gigantic prize check.

"Our winners!" Aunt Gully beamed as she greeted them. "Come right in! I have your table right here."

Fred wore a fresh plaid shirt and pressed chinos with a blue sweater vest. His tie was printed with bright red lobsters. Gladys wore a white polo shirt tucked into black slacks, topped with a black sweater embroidered with pumpkins and purple ribbons. She'd applied a slick of red lipstick.

Well, well, well. A date.

Hector wiggled his eyebrows at me from the pass-through as I went behind the counter and into the tiny office off the kitchen where I hung up my tote bag.

I hurried to rejoin Hector. Aunt Gully set menus in front of Fred and Gladys.

"Is she matchmaking? Why bother? They're already a match," Hector said.

"How about cups of chowder to start off your winner's dinner?" Aunt Gully said.

Hilda stood behind the counter and took photos. "Your sister asked me to," she said. I wondered why she hadn't asked me. Hilda read my mind. "She said you're too wrapped up in *The Nutcracker.* She thought you'd have rehearsal today."

Lorel. I'd forgotten to call her and tell her about the accident. I texted her, then slid the phone in my pocket.

I remembered the plaque I'd seen last night. Gladys was on the board of the historical society.

Fred headed to the restroom as I carried over bowls of chowder. I was itching to ask about the vandalism, but Gladys was already talking to Aunt Gully about it.

I set the bowls down along with some oyster crackers.

Gladys pursed her lips. "I just heard. The inventory is

complete. Only one thing missing." My heart dropped. I knew what she was going to say. "A diary from one of the Parish family members, one of a kind, written by Rosamund Parish."

"Allie, are you okay?" Aunt Gully said. "You look like you saw a ghost."

Gladys jabbed her spoon at me. "You were in there. I saw you go in yesterday with Fern Doucette."

Her tone was accusatory. I swallowed. "We left right after—" Right after Lyman Smith threw us out. "Right after Lyman Smith came in. That was yesterday evening. Everything was fine then. I hope the police talk to him."

"Oh, they have." She smirked and sipped her soup.

"What did he say?"

Aunt Gully shot me a warning look but I ignored her.

"The diary was found in Fern Doucette's bag this morning. The police got a tip." She smiled and my stomach soured with dislike. "Lyman told her that she's not welcome at the historical society anymore."

Poor Fern!

Fred returned from the restroom, rubbed his hands together and sat down. "We're looking forward to this. Gladys has never had a lobster roll before."

I forced a smile. "I hope you enjoy it."

I headed for the kitchen, my mind whirling. *Fern wouldn't steal the diary, would she?*

An empty plastic crate leaned against the kitchen wall. I took it outside to stack with the others behind the shack.

A cool gust of wind blew a paper cup across the gravel. I bent to pick it up and carried it to the trash bin. Then I put the crate with the others behind the shack.

A box was overturned under the kitchen window, just where I'd seen the Peeping Tom last week. Orange and black tinsel dangled from the gutters; Aunt Gully hadn't had a chance to pull down all the Halloween decorations. I sighed, thinking how many hours it would take to un-decorate the shack. The tinsel looked ready to fall, so I tugged on it. It didn't move. What was holding it up?

When I looked up I noticed a tiny black box stuck to the underside of the eaves, held in place with a strip of black masking tape. The tape had caught on the tinsel. I froze.

A red light on the box blinked. It was a video camera, aimed in the window of the shack.

Chapter 39

I dashed into the shack. "You're not going to believe this." I pulled everyone toward the back door, away from the window, and told them about the camera.

"Do you think the Peeping Tom was back?" Hilda said.

Aunt Gully put her hands on her hips. "Enough! Hector, do you have a baseball bat at home?"

"What? For Don O'Neill? Don't you want to wait until after the Celtics game tonight to kill him?" Hector said.

Aunt Gully pushed up her sleeves and started steamrolling toward the back door. I grabbed her arm.

"Wait a second, Aunt Gully. Don't you want to catch him?"

She took a deep breath. "Don O'Neill sent me the nicest note telling me to enjoy the Celtics game tonight. I thought that was awfully big of him after I kicked him out." She folded her arms. "He was just trying to lull me into a false sense of security."

"I have an idea," I said. "Let's set a trap. Aunt Gully, You haven't made a fresh batch of chowder since yesterday, have you?"

Aunt Gully's eyes widened. "Why, I think I know where you're going with this. You devious little sweetheart! No, I haven't."

During the summer, Aunt Gully would have to cook up chowder every day to feed hungry customers. Now that business had slowed, Aunt Gully cooked up a huge pot of chowder every couple of days. She said her chowder was even better now because the chowder had a chance to rest and the flavors mellow.

She opened the window near the stove. "I do declare, it's time to make some chowder," she enunciated clearly. She went to the shelf and pulled down a supersized jar of red pepper and set it down on the counter next to the stove with a thump.

She came back to us and whispered. "I have an idea. I'm going to pop over to Delilah's for a few ingredients."

We high-fived. Aunt Gully went to the office for her purse. "I'll be back soon. Then it's time to make chowder." She waved and stepped outside.

Hector hummed as he turned back to the steamer and Hilda and I plated lobster rolls.

A crash came from the dining room.

One of Gully's Gals stuck her head through the passthrough. "Somebody call an ambulance!"

My heart pounded as we raced into the dining room.

Gladys slumped forward, her head on the table, empty bowl and plate on the floor.

Hilda and I pulled her upright. Her arms were covered with red splotches.

"What on earth?" Hilda said.

I heard a customer giving our address to the 911 dispatcher.

Hector lifted Gladys in his strong arms and lowered her to the floor. Hilda cradled Gladys's head on her lap.

Angry red blotches covered Gladys's neck and face, and her cheeks were swollen.

Fred's eyes were huge behind his thick glasses as he wrung his large, callused hands. "Oh, Allie, I think my Gladdy's allergic to lobster! She said she couldn't catch her breath!"

Hilda bent over Gladys. "She's breathing. You'll be fine, Gladys, just hang on."

The wail of an ambulance approached and moments later it pulled up to the front door of the Mermaid. Thank goodness we were just a few blocks from the Plex, the police department, and the fire department.

I patted Fred's back, then held the door open for the EMTs, and stood back as they went to Gladys.

After the EMTs wheeled Gladys out on a stretcher with Fred trailing forlornly behind, I'd cleaned up the spilled food, straightened the table and chairs, all the while trying to steady my nerves. I'd heard about people being allergic to lobster, but I'd never seen a reaction like Gladys's.

"Hi, Allie." Fern Doucette came in, closing the door softly behind her. She wore a stained GRAYSTONE COLLEGE sweatshirt over baggy black leggings. Exhaustion had drained her face of color and her freckles stood out on her pale skin.

"Fern, are you okay?"

She shook her head no and sat heavily on the chair I'd just righted. "Allie, did you see the news?" She wiped her eyes with a tissue.

I nodded and slid into the seat across from her. I'd reset the table with Aunt Gully's cheerful red-checked tablecloth, candle, and yellow mum, which contrasted with Fern's worried expression.

"I was helping Beltane with an exhibit early this morning when Royal and Lyman dropped in. They went to the annex and came rushing back, saying there'd been a break-in and theft. Royal and Lyman actually demanded that I open my bag. Well, they asked to see everyone's who was there, me, Beltane, and two volunteers who were dusting, but I knew the way they were looking at me that they were searching 'everyone's'"—she made air quotes—"bags just to prove they weren't targeting me. Well, it didn't work. Now everyone thinks I'm a thief. Except for Beltane. She's the only one who's standing with me."

I was starting to see Beltane in a new light. I couldn't believe that Fern would steal or destroy any historical objects. I'd seen how reverently she'd treated Rosamund Parish's diary. "How do you think the diary got in your bag?"

Fern sniffled. "Allie, meet me at the historical society tonight. Seven o'clock. It's the monthly meeting. I need you to tell Lyman and Royal and everyone else that you were with me and that I didn't steal that diary. You saw me put it on the shelf!" She showed me her tote bag, cream-colored burlap with the Virginia Woolf quote stenciled in black: *For most of history, anonymous was a woman.* "Everyone knows my bag. I think Lyman planted the diary in my bag this morning. It was hanging on a peg in the mudroom off the kitchen."

"Of course I'll go with you. But why would Lyman . . ." Of course I knew why. He wanted to get rid of Fern, or at least discredit her, so any accusation she made against him for plagiarism would look like retaliation. Fern threw her arms around me and waved as she left. I stood, pushing in our chairs, wondering what would happen at the meeting that night.

Voices and laughter billowed from the kitchen and pulled me from my thoughts. Aunt Gully started singing. This would be good. I rushed to the kitchen.

Aunt Gully had found a chef's toque and put it on, tilting it at a flirty angle. "And here I am, making my chowder, just like I do every day. With my secret recipe. I need a lot of clams."

She put in half as many clams as usual. Thank goodness she was using a smaller pot because I had a feeling this particular batch of chowder wasn't going to be edible.

Hector came into the kitchen. "I took a quick look at the camera," he whispered, his back to the window. "It's the transmitting kind and appears to be working fine. Hope Don enjoys the show."

"I hope she won't be too hammy. Aunt Gully . . ." I caught Aunt Gully's eye and made a "slow down" motion.

She nodded and tightened the strings on her apron. She started whistling "Get Happy," a Judy Garland tune she sang as a victory song. She was on a roll.

I knew that Aunt Gully usually started her chowder by sautéing salt pork, a step she now omitted, instead heaping the clams with huge tablespoons of butter. She stirred vigorously as she hummed. She added the chopped vegetables as usual, tossing in several extra handfuls of garlic and shallots and a handful of tomalley, the "green stuff" from lobster.

Hilda turned her back to the camera. "Good grief," she whispered

"And now for my secret ingredients." Aunt Gully spoke in an exaggerated whisper. I rolled my eyes. She was talking right at the camera.

She opened a little brown paper bag from Delilah's

shop. I had a hard time acting casual as I plated two lobster rolls and handed them through the pass-through.

Aunt Gully tossed in two bundles of licorice root, the
same spell-casting stuff Beltane had left in the dining
room. Next, she pulled out a bunch of chamomile, scattering the dried flower heads with a flourish. Then, a
dried fish head, and—I almost choked—a chicken's foot.

"Can't forget the pepper!" She shook in a generous
portion of cayenne pepper and stirred. She bent over the
pot and inhaled.

"Ah, perfect! Now I'll just put the lid on and let it simmer for two hours."

Hector pushed through the screen door outside and
bent over laughing. "Oh, Hector," she called in her sweet-
est voice. "If you'll bring me that special cooking tool
we talked about."

Hector wiped his eyes. "Yes, ma'am." He jogged away.

"Special cooking tool?" I said.

Aunt Gully's eyes glittered. "Special."

Five minutes later, Hector returned, whistling, carrying
a baseball bat over his shoulder. We gathered at the back
of the shack. Hector handed the bat to Aunt Gully with
a bow.

"First we'll put on our little play for Don. Ready?"
Aunt Gully said in a low voice.

Hilda and I nodded.

"Roll 'em!" Aunt Gully stage-whispered.

Hilda and I walked to the back of the shack, carrying
a stepladder and carton. "Time to take down these decorations," I said as I set the ladder almost directly under
the camera. "I had a hard time taking down the tinsel.
It's stuck."

"Yes. We must take them down." Hilda sounded like

the computer voice from a very cheap GPS. "It will be time to decorate for Thanksgiving very soon." She climbed the ladder and tugged the tinsel with the same robotic acting style. Hector and I started giggling. Aunt Gully poked us with the bat and shushed us.

"Oh, my! Come look. It's a cam-er-a!" Hilda shouted. Her wooden acting set me off; I had to choke back my laughter.

Hector put his hands on either side of his face and imitated Hilda's pronunciation. "A cam-er-a!" I burst out laughing.

Some Gals peered around the corner of the shack. I put a finger to my lips. Hector whispered to them and waved them back out of camera range.

Aunt Gully barreled over to the stepladder. "God bless America! A camera, you say? Let me see."

Hilda climbed down.

"Stand back, everyone!" Aunt Gully took a practice swing, gauging the distance to the camera.

Hector helped her up the ladder. "Let it rip, Aunt Gully."

She lined up the bat and the camera, and swung. The camera flew through the air and ricocheted off the Dumpster.

The crowd cheered.

Chapter 40

Later that afternoon, I hung a sign on the front door of the Mermaid: CLOSED FOR CELTICS GAME.

Aunt Gully called me over as Bit Markey squeezed into the backseat of Hilda's lime-green Volkswagen Beetle.

"Allie, with so much happening I forgot to tell you. I've got a loaner coming from the mechanic until I get a new van. He said it'll be here in a few minutes."

"What kind of loaner?"

"Didn't say. He said I can keep it until I have time to shop for a new one." She got in and then Hector folded his tall frame into the front seat. Hilda honked as they spun out of the parking lot.

I'd figured I'd call Verity for a ride to the historical society, but this was welcome news. Almost anything would be better than Aunt Gully's old van. For a moment I pictured myself driving a shiny BMW like Lorel's. *Don't get your hopes up, Allie.* Knowing Aunt Gully's mechanic, the loaner would be something practical.

Some Gully's Gals helped me close up the Mermaid, then I sat on one of the Adirondack chairs outside, wait-

ing for my ride. I sighed. I'd be late for the historical society meeting.

New security floodlights lit up the shack; I wasn't sure
if Aunt Gully had bought them with safety in mind or
with the thought that they would set off her decorations.
They threw enough light for me to see all the diners who
drove in, walked up to the shack, and left disappointed. I
stayed in my shadowy spot, glad I'd put on a dark sweatshirt with a hood. I tucked my hair underneath and enjoyed being invisible.

I scrolled through pictures on my phone—lots of
people had posted pictures from Isobel Parish's Halloween party. A sense of unease settled on me as I remembered the moment in the cemetery when the guys standing
on Otis Parish's grave had discovered Max's body. Someone had taken a photo of that moment. I prayed that no
one ever posted it online.

One photo of a group of guests in front of paneled
walls and a fireplace made me sit up: Madame Monachova, Royal, and Lyman stood together holding drinks.
This photo had been taken in the little room where the
bar had been set up at the Parish House.

Madame had on the same simple colonial-style dress
that Aunt Gully and Beltane had worn, but hers was a
lovely pale blue, and she wore no cape. I remember how
warm it had been that night. She'd said she'd left her cape
in the coat room.

Despite the warm night, Royal was still resplendent
in his long cloak, holding what I assumed was a Scotch
on the rocks instead of his Pilgrim hat. Lyman Smith still
wore his costume but somehow it looked different.

He'd switched to a shorter, tighter cape.

That was odd.

I scrolled back through the pictures. In the group

photo at the grant ceremony, Lyman's cape was as long as Royal's. Now his cape was shorter.

I saw us all running after Kathleen after she'd panicked, Madame Monachova in front of me, her cloak flowing behind her as she ran, so long it trailed in the grass. It was too long for her. I'd stepped on it.

My heart rate ticked upward. She had Lyman Smith's cloak.

Slow down, Allie. I remembered what the frat guys said. The capes and coats were all piled together in the coat room. Anyone could have been wearing the cloak that Madame put on. Couldn't they?

Max had been stabbed with a tapered, curved instrument. I remembered seeing the marlinspikes in the case at the historical society as we waited for the grant presentation. One had been missing, on loan.

What had Beltane said? *Last-minute loans . . . maritime tools . . .*

I remembered Beltane and Lyman Smith talking in the garden before the grant presentation. She'd told him she'd put the loaned items in the office.

Who could get into the office? So many people had been at the old Parish House for the grant presentation. The office would've been locked. Fern told me the annex had a security system and only board members had keys.

Royal, Lyman, Gladys, and Beltane made up the board.

Isobel. I still thought it was possible that Isobel could have murdered Max, mistaking him in the dark for her father. She could have gotten into the annex by taking her father's key. But she'd cared for Max, and despite her volatile temperament, she'd simply been too busy to have time to murder him.

Royal. I didn't know his movements the night of the

party. He must have suspected that Isobel had disarmed the security system for someone, for one of her boyfriends, when his files had been stolen. I'd heard him yelling about his family honor. Did he care enough about the Parish family's reputation to take a life?

Why would Lyman Smith kill Max, his right-hand man? Simple. Max knew Lyman's secret—that he plagiarized Fern's work. Something that had happened at the party struggled to surface, something I'd seen, something I'd heard that made me certain this was the right track.

The throaty roar of a downshifting engine interrupted my thoughts. A yellow convertible sports car pulled up to the front door of the Mermaid. I hunched my shoulders. Another disappointed diner. A white pickup truck followed and parked beside the sports car. Aunt Gully's mechanic jumped out of the truck.

Oh, great. A pickup truck. You couldn't get more practical than that.

As I approached I could see into the sports car. Its leather seats looked meltingly soft. I sighed.

A guy got out of the sports car, closed the door, and looked longingly at the closed front door of the Mermaid.

"Hey, Allie." Aunt Gully's mechanic, one of Uncle Rocco's old buddies, came around the truck holding out a set of keys. To my surprise, the younger guy waved and got in the truck. "It's a stick, but your aunt said you both can drive one. Take good care of her. Gully said she'd be happy with the truck but my son's moving to a new apartment and I need it to move his stuff." He winked. "Thought she'd get a kick out of this. It's just like the one in a TV show she used to like, *Hart to Hart*. Raise the top like this." He demonstrated how to raise the roof of the car, then lowered it again. "Have fun and get it back . . . whenever." He grinned.

"Th-thanks!" I waved as he pulled out of the parking lot. I turned back to the sports car, opened the door, and got in. The leather seats embraced me. *I'm never moving. This is a dream. This can't be real.*

But it was. I turned the key and the engine rumbled to life.

The drive to the old Parish House was pure exhilaration. With the top down, it was a bit cold, but I was in a convertible! I had to leave the top down. I had to. I might have driven a little fast, but the car hugged the curves of the road and purred as I pulled into the parking lot of the historical society.

I'd never been a car person. Cars were for transportation, and if you were living in a city, they were an expense and a nuisance. But I was falling hard for this car. *Hart to Hart* car? That was right. It had my heart. Reluctantly, I shut the door of the beautiful machine.

There were just a few other cars in the lot, two practical New England SUVs and a luxury sedan, all black, and one gray sedan I recognized—Fern's.

The black vehicles jolted me back to last night when I was run off the road. The impact. The sickening way Aunt Gully's van had lurched into the ditch replayed in my mind. The joy of my drive over from the shack evaporated.

I shone my cell phone beam on the sides and front end of all the cars, but there were no scrapes. None of these cars had driven me off the road last night. My attacker could probably afford another car and had the battered vehicle tucked away somewhere until the police stopped searching for it. Plus, I'd given the police nothing to go on—dark car, maybe an SUV. In New England, that description fit a lot of cars.

As I approached the front door of the old Parish House,

my mind flashed back to Fern's story of Rosamund Parish. *A woman stood at the door, white bonnet framing her face, worry and fear in her eyes.*

I blinked. *Get a grip, Allie. Check your imagination and stay sharp.* Yes, I was here to help Fern but I was also pretty sure the killer of Max Hempstead was attending this meeting and this killer had a lot to lose. I wondered at the fear that would drive a person to kill another, the hubris of taking a life.

I stepped inside, shutting the heavy wooden door softly behind me. Immediately I felt the disdainful gaze of all the Parishes on the walls, looking out from behind the crackled glaze of centuries-old paint. I followed the quiet murmur of voices to a small room off the kitchen, the keeping room. Royal Parish, Beltane, Lyman Smith, and Gladys Burley sat at a wooden table, Fern Doucette stood at the end.

Old-fashioned table lamps on heavy antique furniture made pools of pale yellow light. The board members had all worn dark-colored sweaters and their expressions were serious. Royal paused, watching me over his reading glasses, as I entered the room.

Fern still wore her gray sweatshirt, her pale hair loose on her shoulders. I thought of a play I'd seen years ago, about an innocent woman accused of witchcraft. The actress had stood just as Fern did now, her chin lifted, her fear warring with anger.

"Sorry to interrupt," I said. "I'm sorry I'm late, Fern."

"Thank you for coming, Allie," Fern breathed.

"Objection. This person is not on the agenda for the meeting." Gladys jabbed a paper on the table in front of her. I was relieved to see her blotches had faded but her eyes blazed with indignation.

Royal and Lyman exchanged glances.

"Gladys, I'm glad you're doing better—" I started.

Royal raised a hand to interrupt me. "Young lady, you can't just—"

"Please, just listen to what Allie has to say. She was with me at the annex last night," Fern said.

Gladys opened her mouth to speak.

"I was with Fern yesterday in the annex," I said quickly. "Professor Smith came into the library. He saw us looking at the book and told Fern to put it back. She did and we left."

Beltane's crow-black eyes shifted to Lyman. "Is that what happened?"

Lyman nodded. "Yes. I didn't want to go into it and embarrass Fern further although she was breaking the rules by taking unauthorized visitors into the annex. After all, Fern isn't on the list of approved researchers. I value Fern's contributions, of course." He nodded at her, still so condescending. "But it doesn't matter. The book was found in her bag. And you, Beltane, were here with Fern this morning . . ." His voice dripped with insinuation.

"Neither one of us went into the library, Lyman," Beltane said in her silky voice.

"That doesn't change the fact that the book was found in Fern's bag."

"And how did Fern do this? When she was with me?" A warning note crept into Beltane's voice. "The police said there was no sign of forced entry and you know as well as I that there are only four keys to the annex."

Royal cleared his throat, looked over his reading glasses. "My key went missing, Beltane. A few days ago."

Fern clutched the edge of the table. "Now you're saying I stole your key?" Her voice shrilled.

"Not at all." Royal's tone was reasonable. He gave Fern a small smile. "Anyone could have taken it." But he left the possibility hovering in the air. Of course, Fern was anyone.

"Wait a minute—" I began.

"No, you wait a minute. If you don't leave, I'll call the police," Gladys said.

"Fine with me," I shot back.

Fern looked at me wildly.

Beltane leaned toward Fern. "Fern, you have to do just that. Speak your truth."

Royal's eyebrows jerked up. "Wait a second, wait a second, we're all getting heated. Let's discuss this at another time. What do you say? We'll discuss it more fully at the next meeting. Gladys, what looks good on the calendar?"

Gladys made a show of scrolling through a tablet. "Why don't we add a few minutes to the December meeting? No, that's a busy time. How about January?"

"Very well." Lyman stood. "I have papers to grade."

Fern looked panicked. "But—"

Royal smiled. "We'll discuss it more fully then."

Beltane rose and took Fern's arm. "Come on, Fern."

Fern whirled on me. "What do you mean you're fine with the police? I don't want to get arrested!"

"Fern, Fern, calm yourself," Beltane said, but threw a glance back at the group at the table as they stood and put on jackets. Beltane's glance was a dagger.

Gladys smiled as she gathered up papers.

Beltane herded us through the kitchen, stopping by a row of hooks by the back door. Fern put on a down vest and Beltane—good grief—a dark cloak with a hood.

"Is that true, about Royal's missing key?" I said.

"Don't be ridiculous," Beltane said. "Fern is being railroaded."

"Well, what do we do about it?" I said.

Fern leaned tiredly against the wall and pushed back her hair. "Nothing, Allie. Don't get me wrong, I'm grateful that you tried but I'm stuck. I need Lyman's recommendation. I can't set him off any further. I need this to go away." She straightened and her hand flew to her side. "Oh, I was so upset I forgot my bag! I have to go get it. Thanks for coming tonight, Beltane, I know you had plans."

She squeezed my arm. "Thanks for trying to help, Allie. I appreciate it. You don't have to wait for me. I'll see you around." Fern hurried back to the keeping room.

Beltane put on her cloak, swirling it behind her back and onto her shoulders. "It was good of you to try to help Fern. But the forces arrayed against her are very strong. I've encouraged her to speak to the appropriate authorities at the college but she won't." Beltane folded her arms. "I'm trying to respect her autonomy, but it's difficult."

Did I agree with Beltane Kowalski?

We stepped outside into the kitchen garden. Lights winked off within the house and outdoor security lights blazed on.

Beltane glanced up at the moon. "Good night," she said, then whirled and hurried down the kitchen garden path. She didn't head to the parking lot, instead crossing the broad lawn toward the trees.

I walked slowly toward the parking lot. I didn't want to run into Lyman, Royal, or most especially Gladys. Lingering in the shadows of the garden, I watched them exit the front door and cross the parking lot. Engines started and the cars pulled out.

I leaned against Fern's sedan. Fern. A woman of immense gifts, a born storyteller, who knew Lyman had stolen from her but didn't have the courage to demand justice. I'd wait for her and try to convince her one more time to go with me to the police tonight. As I wondered what to say, I watched Beltane cross the lawn.

Fern stepped from the kitchen door, pulling it closed behind her. She started to walk through the kitchen garden toward the parking lot, but stopped short. I followed the direction of her gaze. She'd seen Beltane, a shadow crossing the moonlight-silvered lawn. It was a short commute home through the cemetery. Talk about appropriate. Unless . . . there was something else going on tonight. Fern had thanked Beltane for coming tonight when she knew she had other plans. When she'd left, Beltane had looked up.

I looked up. The moon was full.

A ceremony. Beltane must have planned to attend a rite at the Witch's Table. Now she was hurrying to meet her sisters

Delilah's words rang in my mind as I stepped softly across the gravel. *The Witch's Table. A place I don't dare go. The echoes are too strong, too dangerous.*

Fern made a call on her phone, then tucked it into her canvas shoulder bag. She hurried through the garden, opening and closing the gate softly, stealthily—she didn't want Beltane to know she was being followed. She, too, hurried across the lawn.

Fern was a scholar with an interest in women's studies and anthropology. She wasn't going to pass up a chance to observe Beltane's ceremony.

The sound of a car's engine made me turn. A dark car drove slowly through the lot. Was it one of the board members who had just left? Returning? Why? Or was it someone else? I lost sight of it as it went behind the Otis

Parish House but the sound of the tires on gravel was loud in the still night air. I scuttled forward and saw the car draw up to the door of the annex.

The engine cut, the car door opened and shut softly. A shadow moved across a floodlight behind the annex. I ducked behind the fence of the kitchen garden and saw a silhouetted figure, tall and broad-shouldered, halt and watch the women cross the lawn toward the woods.

The figure ran behind the annex. Was there a back door? I crept to the end of the garden fence and peered around, holding my breath, grateful for my dark sweatshirt. I glanced at the figures crossing the lawn just in time to see the dark woods swallow the shadow that I knew was Beltane.

Just as Fern disappeared into the woods, I heard a door close. An oddly shaped shadow ran with surprising speed across the lawn, carrying something long and thin that was almost as tall as the shadow itself. Light gleamed on the end.

I caught my breath. I remembered the frat boys at the grant presentation carrying historical replicas of weapons.

It was a pike.

I ran after the shadow.

I was pretty sure I knew why Beltane was going into the woods.

And I thought I knew why Fern was going.

But the third figure was unmistakably going to kill someone.

Chapter 41

I plunged into the shadows of the woods, then pulled up short. I had to call the police. I pulled out my phone and started to dial, then stopped. *What if he hears me?* Instead I texted Verity: *Call police. Tell them to go to the Witch's Table. NOW.*

My breath was ragged. I took one deep breath and closed my eyes briefly, centering myself. Then I opened my eyes and my senses, feeling myself in space, aware of the air on my body and the contours of the earth beneath my feet, a technique Madame had taught me.

My eyes adjusted to the dark. Gray moonlight pierced the canopy of trees, creating veils of light. Up ahead, I saw a tall shadow slip through one of the veils. A man.

Now he carried the pike as if it were a wizard's staff. He placed each foot carefully, a wolf stalking prey. It was light enough for me to see, and, I realized, light enough for him to see me. I pressed my back against the rough bark of an oak, willing myself to disappear, to melt into the darkness.

Ahead of us both, leaves rustled as Fern rushed, careless, unaware that she was being hunted. She knew the path, had probably walked it several times to her friend Beltane's house, and she was eager to get where she was going.

Warm light flickered through the trees to my right. I remembered that the woods bordered the lawn behind Isobel Parish's house. Light. Safety. Should I run there? Try to get help? I hesitated. Fern wasn't far ahead on the path. The hunter was too close to his prey. I had to stay here in the woods, try to figure out how to stop him.

I crept forward, placing my feet deliberately, careful not to shuffle in the fallen leaves. Too easy for him to turn and see me, to reach me with the ugly sharp point of the pike. I pressed on, hoping that Verity had gotten my message, my mind blank, my heart beating with such force I imagined the hunter could hear it.

Ahead, a low murmur of voices and flickering firelight drew us all.

The voices rose. I imagined what was happening. Greetings, then hands clasped around the stone table.

Farther, farther into the woods we went, my body stiff with tension and the effort of moving soundlessly. Slowly, barely able to breathe, I stalked the stalker.

My phone dinged.

The hunter's head turned, then he spun, the pike in front of him.

I glanced at the screen. Verity. *R U OK? I'm coming!*

I fumbled to silence my cell.

I looked up. In that moment, he'd disappeared.

I froze. He was probably doing the same, in front of one of the trees ahead of me. I hesitated, then fear drove me. He'd heard the phone. I had to move. Without conscious thought, I skirted to the right. My shaking legs stirred up dry leaves.

The chanting grew louder, providing accompanying music to this deadly dance. I considered screaming to warn Fern, but the chanting would cover the sound. The only one who would certainly hear me was the man hunting Fern. I had to reach her before he did, get past him to the safety of the circle, make sure Fern did the same.

I imagined the pike's sharp tip embedded in my chest, or piercing my back, pinning me to the ground. I had no doubt he'd use that pike. He had a lot to lose.

Up ahead, a small rectangle of light caught my eye. No! Just as quickly, the light was extinguished. Fern had checked her phone.

My body buzzed with adrenaline. I felt rather than saw that Fern's hunter was closing in. The chanting continued. He'd strike before they finished.

I dodged behind another tree, and another, my footsteps too loud in the leaves. The chanting grew louder, crescendoed, then stopped abruptly.

In the sudden silence, footsteps whispered through leaves to my left. "Fern, run to the circle!" I shouted.

A light appeared ahead and aimed back at me. "Is that you, Allie?"

"Fern, run!" I shouted so loudly the words rasped my throat.

At that moment a shadow crossed the beam of her cell phone light. Fern screamed. A blur of movement blotted her from my sight. I hurried forward as an unearthly scream tore the night air.

A man shouted. Then a howl, like a wounded animal, made my blood turn to ice. Shadows flitted through the trees. *Where is Fern? Who screamed?*

I darted forward, turning on my phone's flashlight. Several forms, hooded, materialized in front of me.

I ran into something hard, just at shoulder level. A branch? It was smooth. The shaft of the pike stuck out from where it was embedded in the trunk of a tree.

A form thrashed and moaned at my feet. One of the hooded figures brought a lantern and raised it high over Lyman Smith writhing in the leaves and dirt. Two more hooded figures tended to him, one spoke on a cell phone.

Fern Doucette walked slowly toward me, her eyes wide with shock. She grabbed my arm. "He was, he tried to stab me! Allie, when you screamed for me, I turned around. He was right behind me, with the pike. He missed me, but then I was too scared to move."

"So what happened?"

Fern swung her cell phone light. "She saved me. She came out of the trees and stabbed him before he could pull the pike out of the tree to try to stab me again."

Isobel Parish stood over Lyman, panting, a broken sword at her side.

Chapter 42

"So did Professor Smith kill Max with that pike?"

A few days later, Verity, Bronwyn, and I sat in the Adirondack chairs at the Mermaid, sharing a thermos of hot chocolate after the dinner rush. We all wore thick sweatshirts and Verity had a car blanket draped over her knees. Golden autumn was fading and frost was in the forecast.

I shook my head. "No, he used a marlinspike."

"A what?" Verity tossed the end of a wooly scarf across her shoulders.

"Marlinspike. Sailors use them for working on lines—that's rope to you landlubbers. They're tapered, spike-like things, sometimes with a curve. They help you undo knots. Usually they're small enough to fit in your hand, but the old ones the historical society had were a foot long.

"When we were at the grant ceremony, I saw little cards in a display case that told where some items had been loaned. Beltane was mad because Lyman Smith asked for a loan at the last minute. Max and the frat boys got a last-minute invitation to the ceremony, too. It was that term, *last minute,* repeated so many times that got me thinking.

"I think Max had started blackmailing Lyman as soon as he learned that Lyman Smith was getting that grant, which he probably heard from Isobel Parish. Now Lyman Smith had more than his reputation to lose, he could lose that grant money, too. Which, by the way, was a payoff to suppress what Fern had learned from the diary and what they'd learned when they dug up the grave of Uriah Parish.

"As frat adviser, Lyman would've known that Max had been cut off by his parents, that he needed money. He readily agreed to pay Max off because Max's knowledge was too dangerous. I think Fern's wasn't the only student's work Lyman plagiarized.

"But how to silence Max? It was best to do it somewhere removed from the college. The Parish cemetery was perfect. And Lyman knew there was a weapon he could use right in the historical society display case. He just had to borrow it, clean it, and return it.

"It was too easy to make sure Max got that slip of paper right at the ceremony. The note was vague—what grave? But Fern told me Max, Royal, and Lyman had dug up the family cemetery, so there was only one grave that mattered. The grave of Uriah Parish."

"Uriah?" Verity said. "Not Otis?"

I held up my hand. "I'll explain that in a sec."

"Wouldn't Max be scared, meeting Lyman in the cemetery?" Verity said.

I shook my head. "Max worked for Lyman. It was during a big party. He probably wasn't a bit worried."

Bronwyn said, "Max's autopsy also found that he had

a blunt-force head injury. I bet Lyman Smith knocked him out first."

I nodded. "Lyman probably had no idea Max had plans of his own in the cemetery that night. His big prank—leaving Lobzilla at the grave of Otis Parish."

"So Max was probably busy with Lobzilla," Verity said. "Lyman sneaked up, hit him on the head with a stone, and then stabbed him with that marlinspike."

"Lyman got his cape all bloody, but that was easy to fix," I said. "He just added his cape to all the others in the coat room and traded it for another."

"And poor Madame Monachova picked it up," Verity said. "She doesn't see well and the lights were low. Lyman needed a cape, too, and managed to take one that was too short and too small. That's what you noticed in the photos online, Allie."

"So social media captured the killer," Bronwyn said.

"You could say that." I scrolled to the party picture I'd seen earlier. "Here are the pictures from the party. In this one, taken early in the evening, Lyman Smith is wearing that gorgeous long—"

"Historically accurate," Verity added.

"Historically accurate cape."

I scrolled to later in the evening. "And look. He's wearing the cape pushed back over his shoulders. You can tell it's too small and too short."

"Absolutely atrocious!" Verity said.

"Fashion catches a killer." Bronwyn laughed.

We clinked our mugs.

A puppy scampered up to us, tail wagging wildly. "What a sweetie!"

"Oliver!" Johnny Sabino called from a picnic table. In the golden light thrown by a candle stuck in a Chianti bottle, I could just make out Bertha Betancourt sitting across from him. Aunt Gully had spread their table with the red-checked cloth. Johnny's puppy ran back to them as Bertha's laugh boomed.

Verity, Bronwyn, and I shared a look.

"I wondered who Bertha'd invite for her free dinner," I whispered.

"Look at that candle! Aunt Gully's playing matchmaker," Verity said.

Bronwyn turned to me. "So what about Uriah Parish?"

I gathered my thoughts. "All my life I've heard stories about Otis Parish. He's the founder of Mystic Bay. The important guy. But I noticed that when I spoke to Fern, or Isobel, people who knew the Parish history, they mentioned Otis, sure, but they also always mentioned Uriah and Mercy." I told them of Fern's research, the dark deeds done in the Parish cemetery. "Fern said that we only learn the winner's version of history. The Parishes had always suppressed things they didn't want known. But she'd dug up evidence of this part of the Parish story that the family wanted to keep buried."

"Is that why Lyman attacked Fern?"

Verity leaned forward. "I wish I'd seen that!"

"I wish I'd been able to see it better, too." Say what you wanted about Isobel Parish, she'd saved Fern's life. "The Parish family has security cameras all through the woods. Isobel saw Lyman stalking Fern with the pike. She told me that she grabbed one of her old fencing swords and ran after him."

"Wouldn't an old sword be dull?" Bronyn asked.

I shook my head. "Isobel told me she cracked it over her knee and broke it to get a sharper edge." I shivered. Isobel was volatile, but thank goodness she'd been willing to act to save Fern.

"Don't mess with Isobel Parish," Verity said.

"Wait a second," Bronwyn said. "If there were security cameras, wouldn't they have captured Lyman killing Max?"

I nodded. "Isobel told her parents to turn them off for her party. How did she put it? She didn't want her parents spying on her friends."

Bronwyn scoffed. "Even after their theft?"

"I'm sure it was Kathleen Parish who turned them off, not Royal Parish." I pulled my woolly scarf closer against the chilly air. Isobel, Kathleen, Royal. That family would never be the same.

Bronwyn raised a hand. "You said they dug up Uriah. Why on earth did Royal want Uriah dug up? It only confirmed Fern's research."

I nodded. "Royal Parish's ego was so big, I think he discounted the story in Rosamund Parish's diary because it was written by a teenage girl. He thought the exhumation would disprove the diary account. Instead, it corroborated it. That's why Lyman got the grant. Royal was rewarding him for making sure Fern's second paper, the one about Uriah and Mercy, didn't get published."

"I'm still on the marlinspike," Bronwyn said. "What did Lyman do with it after he killed Max?"

I remembered how I'd carried my flashlight in my boot. "I bet he put it in his boot."

"Our forensics team is going over the artifacts at the historical society now," Bronwyn said.

A black sedan pulled into the parking lot. A woman in a black leather jacket over black slacks, her hair slicked back into a tight bun, got out and scanned the parking lot. She spotted us and headed over.

"Oh, no." Bronwyn threw me a look. I swallowed hard. It was Detective Rosato.

"What?" Verity said. "You both look like you've seen Uriah Parish."

Detective Rosato approached, zipping her jacket. "Good evening. Bit chilly tonight."

Bronwyn snapped to her feet. "Detective Rosato."

Detective Rosato nodded to her and Verity, then turned to me. "May I have a word?"

My mouth went dry, but I managed to nod.

"We'll clean up." Bronwyn and Verity gathered our mugs and thermos and headed to the shack, throwing glances back at us.

Detective Rosato took the seat next to me. "I heard about your car accident. How are you doing?"

I relaxed, slightly. "I'm fine, thanks. I was just shaken up."

She didn't say anything else for a moment.

I shifted in my seat. She had started with a softball question. I knew more difficult ones would follow.

The wind picked up and Detective Rosato smoothed her hair.

"What made you suspect Lyman Smith?"

I took a deep breath. "Although he was supposed to keep the story of Otis—well, Otis, Uriah, and Mercy Parish—quiet, although he was a trained historian and was familiar with archaeological excavation"—Fern told me how carefully they'd worked on the grave site—"he told the story of Otis Parish to a bunch of drunk fraternity brothers. He knows kids that age, understands them. The first thing those guys were going to do was run down to the cemetery to see the grave. All those kids running around would obliterate any footprints and compromise the murder scene, and as a bonus, the grave they'd dug up. Lyman didn't even try to stop them from going to the cemetery."

"The scene was well compromised." She cleared her throat. "Tell me about the backpack and the papers."

I swallowed hard. I knew this question was coming. I should have taken the papers to the police as soon as I'd found them.

I told her how odd it had been when Max came to help Professor Nickerson with Lobzilla. How he'd worn his backpack into the crowded lobster shed while he worked. "He just didn't strike me as the nerdy, forgetful type. I thought he left that backpack on because he didn't want to lose it. Then Isobel told me he'd taken the papers. I put two and two together . . ." My voice trailed off. I guess this was the part where she arrested me.

Detective Rosato didn't speak for a long time, admiring the twinkling lights of the houses on the far shore of the river. "We discovered a car registered to Lyman Smith hidden in the woods off Old Farms Road. The damage was consistent with your accident. And a backpack was discovered in his office." She stood and turned to me.

"I could arrest you for so many things," she said. My stomach clenched.

"But you have allies. The Parish family is happy to have their"—she hesitated—"property returned. Quietly."

Property? She must mean the papers.

She walked back to the sedan, raising her hand in a wave.

Chapter 43

As I wiped down the counter in the Mermaid the next day, Beltane and Fern came into the shack. Fern waved, smiling broadly. Then her phone rang and she stepped outside to take the call.

"Hello, Allegra. One cup of chowder, please. To go." Beltane slid money onto the counter, then said, "Is your aunt here?"

Honestly, this woman does not give up.

"Listen, Beltane, why do you keep asking her to join your group? She's not interested."

Beltane regarded me with her unsettling eyes. "She knows the old ways. Especially with herbs. The tisane she gave me cleared up my rash and my doctors haven't been able to do that for years. Her knowledge is encyclopedic. Plus—"

Beltane leaned close. Her breath smelled like coffee and peppermint. "Her aura. It's white."

"Aura?" I gripped onto the counter, tried to steady myself. All this crazy was making me dizzy.

Beltane continued, "All living things are energy. We give off auras. Yours is blue."

"My aura is blue?" *Is that what she'd been talking about?*

She brushed my question aside. "But those whose energies are in perfect balance with the earth, the air, the sky, the spirits, those who have gone into the Beyond and those To Come . . . their auras are white. A signpost to those who can read it. A signpost to power."

Power? Aunt Gully, who had gone to a Celtics game in a T-shirt with a sequined red lobster and red earrings to match? Who had dressed up as Glinda for Halloween?

"Here's your chowder," Hilda said abruptly as she put the cup on the counter in front of Beltane. "Have a nice day."

Fern came up to the counter.

Beltane nodded curtly to me and Hilda. "I'll wait for you in the car, Fern." Hilda watched Beltane go, then returned to the kitchen.

"You won't believe what just happened," Fern said.

"Tell me! Something good, I hope."

"I think so. Royal Parish called to tell me that he was so impressed by my research that the Parish Family Trust has arranged for me to have a scholarship to a special history program in England!"

"Wow!"

"It's amazing." She pushed back her hair. "But moving, uprooting. And mostly, leaving my research here. It's just . . ."

"Out of the blue." The phrase *packed her off* came to mind.

She mirrored my thoughts. "Allie, I'm not a fool. They're getting rid of me. I know too many inconvenient things about the Parish history and their friend Lyman. But if I could get packed off somewhere, this is a place I'd want to go. My mom said she'd come and take care of Prudie while I'm there. My husband is okay with it, too. He says it's too good a chance to pass up."

I thought of the follow-your-dreams speech Aunt Gully would be giving now. "Is this your dream?"

"I think so." Fern's face clouded. "I thought I could have my dream here. Now I just don't know."

"Sleep on it."

She smiled. "If Prudie lets me."

Chapter 44

Three weeks later
Opening night of *The Nutcracker*

Applause carried me from the Opera House stage like a rushing wave as I made my exit at the end of act 1. Madame Monachova waited for me in the wings, leaning on a carved wooden cane.

She held out her arm and embraced me. "Lovely, just perfect," she whispered, her eyes shining.

Cody rushed toward us. In his Snow Prince costume for act 2, he looked regal, but his words tumbled. "Have you heard? Margot's AWOL. I heard someone on Twitter saw her at the airport getting on a private jet."

"What! She's supposed to dance Dewdrop tonight!"

"She was here, warmed up, in her makeup—everyone saw her! Then she disappeared! Serge is in a panic. He wants to talk to you."

As Madame and I followed him, I remembered there were three understudies for the Dewdrop role: Kellye still had her arm in a cast from her fall and couldn't dance. Serge had another dancer learning the part, but she had

had to fly to Dallas for a family funeral. That left Dawn Atkins.

"Dawn's available, right? Where is she?"

"She's on her way but is stuck in traffic at the bridge. An accident closed it and the backup is miles long. The snowstorm started and it's snarling everything."

Bad weather had been predicted, but the theater was full of families eager to start their holiday season with *The Nutcracker*.

"Looks like Dawn might not make it on time."

Madame Monachova smiled. "Not to worry. Allie knows that dance. She can do it." She pulled me close. "You've regained your strength. You must do it."

I swallowed. I did know that dance, in my bones, in every muscle, every tendon. Even though the doctor hadn't officially cleared me to dance on pointe again, I'd danced through the Dewdrop variation dozens of times in the studio at the college, a million times in my mind. I just hadn't done it in rehearsal or in front of an audience of over a thousand people.

Serge rushed to me. "Allie, can you go on for Margot?"

"Yes, of course." We moved en masse to the dressing room—I had barely enough time to change. "What happened to Margot?"

Virginia helped me out of my gown and into the Dewdrop costume. "Done a runner. Can you believe it?" Virginia fastened my bodice as we spoke. "Cody left his GoPro on a table at the top of the stairs at your group house. It was set to be motion activated. And it caught her!"

"Caught her? What do you mean?"

Cody ran into the dressing room.

"Cody! What happened?"

He waved his phone. "Look at this. Remember the motion-activated video camera I got for my birthday? I had the footage sent to my phone and I didn't check it until today. I was so shocked, I guess I wasn't thinking clearly. I showed it to Serge. Margot must've heard us talking about it."

He turned the screen toward me. The time stamp was the day Kellye'd had her accident.

There onscreen was the doorway to our cellar stairs. It was directly across from a table where we all used to drop our keys and phones.

I heard Kellye's voice, then Margot's, their words indistinct. Then Margot moved into the frame and went down the cellar stairs. She bent out of view. A few minutes later, she came back upstairs.

The video stuttered and then Kellye was heading down the same stairs, singing, holding a basket full of laundry in front of her. Just as I had when I fell down those same stairs.

I clutched my throat.

Just as Kellye stepped out of view, we heard a terrified shriek. We all winced, imagining her plummeting down the steep stairs to the cement floor below, her body thudding against the warped wooden steps. Then Margot dashed onscreen, went down the stairs and came back quickly. She shouted over her shoulder, "I'll get help!" She carried scissors and looped something around her hand. The motion made me think of Aunt Gully winding yarn. Then Margot stuffed it all into a shopping bag.

"What was she putting in the bag?" Madame said.

For a moment, I relived my own terrifying plunge down those steep stairs. I'd always thought that I'd tripped on something, but had found nothing on the steps when I checked days after my accident. "Fishing wire. Practically invisible but strong. Margot could've tied that across the steps and attached it to old nails that jutted from the walls. Then she simply cut it and removed it."

"My God, she could have killed you or Kellye!" Virginia swore.

Too many thoughts swirled in my mind. *Poor Kellye!* Margot's treachery. Serge's worry—I hadn't rehearsed at all. He was taking a chance. I was taking a chance. But I knew I was strong enough. Adrenaline coursed through me like a rip current.

Madame squeezed my hand. She thought I was ready.

I heard Aunt Gully's voice in my head: *Back on your toes. Where you belong.*

I took a deep breath. My body relaxed.

Virginia smoothed my hair and jammed in pins. "Ouch!"

She sprayed me with a cloud of hair spray. "You haven't practiced with this crown, and Margot said it was heavy. That bitch."

I laughed. Virginia pulled me close. *"Merde!"* She whispered the dancer's traditional swear/good-luck wish. No one ever says *break a leg* to a dancer.

"We must hurry." Her eyes aglow, Madame Monachova kissed my cheeks. "I don't want to miss a moment."

We all rushed back to the wings, the music and lights of the stage like a doorway to another world. My introduction played.

Serge blew me a kiss. With one last nod from Madame, I stepped onstage.

AUNT GULLY'S NEW ENGLAND CLAM CHOWDER

If you're in the mood for New England comfort food, you can't go wrong with clam chowder. Purists say that New England clam chowder must be made with salt pork, but if you don't have any you can use bacon for a tasty variation. If you like creamier chowder, substitute half and half for the milk.

1 medium onion, chopped very fine

½ cup lean salt pork, cut into small pieces (or 3 pieces bacon)

2 6.5-oz. cans minced clams, drained, but be sure to reserve the liquid. You can also use frozen minced clams—just defrost.

1 small Russet potato, chopped fine (about 1 cup)

1 bay leaf

¼ tsp thyme

½ tsp salt

Pepper to taste

2 cups milk

1 bottle of clam juice (in case you want to add more clam flavor)

Oyster crackers
Sauce pan with lid

Cook and stir the salt pork (or bacon) and onion until the onion is soft (and the bacon is crisp if you used bacon. If so remove it now and reserve. Actually, who would discard bacon?).

Drain the clams, reserving the liquid. Add the liquid, potatoes, bay leaf, thyme, salt and pepper to the salt pork/onion mixture. Heat to a boil, then lower heat, cover, and simmer until the potato is very soft (10–15 minutes). If you need more liquid you can add some clam juice or water.

Add the milk and clams, stirring occasionally until they are heated through.

Adjust seasoning to your taste.

If you used bacon, crumble the pieces to garnish the chowder.

Serve with oyster crackers and enjoy!